D1259489

The
Belchamber
Scandal

The Belchamber Scandal

Frances Murray

St. Martin's Press
New York

The chapter headings are taken from *The Young Woman's Companion* mentioned on page 38, published by Ward and Lock in 1863.

Library of Congress Cataloging in Publication Data

Murray, Frances.
    The Belchamber scandal.

    I. Title.
PR6063.U738B4   1985   823'.914   85-12528
ISBN 0-312-07394-1

First published in Great Britain by Hodder & Stoughton Ltd.

First U.S. Edition

10 9 8 7 6 5 4 3 2 1

For my daughter Frances
at long last . . .

The Governess is a class rapidly on the increase;
it is the only recourse left to young girls
in the higher classes of society who are forced
to earn their own living.

Ladies' Journal, 1840

1

*"An hour in the morning
is worth two in the afternoon."*

The postman whistled as he turned into Aspel Square. It was a still, hazy July morning with a hint of heat to come and he had the great square entirely to himself. The huge windows of the houses gleamed gold on the west side of the square as the rising sun slanted over the bushes in the garden which was laid out with rigid symmetry in the centre. The postman began to run up and down the flights of steps which graced each of the double front doors. Occasionally a mob-capped servant would emerge from the area below the steps and take the letters. At number fourteen the postman went straight down the area steps and into the kitchen where a cup steamed ready on the table for him.

"Mornin'," he said to the girl on her knees by the range. "How's Mollie this fine mornin'?"

"Perky, Mr Beckwith, I thank you."

"How did the funeral at number twenty-one go?"

"Oh," Mollie said, sitting back on her heels, "such poor doin's. Just a plain hearse, no plumes or velvet or anything. No mutes, just the two black horses, old screws both of them and a coachman with crape. Disgraceful in a square like this."

"Many come?"

"Just the one closed cab after. Her and them cousins. No one else. Not even empty carriages like. And when you think of the folk have et their dinners at that house . . ."

"You'd not look for a turn-out . . . not in the circumstances. Him suiciding an' all, poor beggar," said Mr Beckwith tolerantly.

7

"No, I s'pose not," Mollie admitted. "But it weren't much to see. We had the blinds down, that I will say. What a scandal, eh, for a place like this? Her upstairs is never done talking about it. What's embezzlement, Mr Beckwith?"

"Stealing other folks' money, I reckon, only it's done polite and an awful lot more of it than normal. Thousands and thousands, they reckon."

Mollie brought the teapot from the range and refilled his cup.

"Her upstairs is wondering what's to become of Miss Belchamber. Not a penny left, they say, and debts all over."

The postman shook his head and gulped.

"No mother," Mollie mused. "Mind, she's engaged. That was a sixmonth ago. But I ain't seen him there . . . not for a long while."

"Think he'll stand buff?"

"He's no gentleman if'n he don't," Mollie said.

"Mmm," the postman said doubtfully. "Any relations?"

"Some cousins. That's them staying there now. Lady something. Mother's folk, her upstairs says."

"Name of Lester?"

"No," Mollie said, "that ain't it. I can't just bring it to mind."

"Got a letter for a Miss Lester, number twenty-one."

"Never heard of no Miss Lester there. The chaperone, she was a Mrs Thomas. She went off in a great bang after it happened. Couldn't afford to be in such a house, so she said. Let's see the letter, Mr Beckwith."

"'Gainst regulations," he said and sorted it out to show.

"From Bindleton . . . fancy! Where's Bindleton, Mr Beckwith?"

"In the north, someplace."

Mollie looked suspiciously at the envelope.

"I dunno, I'm sure. No one there, name of Lester, that I'll swear to. I've spoke to all of them in the kitchen."

The clock in the hall upstairs chimed.

"Best be on my way," said the postman and gulped down the rest of his tea.

"That you 'ad, Mr Beckwith. Cook'll be down any minute and she don't hold with gentleman callers, she don't . . . ooh, Mr Beckwith!"

8

The postman signified his thanks with a kiss and a squeeze of Mollie's waist and was off and out of the door.

At number twenty-one there was no letter-box. He knocked his usual sharp rat-tat and the door was opened before he could let go of the knocker.

"My, miss, you didn't arf give me a turn!"

He regarded the figure in front of him with interest. She was slightly below middle height and so slender that in another walk of society she might have been called skinny. She wore deep mourning but it was very plain, no crape flounces or jet bead embroidery or black lace veils, her face was pale and framed in wings of dark hair dressed in a very plain style. The hand she held out for the letters was encased in black thread-net mittens.

"Thank you, postman," she said firmly, aware of his interested gaze, and shut the door. Beckwith went down the steps speculating: dark hair and them bright very blue eyes. Would that be Miss Belchamber? It seemed likely and if it was, what was she doing answering her own door at six in the morning. He resolved to ask Mollie and continued round the square whistling.

Miss Belchamber examined the bundle of post behind the closed door. It consisted mostly of bills and abusive letters. She tore up the latter and dropped them into the wastepaper basket and the bills she put with many others like them under a huge paperweight on the desk in the study. The letter addressed to Miss Lester she opened eagerly. A bill for five pounds fell out as she unfolded the letter.

> Blackyetts,
> Nr. Bindleton,
> Lancashire.
> July 19th 1863.

Miss Amelia Lester,
Dear Madam,

In pursuance of our interesting conversation at the Noakes Royal Opera Hotel on 18th instant I write to offer you the position we discussed as governess to my daughters. I agree to the stipulation you made as you may see. Please telegraph the time of your arrival in Bindleton and I

9

will arrange to have you met and conveyed to Blackyetts. The house is, as I told you, some seven miles from the town. I have informed my wife of my decision and she and my daughters join in wishing you a safe journey and a pleasant sojourn with us. As I understand you might be embarrassed for money I enclose £5 journey-money.

Yours faithfully,

The signature was in another hand and illegible but Amelia knew it to be that of Mr Staneley Hoggett, manufacturer of cottons and canvases. She knew a slight irritation that a secretary should have written that last sentence but reminded herself that she was in no position to stand on her dignity. She folded the letter and put it and the enclosure in the pocket round her waist before she went down the back stairs and into the kitchen where the cook, the butler and the pantry-boy, all that was left of the staff, were enjoying a cup of tea. They got up when she came in and offered her a chair and a cup. Then they sat down, their eyes fixed on her in expressions suitably lugubrious.

"Well," she said briskly. "The time's come to say good-bye."

No one replied. Cook shook her head slowly.

"There's a good deal to be done," she went on, "especially for you . . ."

She smiled at the pantry-boy who had given her his chair. He blushed up into his close-cropped hair and mumbled that nuffink wasn't too much trouble; the butler gave him a glance and he faltered into silence. He was given a handful of letters to deliver and rose, ready, like an urban Puck, to girdle London on her behalf.

"No, not yet. I've another letter to write," Amelia told him, "you've time to eat your breakfast."

The other two received their instructions with mournful expressions and heavy sighs.

"Here are your references," said Amelia at last, laying them on the table with a little pile of coins. "I have made them positively glowing, I promise you. As you deserve. I couldn't have asked for better friends."

She paused and looked at them speakingly and Cook sniffed and wiped her eyes on her apron.

10

"But let's be more cheerful. Have you found a suitable situation?"

"As it chances, miss, we have," the butler replied. "We will be together, Mrs Grey and Georgie and me. A very pleasant family, new come to town. Four kept beside ourselves and everything very handsome. In Bedford Square."

"You saw this coming, didn't you?" Amelia asked abruptly.

"In a manner of speaking, miss."

"I wish I had," she observed expressionlessly.

"But we never thought the master would lay hands on himself, the poor gentleman," Cook said tearfully, "that we never. Trouble coming we did see, bills mounting up and visitors at all hours, voices raised and that. But not . . . not . . ."

"No," Amelia agreed. "It was a great shock. And I am grateful to you both for all you have done to help."

"I mean to leave this morning," Amelia added and rose from the table. "I'll see you all again before I go but I'd like to say goodbye now and wish you good fortune."

She held her hand out to Cook who shook it damply.

"If we might take the liberty, miss . . . we'd like to know, Mr Grey and me, will you be all right? I mean . . . that is we think . . ."

Her plump face under the starched cap was creased with anxiety.

"You needn't worry your heads about me," Amelia assured them. "I am going to be able to provide for myself . . . thanks to Miss Aylett . . ."

"Now there was a right good woman," Cook said emphatically. "She wouldn't have run off and left you to stand the nonsense, not she!"

"No."

Amelia thought bleakly of her governess in Highgate cemetery and hoped that she did not know what was happening to her pupil.

"It's kind of you both to be concerned," she said and turned to Grey. "Goodbye Grey and I hope your new employers realise what treasures they have found."

He shook her hand painfully.

"And Georgie I'll see before I leave," she assured him. "Come to the study in about half an hour."

11

Georgie knuckled his forehead and wiped his nose on his sleeve.

Amelia sat at the desk which had been her father's and stared at the sheet of paper before her. She had half an hour to write her letter and it was not going to be easy. However, it need not be long. What she had to tell Oliver Scott could be said very briefly.

> 21, Aspel Square,
> July 20th.

Dear Oliver,

This is to await your return from Spain. When you come back you will hear the news if someone has not already written to tell you which I expect someone has. It is the sort of news which people like to give, I find. Briefly, my father escaped trial for fraud and embezzlement only by shooting himself. I suppose you may have had some notion that he was in deep water. Everyone but me seems to have had 'a good idea' though what is good or was good about it I do not know.

I am now no asset to a diplomatic career. This tale is likely to follow me wherever I go. Moreover, your parents told me some time ago that you could not afford to marry to please yourself and I know this to be true. My portion has vanished with all the rest as it is only right that it should: which makes me poor as well as ineligible.

I know you are too much the gentleman to give me my congé. I like to think also (you know what a vain creature I am) that you might be reluctant to do so. I cannot let you disoblige yourself to such an extent so I am exercising my female prerogative to release you from our engagement.

Enclosed in this packet is your ring, the posy-holder of last Christmas, your miniature and your letters. I part with these last reluctantly for they are entertaining as well as affectionate and, I believe, this is not always the case. Believe me that I shall remember our association with pleasure and hope (vain again) that you will not forget too quickly,

> your sincere friend,
> Amelia.

The letters and the trinkets were already in a little box. She added her own letter, took the ring from her finger and placed it safely in a corner, wrapped the box neatly and sealed it. Not till that was done and she was looking at all that was left of her future, did her eyes fill. She blinked the tears away and wrote the address as neatly as she had written the letter.

"There," she muttered defiantly. "It had to be done and now it is done."

Georgie sidled into the room.

"Good boy," she said. "Take this packet as well. You've taken letters there before. There's no answer . . ." Her voice faltered a little. "No answer," she repeated firmly. "Leave it with the footman and come away. Then, when you've done all those errands for me fetch a cab here for a quarter past ten o'clock. Find a four-wheeler for I'll have baggage. Can you remember all this?"

"Yes, miss."

Breakfast for Amelia and her guests was served in the breakfast parlour at the back of the house. When Lady Wheatley appeared, also in deep mourning, but, unlike Amelia, in full panoply of crape and weepers, her hostess had almost finished. Lady Wheatley greeted her sombrely, as befitted a guest in a house of mourning, sat down in a slither of black silk and accepted a cup of tea with a wan smile. Into the tea she proceeded to dip slices of thickly buttered toast, a custom from which Amelia preferred to avert her eyes.

"Now, my dear Amelia," Lady Wheatley began, "we have to talk very seriously. You are left shockingly, are you not?"

"Yes, cousin," Amelia agreed meekly.

"I can only say," her cousin observed through a mouthful of toast, "that your father might have thought of *you* before he . . . but I must not enlarge on that . . ."

"No, cousin."

"There is no portion for you, I understand?"

"No, cousin."

"This Mr Scott . . . do you suppose he will fulfil his obligations to you without a portion?"

"I daresay not, cousin."

"I fear you are right. It is a great deal to ask of any man, I must say. He asked you when you were an heiress, as you

13

thought, the only child of a very wealthy man and now you are not only penniless but quite disgraced."

She shook her black cap gloomily and buttered a third slice of toast.

"I very much fear he will back off."

"Yes, cousin."

"So . . . we must consider the possibility that he will not come up to scratch. A third son, when all was said. I thought at the time you could have looked for a better match but there it is. We must consider what is to be done with you."

"I have, cousin."

Lady Wheatley stared tight-lipped.

"Have you indeed? My good girl, you are too pert by far. I have had occasion to observe this before. When you are with us you must endeavour to avoid such remarks."

"With you, cousin?"

"Yes. I have decided, that is Lord Wheatley and I have decided that you will have to make your home with us. It is not convenient and it will occasion us considerable expense which we cannot, of course, expect to recoup, but nevertheless we feel that it is our Christian duty."

"I am obliged, cousin."

"So I should imagine. I will expect you to discharge this obligation by making yourself useful in the schoolroom. You are perfectly well-qualified to do so. Your father, so it seemed to me, squandered an inordinate amount of money upon your education."

"In the present circumstances it seems to me money well spent."

"How you do take one up," snapped Lady Wheatley irritably. "It is just what one disliked in your father. At all events you have a good command of languages and this is what I wish for Laura and Beatrix. Lord Wheatley expects to go with the Commission to Paris and I would like the girls to accompany us. I mean to dismiss Miss Smout. She was all very well for the girls while they were young but now they have reached an age when they need much more than she has to offer. Doubtless you will be glad of an occupation."

"Doubtless. And when Laura and Beatrix no longer require a governess? What then?"

14

Lady Emily shrugged.

"Laura may be able to give you a position. I expect her to marry well. She is very pretty and of course her portion will be considerable."

"Fortunate Laura."

"If she has no use for you you could make yourself useful at Wheatley Hall. The housekeeper, Mrs Amber, is getting no younger and I understand you have kept house for your father since you were sixteen. Nearly ten years, I declare. This house is not to be compared with Wheatley, of course, but you could learn what is required, doubtless?"

"Doubtless I could, cousin."

"Well, that is settled. We intend to leave for Hertfordshire tomorrow morning. See that you are packed and ready to leave with us."

"I am packed already, cousin."

Lady Emily wiped her buttery mouth.

"Upon my word, miss, you take a lot for granted!"

"As you do, cousin."

"I beg your pardon?"

"You have just taken for granted that I will work for you for the rest of my life in return for a roof and my keep. You have also taken for granted that you can remain here for another night. Well . . . " She rose and brushed crumbs from her skirt. ". . . you are wrong on both counts. This house will be closed up from midday today. The servants are paid off, the furniture will be removed this morning."

"You cannot be serious!"

"Oh, but I am. If Lord Wheatley does not get up within the next half hour he will be carried to the Repository on a mattress in his nightshirt."

"But we have engagements . . . business . . . we cannot leave today."

"This is London. There are plenty of hotels, you know. I daresay if you were to ask Grey he would tell you which is the cheapest."

"Iniquitous!"

"My father's creditors would not agree. The sooner the house is sold, the sooner they may be paid something. They have waited a long time, as you have repeatedly told me."

"Ingrate . . . insolent ingrate. I cannot think why we put

15

ourselves to the trouble and expense of coming to this house at such a time . . ."

"I think you will find the answer in your trunk," said Amelia icily. "From what I can discover you came to see the pickings there were. Pickings such as the Sèvres jar and the ivories from the drawing-room. Do you think I am blind? They are on my inventory and that of the lawyers so they had better reappear. So had the Dresden shepherdess and the Chinese bowl."

Lady Wheatley went scarlet and spluttered crumbs.

"Are you accusing me of . . ."

"Yes," said Amelia. "I am. They are in your trunk. I looked."

"I don't deny I have taken a keepsake or two . . . your dear mother was my aunt, a most beloved aunt. Would you grudge me a keepsake or two?"

"Yes . . . I would most certainly grudge you those. They are worth a considerable sum. And if I didn't grudge you them the creditors would. Besides, my mother never saw them. They were bought long after she left us."

The contempt in her voice stung the older woman.

"Then, all I have to say to you, miss, is that you need never look for help at our hands. As far as we are concerned you can die in the gutter."

"I can work," Amelia said quietly. "As you intended I should. But I would like to be paid for what I do. It is a reasonable preference."

There was a sound of loud voices and stamping in the hall.

"The men from the Repository," Amelia observed. "I trust Lord Wheatley is astir. I wish them to clear the upper part of the house first."

Lady Wheatley went hurriedly from the room with a waddling gait very unlike her usual swanlike glide. Amelia followed her into the hall. In a corner was a dome-topped leather trunk and two small bags and a dressing case.

"Thank you, Grey. Is everything going as it should?"

Grey bowed his assent and held her cloak for her.

"Your cab is waiting, miss. May I venture to wish you a happy change in your fortunes, miss?"

"Thank you, Grey, you are very kind . . ."

16

"Where do you think you are going?" Lady Emily demanded from the staircase. "You don't mean to leave just like that with nothing settled . . ."

The front door swung violently open and admitted half a dozen brawny men in aprons with rolls of sacking under their arms.

"Ah," Amelia greeted them with a smile. "You know you are to clear the upper floors first?"

"Amelia!" shrilled her cousin. "I insist on knowing where you are going!"

She followed her down the steps to where the cab was waiting. Georgie was feeding an astonished horse with bread.

"Thank you Georgie and goodbye."

Lady Wheatley caught the glint of a half sovereign.

"Well, really! A sixpence would have been ample. What would the creditors have to say to that, miss?"

"Like me, they can say goodbye," Amelia told her. "I have a long journey in front of me."

She climbed into the cab.

"But where to?" demanded her cousin.

"To the gutter . . . who knows?" Amelia said frivolously.

"But the house . . . all the things . . . these men . . . you can't leave me to . . ."

"Everything necessary is done," Amelia soothed her. "The agent knows, so does the attorney. Grey will lock up in an hour or so and take the keys round to the agents. There's nothing for you to do . . . expect restore your keepsakes. And pack of course. I see Cousin Wheatley is awake."

A night-capped head was peering bewilderedly from behind the curtains of a window on the second storey.

"Now that *is* fortunate," observed Amelia sunnily. "I should not care to think he had been rolled up in a feather bed and never heard of again."

The driver put his head in the door at the other side.

"Where to, miss?"

"Waterloo," she said after a tiny hesitation, "yes, Waterloo. And would you be good enough to hurry. I have a train to catch."

"Right, miss . . . Waterloo station and 'urry!"

He slammed the door and heaved himself on to the box. In

17

a few seconds Lady Wheatley found herself in the uncomfortable state of having a great deal to say and no one to say it to. The emergence of the great mahogany table from the dining-room, its sacking-wrapped legs sticking out sideways like those of a dead animal, roused her from her trance of frustration and she hurried inside to relate these hideous events to her husband. In the hall she saw the foreman of the removers with a set of neatly written pages in his fist.

"Is that the inventory?"

She looked through it quickly and saw to her chagrin that all her 'keepsakes' were indeed listed. Upstairs in the dressing room she opened the trunk but once the highly desirable objects were visible she hesitated. After all, she argued with herself, it was just as likely that Amelia would have taken them . . . much more likely in fact, the penniless little hoyden; if they were missed . . . and they might not be for the list was pages long . . . she would herself deny all knowledge. Amelia would take the blame and serve her right. She slammed down the lid and went to rouse her husband into unwelcome and unwonted activity.

Some time later while she was supervising the carrying down of her trunk to a waiting cab a young man came running up the steps to the house. The door was open and he came in without ceremony. In the street a groom was standing to the head of a sweating and snorting black horse.

"Where is Miss Belchamber?" he demanded in what Lady Wheatley considered to be a wretchedly abrupt fashion. She stared pointedly at his hat until he was constrained to remove it.

"My name is Scott . . . Oliver Scott. I am engaged to Miss Belchamber."

"Am I to understand that you still wish for the wedding to take place?" Lady Emily demanded. "After everything that has occurred? Such a scandal."

Mr Scott glared at her. "You must be the cousin," he said. "I would like to know what you take me for?"

"A most imprudent young man. The least she could have done in the circumstances was to release you from your engagement."

"Well, that is just what she has done and I very much want

18

to see her. Poor, little soul . . . does she think that I would leave her in the lurch?"

"If that is the case," Lady Wheatley told him loftily, "it is a great pity you didn't put in an appearance sooner. Sir Octavius has been dead these six days. And as it was, most regrettably, common knowledge I can only suppose . . ."

"I was in Spain, dammit," interrupted Mr Scott, flushing with annoyance. "I sailed as soon as I received my mama's cable. I arrived less than an hour ago and found my mama in a great taking . . ."

"I cannot blame her . . ." sniffed Lady Wheatley.

". . . and *this*." He shook the letter at her. "I must speak to her. Where is she?"

"The poor little soul, as you call her, has an inordinate confidence in her ability to manage her own affairs."

"Balderdash! From what my mama says there isn't so much as a crooked sixpence left for her. She *has* no affairs."

"Nevertheless, she has rejected – most ungratefully, I may say – our offer of a home at Wheatley."

"Has she, by Jupiter!"

"And what is more she has left. She left an hour ago. Nor did she see fit to vouchsafe to me, her nearest relation, what her destination was."

Mr Scott chewed his lip uncertainly for a second and then his eye fell on Grey.

"Grey . . . did she say anything to you?"

"No, sir."

"Labels on her trunks?"

"No, sir. She told me that she would have them put on at the station."

"And you've no notion at all where she may be?"

"None, sir . . . or I'd tell you directly."

Mr Scott looked about as if he expected to find an answer on the wallpaper.

"She tol' the cabbie, Waterloo."

Georgie, who now found the eyes of all the party firmly fixed on him, blushed right into his scalp for the second time that morning.

"Waterloo," he repeated. "You 'eard, mum, you was standin' right by the door."

"I do not recall," lied Lady Wheatley.

Mr Scott gave her a look of acute dislike and ran down the steps.

"Young man!" she called after him.

"I'm in a hurry, ma'am."

"I cannot let you go without an attempt to bring you to your senses. You tell me she has released you from your obligations. No blame will reflect on you if you accept that. You cannot marry a criminal's daughter without the most serious repercussions on you and your family . . . it would be a foolish act . . . foolish beyond permission . . ."

Mr Scott did not turn his head. He scrambled on to the box of his tilbury, told the groom to stand clear and drove off at a dangerous pace.

"High-nosed old dragon," he said between his teeth. "A home at Wheatley, indeed. As if I didn't know how she would be treated there. Wheatley is a bacon-headed place-hunter and she makes every penny a prisoner. I wouldn't want to go to Wheatley even as a guest. She'd be an unpaid servant . . ."

"Yessir," agreed the groom who had managed to scramble to his seat, but only just, "nice young lady, sir. Got a good head on her, wouldn't you say?"

Scott and his groom were used to discussing his most private affairs.

"I must find her. And hell and the devil confound it, I've only got four days. We sail for America on Monday."

"Yessir."

"I suppose she's engaged herself as a governess or a companion or some such thing," Scott speculated. "What else can she have done?"

"Yessir, watch that cart, sir. They'll be able to tell you at Waterloo which trains have left in the last hour or so, sir. And you can do wonders with the telegraph, these days, sir. Mind that dray, sir, he's turning right . . ."

As he made his hasty and hazardous way through the London traffic Oliver Scott's mind was not wholly on his driving for he knew very well what he was doing was no more than a chivalrous gesture. It had no substance. He could not marry Amelia if he did find her and there was no help she could expect from him unless it was a temporary refuge with his family until an agreeable position was to be had: and his mother was unlikely to make her welcome. He had left her in hysterics at the mere idea of his going in search of Amelia. His sister perhaps, if that stiff-rumped ass of a husband didn't cut up rough . . . but whatever he did it must end in the same way. Amelia was right. She always was. She was no longer the accomplished heiress who would ornament embassies abroad; she was penniless and bearing the stigma of a singularly unpleasant financial scandal. To marry her would be to commit professional suicide. In any event, he must marry money. He could not let his considerable affection for the girl affect this hard fact.

"Hell and the devil," he exclaimed again, "I can't just let her disappear without a word . . . it wouldn't be the thing at all, dammit!"

But the thought intruded persistently, perhaps it would be kinder; if he did find her she might think . . . while all he would be able to do would be to shake her by the hand and assure her of his lifelong friendship and for all the good that could do her . . . At that point his attention was recalled to his driving when the groom unceremoniously grabbed the reins to avoid a collision with an omnibus.

In any event their drive to Waterloo was wasted effort. As Amelia's cab trundled out of the square she had put her head out of the window.

"Driver!"

"Yes, miss?"

"I'm afraid I made a mistake, driver. I ought to have said Euston Station, not Waterloo. I am very sorry."

She withdrew her head and the driver, muttering that women was a curse, so they was, dunno where they're a-goin', don't care a button how they puts a bloke about, managed to turn his cab to the dismay of the traffic and head in the opposite direction.

21

2

"Good Counsel is above all Price."

From Bindleton to Blackyetts was a matter of some seven miles over a good road. Amelia covered this in a dog-cart drawn by a sluggish cob driven by Jem Matthews the second coachman. The cob was grass-fat and lazy and jibbed continually at the hills. Amelia thought Bindleton itself small, grimy and unattractive: five mill-chimneys sprouted high among the huddled blackened terraces and on the highest, picked out vertically in yellow bricks was the name, Hoggett. Jem jerked his head at it.

"That's ourn," he announced. "Hoggett, Cottons and Canvases. The rest on 'em's just small fry. Come *hup* ye . . ."

He bit off an adjective and smiled apologetically over his shoulder. Amelia smiled merrily back and Jem nodded in friendly style.

The road left the narrow, mean streets where unkempt women gossiped in groups on the doorsteps and stared inimically at the dog-cart; it climbed gradually, though not gradually enough for the cob, out of the hollow where the little town lay on either side of the black and stinking river and came to a tidy suburb of raw, new villas. Their gardens stared and pulsed with colour, geranium red, delphinium blue, glaring yellows and oranges which swore at the fresh bright brickwork and the red-tiled roofs. Unhappy little trees tethered to posts promised a more graceful and shady future. After this the road climbed steeply and the sweating cob snorted and whickered his displeasure.

"Should I get out and walk for a space?" Amelia enquired.

"Oh, no, miss. He's a lazy bug . . . beggar, this 'un. Needs the grease sweated off him. Come *hup*!"

The top of the hill opened up a fine vista of rolling, green, summer-lit country but the high-flowering hedges made it difficult for Amelia to see.

"Driver . . . driver!"

"Miss?"

"What's your name?"

"Matthews, miss. Jem Matthews. The young ladies and gentlemen calls me Jem, mostly. I has the drivin' of them."

"Then, Jem, do you think I might come and sit on the box beside you? I can't see at all from down here and I'm pining for a sight of the countryside."

"For sure, miss," he returned in pleased surprise.

He halted the cob who made no objection, and offered a hand when Amelia came to the box.

"Oh, but that is better," she said when they had set off again. "This is splendid country. I've been in London all this summer."

"You'll know a differ here, I wouldn't wonder," Jem observed.

"I hope so. London in the heat is intolerable."

The cob trotted sulkily along the flat road on the ridge. Jem gave this new miss a sidelong glance and decided to chance a question.

"Your last post in London, miss?"

He waited for the reaction. It was unexpectedly friendly.

"My home is . . . was there. This is my first post."

"Your first! Oh, mercy on us!" Jem exclaimed and then bit his lip. Amelia looked at him in surprise.

"Why . . . what is wrong with that?"

Jem glanced at her sideways again.

"If you'll pardon the liberty, miss . . . but this ain't no place to start out on teacherin'."

"Why ever not?"

"Miss, you don't know what's awaitin' up there. A right lot of little devils they are, beggin' your pardon, miss. You wouldn't credit the governesses they've 'ad. They comes and they goes reg'lar as Sunday. It's nobbut July and you're the fourth I've driven over this road since the New Year. T'Master's at his wits' end, so they say."

"Dear me," observed Amelia, rather faintly.

"Mr Booth, he's the butler, *he* says as how the Master told

23

the Mistress that you'd be able to do the trick like and we all thought you'd a bin teacherin' a longish while. But your first post . . ."

He shook his head doubtfully.

"Are the children so difficult?"

Jem's whistle and comic expression of dismay made Amelia chuckle.

"Miss, I promise you, they ain't no laughin' matter . . ."

"Tell me about them," she invited.

"If'n it ain't a liberty, miss. The last 'un, Miss Dymoke, parson's daughter she were and all on her high horse, like, she called me pert and forward when I tried to warn her. She didn't last the month. Down to the station for the midday train it was, and a veil over her face so's I couldn't see she been a-cryin'. A life of it, they'd led her, I promise you."

"I'd be grateful," Amelia assured him, "more than grateful . . ."

Jem cracked the whip a fraction of an inch from the cob's flank, just to remind him of his obligations.

"I dunno where to start, miss, I'm sure."

"But surely they can't all be as bad as you say?"

"No, miss. The two littl'uns, Miss Amy and Miss Jane, they're nice little critters. Mind they're young yet, four and six, I reckon. They're the missus's childer. She's the second Mrs Hoggett. Been married a matter o' seven year. Eighteen she were and him more'n thirty year older. But she were pleased enough by all 'counts."

"Then the others are her stepchildren?"

"Right, miss . . . six on 'em."

"Eight altogether," she commented, a little startled. Mr Hoggett had mentioned that she would have five pupils in all.

"Nine, near enough."

Jem glanced at her.

"Missus is in the straw again, if you'll pardon the expression, miss. That's for why we got this fat old slug, 'ere. The carriage pair's bein' kept at ready 'case we needs to fetch doctor in an 'urry. The month-nurse is there already and a fair termyjant, *she* is. Fights all day with Mrs Sands, the nurse. Lord, but the fur flies most days. Mrs Sands, she had

Master Staneley from the month and she stayed on for all the others. Oh, and proper tongue-pie she can bake, I tell you."

"Master Staneley's the eldest?"

"Sixteen past and a terror. Set on the army, he is. Fair haunts Harry Passmore in the garden askin' questions about the Roossian Wars. Harry's an old soldier, d'ye see, in the cavalry."

"Who comes after him?"

"Miss Louisa. Proper little horsewoman," Jem said admiringly. "Rides anything on four legs. She can drive too, like a right 'un. *She'd* not let this brute away with it, like I'm a-doin'."

The whip stung the cob out of the amble to which it had resorted while its driver was distracted.

"More like a lad than a lass, is Miss Lou. But the trouble is, miss, that you can't keep her out the stables. We see more of her than the schoolroom and her language . . . well, it's a bit ripe. We does our best but horses is contumacious critters, there's no denyin', and she hears what she shouldn't. Miss Dymoke was everlastin' at the door callin' her and Miss Lou'd hide in the hay-loft and tell us to say nowt."

"Are her sisters like her?"

"No, miss. Miss Alice's a pert pretty lass and a proper lady, but that set on her own way you wouldn't believe. Miss Dorcas . . ." He sighed. "Ah, well . . . she's different."

"How is she different?"

Jem shook his head. "If she'd been born in a cottage, miss, they'd call her a natural and ha' done. Ninepence in the shilling, that's what she is . . . but they'll not admit it, not they. Takes terrible tantrums, Mrs Sands says. Fits my mother'd call them."

A hoyden, thought Amelia, a pretty mule and a simpleton: Hoggett, Mr Hoggett, she corrected herself sternly, had been less than frank with her. Doubtless, he had thought that she would be unlikely to leave no matter what she found waiting for her.

"That leaves two . . . boys, aren't they?"

"Master Fred, he's all right, follows his brother like a tantony piglet in and out of trouble and more often in than out. But he's *navy*-mad. Ran off to Scarborough once to see a man-o'-war and didn't come back till daylight. Master was fit to be tied."

He glanced at her and found to his surprise that she was smiling.

"Mind, you'll not have owt to do with them terrors. There's a tutor for them. Mr Bethune. He don't live in, like. The Rector at Bindlewick's his father and he rides over most days from the Rectory. He's a likely one, Mr Bethune . . . he don't have much trouble." Jem's expression indicated that he had reservations about the tutor, but if he did he wasn't going to say what they were. "'Ceptin' with Master Albert," he added.

"I understand Master Albert is something of an invalid?"

Jem didn't answer at once but his goodnatured face looked grim.

"Not bed-rid . . . crippled like," he said and then burst into speech. "Crook-backed and bad-hearted, miss. I'll not hide my teeth. He's a real bad'un"

"Surely not? How old is he . . . eleven, isn't it?" asked Amelia, rather shocked at the dislike in Jem's description.

"Miss, I reckon folks is like horses . . . every now and then you gets a rogue and there's no doing anythin' with un. Master Albert were crippled at birth, like. There was a carriage accident, before my time it were, over by Bindlewick, and his ma, she were thrown out and fell badly, so the bairn came a month before his time. His ma died, God rest her, the poor lady, and Master, he couldn't look at the babby. You'd think the critter knowed it for he grew up just wicked and no one able to beat the badness out of him, he was that feeble and twisted. Now, Master Staneley, he'd shame the devil with his tricks but he don't mean no harm, miss, and nor don't Master Fred. But that Albert . . . miss, he'd do you a mischief for to pleasure himself."

Jem was a talkative man, given the opportunity, and Amelia, very willing to give him the opportunity, learned a great deal about the household of which she was about to make part. The father, she discovered, spent little time with the family; much of the year he was away on his travels, for Hoggett's Cottons and Canvases were sold the wide world over, thanks mostly to the efforts of Mr Hoggett.

"He was expectin' Master Staneley to follow him into the

business but I reckon he's given up the idea. Master Staneley, he don't want nothing but the army and Master Fred's the same 'cept that it's the navy he's set on . . ."

Jem was uncharacteristically reticent about Mrs Hoggett, barring the comment that she'd been a rare pretty lass, but it appeared that when not about to give birth she was considered to be the shining light of Bindleton Society and rarely spent an evening at home.

"Speak as I find," said Jem, "I've never 'ad a cross word but then I don't set eyes on her from one week's end to the next 'ceptin' she's a notion to take the young ladies for a drive. But they do say in the Hall as how she's rare and hard to please."

They turned in at the wrought-iron gates, the cob scenting his stable and for the first time picking up his feet, and Jem negotiated the turn into the gravelled sweep.

"That's Mr Bethune on the steps," he mentioned.

The house was vast. It had been built some ten years earlier in the fashionable Gothic style and was bedizened with turrets and battlements and arrow-slits. The windows were heavily leaded inside elaborate stone tracery and the porch before which they had drawn up resembled a game pie, so crenellated and machicolated it was. Amelia, surveying the imposing stone frontage with a mixture of admiration and amusement, caught a brief glimpse of faces at a turret window. They vanished as soon as she looked at them directly. She then turned her gaze on Mr Bethune, waiting to greet her and hand her down from the dog-cart. He presented a somewhat incongruous appearance in the midst of all those gothic splendours: he was slight, no taller than herself, and dressed as fashionably as any of her acquaintance in London. 'Either his father has money,' Amelia thought, 'or Hoggett pays him very much more than he means to pay me. He couldn't dress like that on eighty pounds a year and washing . . . ' She accepted his hand and alighted nimbly from the box.

"Miss Lester, I understand. A great pleasure to meet you . . . a great pleasure."

Mr Bethune regarded her appreciatively and kept hold of her hand just a little too long. Amelia withdrew it and smiled.

"Mrs Hoggett has requested me to make you welcome,"

he continued. "She is indisposed for the moment . . . rarely leaves her room. She does not find herself well enough to see you tonight. I trust you understand?"

"Very well," said Amelia. "I understand there is a happy event impending."

Mr Bethune looked taken aback.

"Did Hoggett mention . . ."

"Mr Hoggett said something of the kind," she agreed.

"Hoggett has no delicacy," he observed, "though I suppose the whole countryside knows that it is impending . . . it has been impending this fortnight and more. We are beginning to wonder whether the creature will be like Richard III, a whole year . . . impending."

He gave her a bold glance to see how she took this sally and then picked up her dressing case and motioned her towards the steps. When she paused at the top of the flight and looked back she found him examining the case with interest.

"An elegant piece," he approved. "Russia leather and gilt. Very pretty, upon my word."

'Too pretty for a governess' was the implication and Amelia did not miss it. Nor did Mr Bethune miss the discrepancy of initials.

"A.B.," he observed. "Is your name not Lester?"

"It is a keepsake," she mentioned and smiled again.

As she waited for him to join her at the top of the steps she realised she had taken rather a dislike to him and wondered why. He was not unhandsome in a smooth polished style as if he daily practised his smile in the looking-glass. His eyes were hazel, almost green, rather protuberant and wide-set; plentiful whiskers disguised, to some extent, a long narrow jaw but did not cover a small mouth, very red and full. He turned away and handed the case to a maid who was hovering at the foot of the impressive staircase.

"Baxter is the schoolroom maid," he said. "She will look after you. Show Miss Lester to her room, Baxter. And now, I have duties I must perform before dinner, Miss Lester. I will see you again then."

He bowed perfunctorily and hurried away towards a door from behind which a noise of argument verging on mayhem was faintly to be heard. Baxter, elderly and a little untidy, bobbed a curtsy and scuttled upstairs. The inside of Blackyetts was even more imposing than the outside; there was an overpowering impression of opulence, fumed oak and stained glass. The doors were carved in linenfold and framed in pointed gothic arches and there seemed to be a great many of them. Baxter, with an occasional anxious glance over her shoulder, led her along a dark thickly carpeted corridor. At the end of it was yet another gothic arch and another carved door.

"This is the young ladies' wing, miss. Your room's on this floor. The schoolroom's below and the young ladies has rooms up there."

'Up there' was a spiral staircase built into a smaller turret. A shuffle and a stifled giggle suggested that the young ladies were just out of sight on the first twist. Amelia followed Baxter into her room. It was not large and, compared to what she had seen of the rest of the house, rather sparsely furnished. Baxter laid the case reverently on the dressing chest.

"Miss Amy and Miss Jane are with Nurse in the nursery," Baxter informed her. "Mrs Sands' compliments and she would be happy if you would care to join her for nursery tea in fifteen minutes."

The inspection continues, thought Amelia, and smiled a little.

"Shall I come and take you along, miss?"

"I would be very glad, Baxter. It seems such a maze."

At once the maid relaxed and tittered a little.

"Oh, it isn't once you knows it, miss. It's like a box, see."

She went to the narrow window. Evidently the architect had expected attack even from the interior of his castle. With some difficulty they both leant into the space. It overlooked a large enclosed courtyard.

"That side's the front with the drawing-rooms and parlours and that. Then this bit's the schoolroom and the young ladies. There's another tower place just like it and that's the Master and the Mistress. Them's guestrooms and the young gentlemen and on this side it's Mrs Sands' nurseries. You'll soon find your way around, miss."

"Thank you, Baxter. You're very helpful."

There was slight surprise in her voice. Amelia knew from her own governess that the servants did not always treat governesses well.

"A pleasure, miss, I'm sure. There's hot water and that over here in the corner. Matthews will be up with your trunks and I'll be back in a jiffy and take you along."

She went, leaving Amelia to sort out her impressions and wash her hands and face clean of the dirt from the long train journey, and make use of 'that'.

Very much later, in the high narrow bed with a huge moon peering in through the arrow-slit, Amelia lay and reviewed her first evening as an employee. Nursery tea had been something of an ordeal. Nurse had been terse; not quite hostile but with judgement very much reserved. Amelia had addressed her as Mrs Sands (Baxter had delicately indicated this preference) and admired her arrangements which were indeed admirable. Amy and Jane had proved delightful, eagerly friendly and restrained from monopolising her attention only by Mrs Sands' occasional sharp rebuke. Louisa had made an appearance, still in her habit and smelling faintly but unmistakeably of the stable. She had been unable to talk about anything but her mare, Coppertop, her breeding, about which she was unexpectedly knowledgeable (Amelia, no parsonage miss, was a little surprised at the extent of her knowledge and wondered what Miss Dymoke's reaction had been to this talk of dams and sires and the duties of stallions), her performance and her health. She spoke directly to Amelia only once.

"Do you ride, Miss Lester?"

"I do."

"Oh . . . how unusual. All the others were frightened of horses, silly creatures."

It was plain she did not believe a word.

Amelia enquired for Dorcas. Mrs Sands replied briefly that she had been sent to bed and would not be introduced to Miss Lester till the morning.

"Thank goodness for that," Alice had observed, speaking for the first time. She had not acknowledged the presence of the new governess at all and had read an impressively large tome during the entire repast. Amelia, stealing a glance at the title, was amused to discover that it was Volume II of the Encyclopaedia Britannica.

"That will do, Miss Alice," Mrs Sands had said fiercely.

"Well, it's much nicer to have tea without having to look at her chewing with her mouth open and dropping things from her mouth . . . ugh! She's in bed because she had a tantrum. I told her the new governess was coming today and she had a tantrum right away. Dorrie doesn't like governesses. She's so stupid they can't teach her anything."

"Then I'll look forward to meeting her tomorrow," Amelia said hastily, forestalling a tirade from the nurse.

"It'll be the last time when you will look forward to meeting Dorrie," sneered Alice and went back to her book. "She is the most dreadful nuisance."

"She wets herself . . . and she's older than me . . . " Jane had announced smugly and was promptly dismissed from the company for such vulgarity. Louisa then announced her intention of seeing if the boys were released from their lessons and departed without ceremony. Shrieks from the courtyard indicated that she had encountered her brothers and that they were throwing sticks for the dogs under the windows of their indisposed stepmother.

"Out of hand, that one," was Mrs Sands' sour comment. Amelia quailed slightly at the thought of trying to tame such an Amazon. Louisa was a strapping girl, nearly six feet tall and strong as one of her beloved horses.

Before dinner she had paid a visit to the schoolroom and found it unexpectedly wanting. There was a battered globe which would not turn in its frame, a shelf of equally abused books, half of which lacked spines and the other half lacked pages. They were scribbled upon, too, and the pages grimy and dog-eared. There were none of the books which had been used in her own schoolroom. The slates piled on a broad window seat (the architect had evidently not expected the ground floor of his castle to be attacked) were chipped and useless and the slate-pencils reduced to stubs. Amelia, discouraged, turned to the piano. She was, she knew, expected to instruct them all in the elements of music. This was going to be difficult on an instrument which was out of tune and had four dumb notes. In one drawer lay an inextricably tangled mass of embroidery silks and wools and a number of uncompleted pieces of embroidery, blood-spotted and unappetising.

In another were drifts of pencil drawings and water-colour sketches, crude and unskilful for the most part, except for a strange vision of the house looking overweighted with its top hamper of turrets and battlements. The colours were strangely chosen but were direct and powerful. Another, by the same hand, depicted a carriage accident and had the same disquieting combination of grimness and comicality. These she propped up on the chimney piece to cheer the dismal room and wondered which of the succession of governesses had done them. Other drawers contained nothing of use: the furniture was stained, scarred and uncomfortable and like the rest of the room needed a thorough cleaning. As for the carpet, better none at all than the greasy rag which lay underfoot thick with crumbs well trodden in and other marks and stains. It even smelled as evil as it appeared. Amelia's nostrils curled and she marvelled that such a room could exist in a house where, it was plain, money had been lavished on the other apartments.

However, the grimmest memory of what had been a discouraging introduction to the household was her first meeting with Albert. Amelia had found him in her bedroom. She had gone there to dress for dinner and her heart had leaped in her breast when she saw him investigating the closet, fingering the clothes which she had hung there. When she came in he had done no more than glance casually over his shoulder at her and shut the closet door. He had then limped towards her looking at her as if she were a botanical specimen. He was mouse-coloured and unremarkable except for his slightly hunched shoulder and the inturned leg . . . and the expression on his face which was compounded of contempt and malevolence. Until this encounter Amelia had thought that Jem Matthews had been exaggerating when he spoke of Albert.

"I'm Master Albert," he had announced. "You have to do as I say because I am sickly. I killed my mother. I expect they told you. They always do."

"Good evening, Albert," she had managed to say calmly. "Have you a commission to inspect my wardrobe?"

32

"I always do," he replied indifferently. "Clothes tell you lots of things. All kinds of things. You've got a great many for a governess."

"How many should I have?" she asked.

This rejoinder brought no response but an edged, narrow-eyed look.

"Was this simply a visit of inspection, or did you have a message?"

"I don't carry messages to servants," he told her arrogantly.

"Then, leave at once. I wish to change for dinner," she told him.

"Don't give me orders. I take orders from nobody."

Amelia, her heart beating like a drum with anger and dislike, took him firmly by the narrow shoulders and marched him to the door. In the corridor he turned and looked at her, small and deformed, but with an aura of resentment and animosity which chilled her to the bone.

"Your gowns are too fine," he told her. "Stepmother won't let you wear them."

Amelia said nothing but turned back to go into the room.

"She made one of them wear a tucker right up to the neck. She told the other to take the flowers off her bonnet."

With that lowering pronouncement he had taken himself off.

Amelia lay awake for some time. She made a determined effort to compose herself for sleep by making plans. On her bedside table lay a long list of requests which she intended to lay before Mr Hoggett at the first opportunity. These ranged from a formidable number of books to a length of cotton cloth. She had decided that embroidery could wait upon plain sewing and the first enterprise would be new curtains for the schoolroom window. As she drifted at last into sleep she spared a thought for Cousin Emily, wondering where she and Lord Wheatley had finally laid their heads. Of Oliver Scott she determinedly did not think at all which, in view of the intensity of the enquiries he was making for her despite the protests of his parents, was a little unfair.

In the Servants' Hall over a final nightcap the verdict was being handed down:

"This one's a proper lady," Baxter opined. "She don't try to make you feel low. Got such a nice smile."

"She won't stay no more than any of the rest of them," Mrs Lucas, the housekeeper, said. "Blackyetts is no place for a proper lady. Such ongoings."

"In my opinion," said Mr Booth, the butler, "she is the most likely yet. I was most favourably impressed by the way she went on at the dinner table. Miss Louisa kept in her place but in the pleasantest fashion . . ."

"What? No 'orse-shit with the roast?" asked Jem irrepressibly.

"Matthews!" reproved Mrs Lucas while Cook bellowed with laughter.

"Indeed, she kept the conversation in quite unexceptional channels," the butler continued. "Even Master Staneley stopped shouting and didn't gulp his food down like a starving lion. Mr Bethune allows him too much licence at table but Miss Lester sets an example."

"It's early days," Mrs Sands said. "New brooms sweep clean. Her dresses are too fine. Whoever heard of a governess in a blue taffeta gown?"

"Well, well," sighed Mrs Lucas. "Let us hope for the best, for the children will be spoiled beyond recall if someone doesn't take them in hand."

"She's too pretty for the Mistress, I'll lay," Cook broke in. "If that Mr Bethune as much as casts an eye her way she'll have her down the road in two shakes of a lamb's tail. See if she don't!"

A series of speaking glances were exchanged. Cook was, as they all knew, prone to vulgarity. She was also prone to hit the mark.

3

"Redeem misspent time by industry."

It was plain from the beginning of the first morning's lessons that Amelia was not going to find the education of the Misses Hoggett an easy matter. All her predecessors appeared to have been able to do was to eliminate the provincial accent from their speech. They were not accustomed to regular hours and they did not intend to become so. Louisa declared that books and sewing and music were all so much 'fuss and feathers'. She didn't care for them and didn't expect to need them. She intended, she said, never to marry but to live at home and breed horses. Coppertop the incomparable was to be the foundation of a stud farm.

"Who'd want to marry me?" she demanded scornfully and Alice muttered that there weren't many brave enough or tall enough, come to that, but Amelia pretended not to hear.

"I don't mean to pretend to be silly and feeble and fluttery just to snare a husband . . ."

Amelia bit her lip at such an idea.

"I don't care for men anyway. They laugh at you if you want to try anything real and think you're just silly for wanting to try. They're toads most of them and I just don't see why all girls are on the catch for them."

"Wouldn't you like to have children?" asked Amelia gently.

"Pooh," said Louisa, "I'd rather have a foal, any day . . . much prettier and much less trouble. Did you know, Miss Lester, they can walk and run almost the very minute they're born?"

There was a chorus of protest at this heresy from her

youngest sisters while Alice said primly, "All *proper* ladies dote on children."

"Then I know a goodish few who ain't very proper," Louisa retorted. "They never take much to do with their children. Even their very own."

The younger children frowned in puzzlement.

"And my Coppertop won't make all this to-do before she drops her foal," Louisa continued defiantly. "She won't lie down all day with the blinds drawn and eat nothing but soup and jelly and chicken and get people to wait on her hand and foot, write her letters, even . . ."

"Hold your tongue, Lou," snapped Alice and glared at her.

"Well, nor she will . . ."

Amelia ended the silence which greeted this revealing interlude by observing in what she realised were depressingly gubernatorial tones, that horses were indeed peerless creatures and Louisa was far from being the first to think so. Had she read Shakespeare on the subject, or Dean Swift? Louisa shied violently at the name of Shakespeare but the Dean struck a chord, even for Louisa.

"Ain't he the Lilliput fellow?" she suggested.

"Gulliver visited the Houyhnhnms, too," Amelia informed her. "That was a country inhabited entirely by horses."

Louisa stared her disbelief. Amelia, striking while the iron, if not hot, was at least slightly malleable, produced a copy of *Gulliver's Travels* which she had purloined from the library earlier. It was splendidly bound but as she was tolerably certain that the pages had never been cut she handed it, together with her own ivory paper-knife, to an open-mouthed Louisa, recalling as she did so certain passages which might be . . . but it was doubtful if even Dean Swift could shock Louisa.

"See what you think of that."

"Now?" protested Louisa. "They're trying out a new cob this morning . . ."

"Now," Amelia told her firmly. "Afterwards you shall write a letter to the author saying how you like the book."

"Shall I?"

"Yes."

Louisa glanced down discontentedly at the volume and her

eye was caught by a splendid engraving of a horse, cunningly displayed by Amelia. She pouted but sat down on the window seat and began to read, tracing the lines with one, rather grimy, forefinger and mouthing the words silently.

"Dean Swift is dead," Alice announced acidly when Amelia turned her attention to her. "He died mad in 1753. How can Lou write to him?"

"Easily enough. By the exercise of a little imagination," Amelia replied politely. "I shall discover whether she has any and, incidentally, whether she can write a letter."

Alice made a face.

"And now, what about you?"

"You have no call to bother yourself about me," stated Alice loftily. "I mean to educate myself. I need no assistance that you can give."

"Well . . . how very laudable. Tell me, have you a plan for this exercise?"

"I intend to read as widely as I can. Father told me I might read anything in the library . . . except the books in the locked cabinet."

Amelia looked suitably impressed.

"And may I enquire whether you propose to write extracts of these books or anything of that nature?"

"I write novels and poetry," Alice returned.

"I look forward to reading them."

"They're private," Alice said indignantly.

"You do not intend to give them to the world?"

"No . . ."

"How very singular. You are quite unlike any writer I have ever met. They all thirst for publication."

"I don't believe you have met any," said Alice rudely.

"Why not?"

"Governesses don't know people like that."

"Why should they not?"

"Because," snapped Alice irritably, "if they did they wouldn't be governesses."

Amelia chuckled, which did nothing to soothe Alice.

"What would they be, then?"

"Proper people . . . people like us."

Amelia laughed aloud.

"I'm afraid your scheme of education has not been too

successful, so far," she observed. "You will write me a description of what you consider to be a well-educated woman."

"Why should I?"

"Because it would amuse me to read it."

Alice glared at her.

"How do you know it would?"

"I don't of course," Amelia admitted. "Not until I have read it . . . and you have written it."

"I promise you," Alice spat at her, "you won't be amused . . . not a bit!"

Amelia presented her with a sheet of paper, a pen and a bottle of ink.

"There. Now, strive not to amuse me."

Alice took the pen and dipped into the ink with great energy.

"*Dîtes-moi, petite, est-ce que ton idée de l'éducation n'inclut pas l'enseignement de la langue française?* "

Alice looked blank.

"Evidently not," said Amelia and repeated the question in German and Italian with just as negative a response.

"Your previous governesses did not try to teach you any languages?"

"We learned verbs and things."

Amelia winced.

"I see. Well, continue your essay."

Alice's pen flew untidily over the paper, interrupted only when its holder cast a baleful glance at Amelia.

Jane and Amy were easy to deal with: the new governess's prettiness and good humour had won their hearts immediately. Anything she asked they were ready to perform. Jane was set to make pothooks on a piece of paper which Amelia had ruled for her the night before. Amy was set on to a copy provided by Amelia from a book discovered on the schoolroom bookshelf. It was compendiously entitled *The Young Woman's Companion in all her Social Relations Embracing Practical Instructions in Plain and Ornamental Needlework, Letter Writing, Sick-Room Management, Dress and Clothing, House Furnishing, gardening, etiquette and every other variety of household economy in the nursery, Kitchen and Parlour with Copious Notes of the Months, Complete History of Domestic*

Manufactures, Moral and Religious Readings in Prose and Poetry and Four Hundred Golden Rules of Life. These Golden Rules appeared at the head of every page so that a homily on Early Rising might be prefaced by the Rule, 'An Evil Lesson is soon learned', or 'Time and Thinking tame the Strongest Grief' preface a detailed description of how to instruct a servant to blacklead a grate. Amelia had smiled a little at it but pressed it into service as the only book on the shelf which she was prepared to handle. She chose the Golden Rule 'Be What You Seem to Be' and wrote it in an elegant formal script at the head of a piece of paper and set Amy to rule lines so that she might copy it. Amy was pleased enough and began work with a ruler and her tongue peeping from her mouth. Alice looked up from her scrawling to remark ill-naturedly,

"The babies have slates."

"Amy is not a baby and she is going to have paper," Amelia told her. "This way she can keep her copies and see what progress she makes."

Alice muttered something cutting about waste and returned with redoubled zeal to her unamusing essay. Amelia then turned her attention to Dorcas who had been staring motionless at the pictures propped on the chimney piece. The child was, frankly, an unattractive sight; she was lumpy and squat, not quite deformed, her face fat, sallow and pallid at the same time and framed in thin, greasy hair scraped back into a tight skinny braid. Her eyes were a very pale blue and had a curiously opaque look; much of the time she seemed to be looking at something which no one else could see. It made her an eerily uncomfortable companion. The shapeless nose was running and the mouth hung open with a string of saliva hanging from it. Amelia stifled a feeling of distaste and produced a handkerchief. Dorcas endured the mopping up as if it were being done to someone else and kept her pale gaze, all the while, on the pictures.

"Mine," she said in a deep, hoarse little voice. "Mine."

Amelia couldn't believe her ears.

"You'd like to have them, Dorcas?" she enquired.

"Mine," Dorcas said again. "House. Carr'age. Mine."

"Did you draw them?"

"Mine . . . " the child nodded frantically.

Alice looked up again, disgust in her face.

"She drew them. She's always scribbling away at drawing, wasting good paper and paint. *I* think they're quite dreadful . . . but it keeps her quiet. She isn't fit to learn anything proper."

Amelia turned on the elder girl with a surge of anger which surprised her.

"Don't ever speak of your sister in such a way again! And certainly not in front of her. You've made her cry."

Alice shrugged and sneered.

"She doesn't understand. She's an idiot. Even you must be able to see that."

"An idiot couldn't do this. They're the . . ."

"They're ridiculous. An ape could draw better."

"You're wrong. They are strange, certainly, but . . ."

"Well, they make me feel queasy," Alice said viciously. "And they'd make all normal people queasy. Just look at her . . . she makes me queasy too, horrid drooling ugly *creature*. She shouldn't be allowed in here with us."

"Take your work to your bedroom," Amelia said quietly. "Don't come back till you've finished it . . . and written it out in a fair copy. I won't read that scrawl."

Dorcas had collapsed on to the floor in a curious, boneless squatting posture, rocking to and fro, her whole fist thrust into her mouth and the tears pouring down her cheeks.

"Why should I?" Alice demanded indignantly. "I didn't say anything that wasn't true. She *shouldn't* be here. Step-mama says so herself. You can't teach her anything, you're here to teach me and the others. Send *her* away."

"You will go to your room," Amelia stated in a voice which hinted menacingly at the eruption of fury, raging within her. "I loathe and detest wanton cruelty. I do not wish to be in the same room as you, nor do I want you near your sisters until you understand what you are doing and saying. You are a most undesirable model for them. Please, go away this instant."

The contempt in that last command burned Alice like acid. She looked around at her sisters, expecting support, but Amy and Jane, taking their cue from Amelia looked at her in silent condemnation and Louisa sprawled ungracefully on the window-seat, one foot on the floor and the other jammed against the side of the seat, looked up and said, "Miss is right. You enjoy being nasty to Dorrie and that's what's disgusting, not poor old Dorrie. She can't help dribbling. It's you makes her have tantrums. Poor little beggar. She's all right when you leave her alone."

Alice stared round as if unable to believe such treachery, left her pen and paper on the table and rushed from the room sobbing.

"I say, Miss Lester . . . this book, eh? It's a goer, ain't it? I mean *horses* running things. They're *good*. They're not spiteful, eh? Like Alice. *He* thinks horses are better than people and *I* think he's right."

"Now that does please me," said Amelia. "You can't think what pleasure it gives to introduce someone to a really good book and see them enjoying it."

"My Coppertop would have been a splendid Queen Hou . . . houn . . ." Louisa went on. "I can just see her. This man ought to have met her. Will you come and see her, this afternoon? She's the sweetest creature, gentle as a lamb. If you really can ride I'll let you ride her . . . if you like. And I'll have a go on the new cob."

Amelia, valuing this offer at its true worth, expressed her delight at such an honour and saw Louisa return to the Houyhnhnms. It took little time to comfort the downcast Dorcas and set her to work upon a drawing. Amelia was determined to *see* her draw. She still could not quite believe that Dorcas had done those strangely skilful pictures. Louisa helped by demanding, 'a picture of the King Horse and the Queen Horse and mind you make the Queen a chestnut like my Coppertop'. Amelia watched incredulously as Dorcas meekly agreed to this request and, tongue protruding, began to draw with a confidence and directness which seemed to have nothing to do with the gross ugly girl who held the pencil. The word 'possession' jerked into Amelia's mind and was instantly suppressed.

"Was Dorcas always . . . like this?" she asked Louisa very quietly some twenty minutes later when there was a lull in the demands on her from Amy and Jane. Louisa put the book down and frowned, then she shook her head uncertainly.

"Mama . . . our real mama, took Dorrie in the carriage to

see Grandmama at Bindlewick. The coachman got drunk with Grandpa's man and the carriage overturned on the way home. Mama was hurt and Albert came much too soon. Mama died afterwards and Albert was never right. I think it began then."

"Was Dorrie hurt?"

"They said not," Louisa said. "But after that she got different and kept staring at things and having fi—tantrums. Before the accident I think she was just like the rest of us. But I was only four . . . I don't remember very well. One of the horses had to be shot."

She sighed.

"It was a horrid time, Miss Lester, I don't like to think about it. Papa couldn't bear to see us. He used to come into the nursery and then he'd cry . . . then he started to go away and stay away for weeks and weeks at a time. After he married stepmama we thought he might stay with us more . . . but he didn't, not for long."

Amelia patted her hand and they sat watching Dorcas drawing.

"No coachman of mine will be allowed to touch liquor," Louisa said fiercely.

"She shall draw as much as she likes," Amelia decided. "Later I shall try her with her letters again."

"Nan won't approve," Louisa confided.

"Why ever not?"

"Nan will have it that there's nothing wrong with Dorrie. She says she's just the same as the rest of us but a little slow. How she *can* say such things. She has to change her three or four times a day, you know. In fact, it's probably time . . . oooh, I'm sorry . . ."

"Why?"

"The others didn't like me talking about chambers and privies and manure. You'd have thought we didn't have to go at all."

"Well, I'm grateful," Amelia said. "I'd have been more grateful if you'd mentioned it half an hour ago."

A pool had spread over the boards below the chair where Dorcas sat. The state of the banished carpet was now explained. As if at a signal Mrs Sands knocked at the door and came in without a bidding.

42

"Miss Amy, Miss Jane, time for your milk. Miss Dorrie, dear, you'd best come too. Oh, Miss Lester, she's been at that dratted scribbling again: she did ought to be learning her letters and figures like the others. And where is Miss Alice, may I ask?"

"Gone 'way," grunted Dorcas and nodded emphatically. "Gone 'way. Bad."

Mrs Sands looked enquiringly at Amelia but it was Amy scrambling down from her stool who answered.

"Alice was nasty to Dorrie and Miss Lester sent her away. Miss Lester thinks Dorrie's very good at drawing, don't you, Miss Lester?"

"I do, indeed," Amelia agreed.

Mrs Sands sniffed suspiciously but softened unrecognisably when Dorrie beamed up at her.

"Nice," Dorrie said and pointed her pencil at Amelia. "Pretty."

"Hmmm. Handsome is," said Mrs Sands inevitably, "as handsome does. I'll send Baxter over to mop up, Miss Lester."

She looked at Louisa reading in the window-seat.

"And if you've kept Miss Louisa at her books for a whole morning, you're doing none so ill at that."

Basking in this qualified approval Amelia went in search of Alice. Alice, it proved, had not gone to her room. She had gone instead to the library where she knew her brothers would be (or should be) having their lessons. There, in the accustomed absence of the tutor, she poured out her woes.

"Dorrie *is* an idiot," she stated tearfully. "She *is*. What's wrong with telling the truth? The bible says the truth shall make you free."

Frederick had been unsympathetic.

"There's truth and truth," he said "And in any case, no need to whack people over the napper with the truth. And Dorrie isn't quite an idiot, you know. Not like that horrid beastly *thing* that begs outside the station."

"Oh, Fred, she *is*!" Alice insisted hotly. "You don't have to be in the same room the way we do. She stares and makes funny noises and dribbles and . . . oh, worse than that . . . you don't *know*!"

43

"Dorrie knows what people are saying to her," Fred said. "And you say horrid beastly things. I've heard you."

"It's that Miss Lester that says horrid things!" cried Alice. "I hate her already. I'm going to get father to send her away."

"He won't," Staneley said, looking up from a very much crossed-out translation.

"He will if I ask him," Alice replied, conscious of her powers of persuasion. "He sent Miss Goole away, didn't he? And Miss Flower, and that awful Mamsell that didn't even speak proper English . . . and Miss Dymoke."

"None of them were the slightest use anyway," Fred put in bluntly. "The schoolroom was always in an uproar."

"Because of you mostly," added Staneley and scoffed when Alice burst into tears all over again. "See? You don't much like the truth either."

"I think you're mean beasts! You have someone nice, down here, and he lets you do just as you like but we have to endure this horrid creature."

"If this Miss Thingmajig has got your measure," Fred observed shrewdly, "Papa won't turn her off – not just before he goes to America."

"And you're just a scrubby little pig!" she stormed. "You wait! If papa won't do it, I'll get stepmama to do it instead!"

She ran out of the room and took refuge in the depressing apartment at the back of the house, known as the sewing-room for no very good reason except that sewing was done in almost any other room. There she had a store of books in the back of a cupboard and she forgot the injustice of her banishment in considering the vicissitudes of *Sylvia's Lovers*.

When Amelia by enquiry tracked her as far as the library she found Staneley and Frederick had abandoned all pretence of lessons and were playing battledore and shuttlecock over the table with a book apiece and a screwed up ball of paper. Amelia watched from the door half-smiling at their skill: it was a skill which argued considerable practice. The shuttle-cock flew her way. She caught it deftly and unfolded it to reveal several false starts at a Latin exercise. She screwed it up again and tossed it back to the players.

"Probably the most appropriate use for that," she said. "Has your sister, Alice, been in here?"

Staneley and Frederick looked at one another and a faint wink was exchanged. It was a situation to which they were accustomed. Amelia caught this as readily as she had caught the shuttlecock.

"Alice?" mused Staneley, as if he had never heard the name before. "Alice . . . ?"

He stared around as if she might be concealed somewhere and the two brothers began hunting around, opening cupboards, lifting the heavy chenille cover on the table and peering behind the books on the shelves. Amelia watched them straightfaced for the time it took for them to weary of this pantomime.

"Behind the clock?" she suggested solemnly. "Under the desk?"

Earnestly they both converged on the desk: this was a huge piece of furniture with a glassfronted book-case above it, full of bound ledgers, and below a ponderous knee-hole writing table with a column of drawers on either side. At it, perched on a large edition of the Complete Works of William Shakespeare, sat Albert working at his sums. With a whoop Staneley lifted him high into the air while Frederick crawled right under the desk and emerged shaking his head mournfully.

"Leave me alone!" Albert protested shrilly, "put me down this instant!"

Dumped again with scant respect on to the calf-bound bard, he glared viciously at them and the by-now laughing Amelia.

"She'll be in the sewing-room, reading rubbishy novels," he spat out. Amelia raised her eyebrows and after a glance at his work which he covered with insolent deliberation she left him alone. The other two followed her back to the table which was littered with their abandoned books. She considered these in silence for a few moments while they fidgeted. Albert watched malevolently.

"You know, Albert should be working at the table. There's too little light over there without a lamp. He'll strain his eyes."

"Then I'll be blind as well as crooked," Albert told them. "And it'll be their fault. I can't do anything over there with two great oafs prancing about."

"Little toad," remarked Frederick, without heat.

"Where is Mr Bethune?" Amelia enquired.

There was no immediate answer.

"Well?"

"He's writing letters," Staneley said, considering his boots.

"Oh, I see," Amelia said and turned to go. Frederick, rather belatedly, scrambled to open the door for her.

"Upstairs," came from the desk and Amelia hesitated.

"In stepmother's boudoir," Albert added. "Like he always is."

"Stepmother," Staneley explained awkwardly, "has a large correspondence."

Albert gave vent to an odd sound which could have passed for a laugh and applied himself once more to the Rule-of-Three.

"If he trusts you to work on your own," Amelia suggested gently, "perhaps you had better not take advantage of his absence."

The two elder boys looked at one another.

"He don't mind much what we do," Frederick assured her. "Really. He'll set us stuff to do before he . . ."

"Takes French leave," Albert put in.

"But he won't get in a wax if we don't do it. And if we do and it's wrong . . ."

"And it usually is," said Albert.

"If it is, he just laughs . . ."

"If he's won," Albert said, "if he's lost he don't laugh much."

Frederick slapped a large grimy hand over Albert's mouth and held it there despite all his wrigglings and clawings.

"Don't take any notice of him, please," Staneley begged, "we do work quite a bit, really we do . . ."

Albert jerked free of Frederick's hand.

"He don't give a button whether they work or not," he jeered. "He says they're ape-ignorant and so they are. All they think of is soldiers and ships and uniforms and fighting. Stupid stuff."

Amelia began to wonder how it was Albert had survived as long as he had.

"Hold your tongue," Staneley snapped, "or I'll box your ears again."

"Father will beat you," Albert told him and put out his tongue.

"Wanting to be a soldier or a sailor is nothing to be ashamed of," Amelia said. "What do you want to be, Albert?"

He stared at her scornfully.

"Why should I tell you?" he returned, his lips in a thin, unchildlike line.

"He'll make a fine toad in a drain," Frederick suggested, "or a freak in a circus."

"Oh, leave the little blighter alone," said Staneley uneasily.

"Whatever I decide to do I'll show you two something," Albert burst out. "When you're strutting about in your fancy uniforms with empty pockets I'll be *somebody*, you'll see! Brains are better than brawn. And don't you come begging to me for you won't get a penny. Not a penny!"

The two older boys laughed at his intensity.

"I hate you!" Albert shouted and scrambled down from his perch. "I hate you till it hurts. You make me feel sick I hate you so much!"

He lurched to the door, his pale face twisted with anger, and stared up at Amelia.

"And I hate you too. I'll get you sent off like all the others. You see if I don't!"

However, that evening the prospect of dismissal seemed very distant. Mr Hoggett came home in the middle of the afternoon, noted a good deal with his darting, narrow, deepsunk eyes, so like Albert's; he made a number of searching enquiries and then summoned Amelia to the library not long after dinner.

"Sit down, Miss Lester. Now, tell me, what do you think? Will you stay?"

Amelia sat very straight with her hands folded in her lap.

"As to that, as you know very well, Mr Hoggett, I have very little choice."

He nodded.

"I daresay, but if you'd not made a fist of it today I'd have found you another place quicker than winking. Now . . . you'll have no trouble wi' t'girls, I allow. Our Lou's decided for you, and Amy and Jane, and I reckon you can stand owt young Alice throws your way."

He got up and stood with his back to the fireplace.

"But there's Dorrie. Now, she has me in a right puzzle to know what to do for t'best. My wife, she's for sending her off. She's got the name of a place where she'll be cared for right and kind-like. But, I'll not bite me tongue, Miss Lester, I don't like the notion above half. She's flesh and blood when all's said and my flesh and blood at that and I don't rightly care to have her live out her life amongst strangers. Come now . . . you're looking at the lass wi' a stranger's eye . . . what d'ye say?"

"After one day?"

"A minute or two must have been enough."

"I think . . . " Amelia faltered, "she's very backward, Mr Hoggett, she's younger in some ways than little Janie . . ."

"Aye," he sighed, "aye . . . she's growed none sin' the accident that killed her mother . . . in her mind, I mean. Eeeh, but she was a jolly little thing afore it 'appened. Howsomever, she's none dangerous, is she?"

"Lord, no . . . " Amelia exclaimed. "The poor little soul couldn't harm a fly. And I've brought these to show you."

She produced Dorcas' drawings and laid them on the table.

"By gum," breathed Mr Hoggett and examined them with care. "Straightout odd, these are. You'd not know whether to laugh at them or shudder. Like a dream . . . a bad dream, maybe . . . and yet, I dunno. You'd never pass them over, any road. Our Albert's are they?"

Amelia shook her head.

"Dorcas did them."

"Our Dorrie's? I don't believe you. She couldna. They're coddin' you."

"I watched her draw that myself. She had no help at all."

"Well, well . . . I'll be kerflummoxed!"

He stared at them again, obviously uncertain of his feelings.

"And yet," he said at last, "they're like her. She seeing like a babby but drawing more growed-up, like."

Amelia eyed him with respect. After a while he pushed them aside and nodded.

"She stays," he said, "and be damned to her being a handicap to the others. They can lump it. What do you say?"

"I agree. I'd let her draw all she wants to for now and if she isn't . . . isn't . . ."

"Isn't teased and tormented. Aye . . ."

"She'll come along a little, perhaps. Speak a little more. But I don't suppose she'll ever be a lot better. But I don't know anything . . . you ought to ask . . ."

"I've asked more doctors than you can shake a stick at and they all say just what you do. She'll get no worse and no better, and she'll like as not live a long life."

He sighed deeply.

"If thou'lt have an eye to her, that'll take a weight from my mind. She'll stay. I'll tell the missus before I leave. She'll kick up all kinds of dust but she'll need to lump it. Now, lass, is there owt else?"

Amelia put before him her string of requests for the schoolroom which made him open his eyes and whistle.

"I know it seems rather a lot," she said apologetically, "but the room is not all I would wish it."

"I don't grudge a penny piece, don't think it," he assured her, "it just beats me how it came to be in such a state."

He scribbled a note at the foot of the list.

"Give that to old Booth. He'll see all's done as you want it. What's this?"

"Books," Amelia explained. "I need some school books."

"Send the list to Remington's in Manchester and they'll have them here before the cat can lick her ear, I promise you. Jem'll fetch them from the station."

He scrawled another note and put both the note and her list into an envelope which he addressed and sealed.

"Give that to Booth to put in the post first thing. And now I'll tell you a thing you'll be the first to know in this house. I'm packing them two young devils off to school. It's no use to hope they'll follow me into t'mill and Stan Hoggett is a man as faces facts. I've faced 'em. It's to be school for them until the corners is knocked off and then they can think about what they'll be at. Not that they've any doubts, *as* I don't doubt you've discovered."

"I should think they'll be delighted," she said frankly.

49

"Aye. And I'd be obliged if you'd oversee the business of getting them off. Clothes and bats and boots and all the things they'll need to have. I've lists as long as your arm. T'Missus ain't up to it in the circumstances and if it's left to nurse she'll fill the trunks up with cough-cures and woollen shirts and such."

"A pleasure."

"They're doing none good here, from what I can discover, and they'd be like fish out t'watter down at Hoggetts. I've a good friend in Lord Benchley; he has the big house up the way . . ."

Mr Hoggett jerked his head to the north.

". . . and he's franked them into a place at Perchards. They'll be licked into shape there, I shouldn't wonder, and come home right down ashamed of their old dad."

He laughed at such a prospect.

"And what about Albert?" Amelia enquired.

Mr Hoggett's good humour evaporated.

"That Bethune can stay and teach him. He's not fit for the rough and tumble of a school . . . even a day school. I daresay he'll do better on his own without those two young devils to lead him a life of it. He's a dab at figures that I will say for him and I'll find him a place under my eye when the time comes. If he lives to grow up."

He frowned. "Now, lass, I'm to be gone a sixmonth. I'm leaving those girls in your hands. I reckon you can see after things, young and all as you are. If Stan Hoggett's owt it's because he's a judge of folk. You don't lack for wit or gumption and given a fair deal you'll hold your own. I wish I could have given you longer to settle in but I've put this trip off time and again because I didn't want to leave the school-room at sixes and sevens, like. Now, if there's owt you think I should know, write to me here . . ."

He gave her a slip of paper with the address of a New York bank.

"You put Private and Personal on it and it'll be sent on to me quick. And you bear in mind, lass, that Stan Hoggett knows more than you think about most things. Rough I may be, but no one ever called me stupid. If owt goes wrong, I'm to be told. Understand me?"

She nodded and folded the slip of paper.

50

"Right then. I'm off before daylight so I'll bid thee good-bye now."

He held out his hand.

"Don't look like you've been hit on the head, lass. You'll do, see if you don't – and you won't find me ungrateful neither."

However, Amelia undressing for bed could not share his confidence. When, a little later while she was reading, she heard a commotion over in the turret where Mrs Hoggett lay awaiting the new arrival she thought at first that the baby was to be born just as its father left. Then, faintly, she found she could hear a shrill voice raised in anger and protest and knew that Mrs Hoggett had taken something in bad part: whether it was the departure of the boys or the non-departure of Dorcas she had no way of discovering. Uneasily she wondered whether her own part in the decision to keep Dorcas at home would be made known to her new mistress. If it were, she might well be in for trouble.

4

*"All women are good for something
or else good for nothing."*

The days after Mr Hoggett's departure were far from easy for
Amelia. In some respects she was glad of this because, at
night, she was too tired to lie awake and grieve for her father
and for what might have been. Her previous life began to
seem to her like a dream, or a novel written about somebody
else, someone quite different to the hard-pressed governess,
someone who had travelled all over Europe, lived in total
comfort and done no more than keep house for an indulgent
father, a labour made easy by a large household of servants
who had vied to spoil her. Looking back on that time she was
astonished at the heedless frivolity of her life, entertaining
guests for her father, accompanying him to other houses,
riding or driving the finest horses, ordering and wearing the
most elegant of clothes and jewellery. She had been like a
child, glad and confident, playing on the slopes of a volcano,
unaware of what waited below the surface. Her father had
seemed so fond and proud of her: it was still unthinkable that
he should have left her as he had done. Her mind flinched
away from the nightmare memory of Grey, his face
bleached to the same colour as his name, barring her from the
study where the flies buzzed and buzzed above a sprawled
shape.

Had he not thought of her before he used that gun? If he
had, had it been that Oliver would look after her? The
thought came to her that if he had thought that he could not
have known her. There had been times when he had said
things which jarred: the night that Oliver had asked her to
marry him was one. He had been so pleased and happy for

her and then he had said, 'She takes after both her parents, Scott; her mother was divinely pretty and almost witless whereas I am as ugly as Socrates himself and have all my faculties. My Amelia has her mother's looks and my brains. She'll never bore you as her mother bored me. Olivia was a beauty, a dear girl, but she had no conversation . . . and she was the worst housekeeper that ever lived.' Amelia could not remember the mother he spoke of so slightingly but she saw Oliver wince at this comment and did not blame him.

In any event, Miss Aylett had been her mama for all real purposes. Every night and every day for the time she had been at Blackyetts she had remembered and blessed Miss Aylett. Perhaps somewhere Ailey was still watching her in that impersonal way she had, allotting praise or criticism in the same calm, affectionate manner. If she could be half so good a governess as Ailey she would be better than anything the Hoggetts had ever dreamed of, she thought defiantly. Ailey's death had been the worst thing which had ever happened to her until her father killed himself: but, at least Ailey had not had to endure the horror and the shock of that. Would it have been such a shock to Ailey? Amelia had often wondered whether Ailey had liked or even respected her father. Papa had been very barbed when he spoke of her. The 'upright one' he called her, or 'the inestimable Aylett' and to her face it was always 'Aylett' as if she was a servant and not a trusted friend. Yet, Ailey had stayed on, even after the schooldays were over, as a chaperone, as an adviser; she had died slowly and painfully in her father's house, a dependent still.

Amelia, toiling over the classwork she was preparing for the next day, breathed a little thankyou to Ailey who had made it possible for her pupil to be independent too. Had Ailey guessed they were living on the slopes of the volcano? At all events it was due to her that Amelia could offer three modern languages, a good deal of Latin, music, drawing and a sound knowledge of other desirable subjects to a prospective employer. It was from Ailey she had grasped some of the principles of imparting that knowledge, from Ailey she took her assured manner. Would she end like Ailey? Would she become an elderly spinster, fiercely, protectively attached to someone else's child? The thought chilled her and she looked about the cheerless room feeling an intense depression and wishing desperately she could talk to someone . . . someone like Ailey. Even Oliver, who had loomed so largely upon her life's horizon only a month ago, had faded in her memory, become insubstantial compared with the memory of Ailey. Ailey was part of what she had become.

Ailey would have understood the amount of sheer will-power needed to control these spoiled children, never mind teach them anything useful. She was lucky if Louisa put in an appearance in the schoolroom one day in three. She was not insolent and disobedient like Alice. Once found, she would come with a fair grace but she preferred to go her own way and that way was usually to the stables, heedless of anything Amelia might say. Alice, thoroughly alienated by that first encounter, would obey her in nothing and did her best to prevent the two little girls from doing what they were bid, threatening them with horrid vengeance if they wrote their copy or sewed their samplers or learned their poems. Luckily, they had come to like Amelia. For what with Mrs Sands ignoring any schoolroom regulation if it interfered with the nursery routine and Alice's active subversion they might have gone quite out of her control. Dorcas was quiet and biddable but she needed constant watching. If Amelia left her in order to go to the library in search of Alice or the stables in search of Louisa she might be sure of finding Dorcas wet or worse when she returned. If she left Alice to her own pursuits in the library a note would arrive from Bethune, usually by the hand of Albert, requesting her removal as her presence distracted the boys. Alice's refusal to budge led, as a rule, to a physical struggle watched by both Albert and the tutor with evident glee. Nor could she depend on winning that struggle for ever: Alice was a tall strong girl and she was growing still. The prospect of months of conflict and struggle ahead suddenly overwhelmed her. She put her head down on the table and clung passionately to the thought of Ailey.

"Are you crying?"

Amelia raised her head and saw Albert staring at her from the other side of the table. She tried to control the surge of dislike which he evoked. No child can be as detestable as Albert seems, she told herself sensibly, and it is nonsensical to be a little afraid of a boy of eleven, even if he does look like a malevolent goblin.

"No," she replied indifferently. "I was tired. Your mother sent over a great deal of sewing."

"You are a liar. There are tears on your cheeks. You were crying."

The triumph and pleasure in his voice was obvious.

"I need not tell you all my thoughts," she said gravely. "And it is no lie that I was tired."

"Go away, then. Leave this house. No one wants you."

Amelia got to her feet and chose a book from the shelf.

"Go to bed, Albert. It's late. All the rest of the children are in bed. I don't know what you're doing here."

"This is my house. I'll go where I wish."

"Good night, Albert."

"They've sent Jem for the doctor," he informed her. "The baby's coming. And when it's here, stepmother will be coming downstairs again. She'll send you off. You'll see. She doesn't like you. She says you put on airs . . . she says Papa had no business to bring you here without consulting her. She says you're uppity and she will need to put you in your place."

Amelia considered the sour resentful face and wondered whether she would ever be able to make this wretched creature tolerate her presence. Liking was simply not in him. Albert shifted uncomfortably under her steady gaze and glared back.

"She thinks you . . ."

"Go to bed, Albert. I detest eavesdroppers and eavesdropping appears to be your favourite pastime."

"You'll be sorry you didn't listen to me," he snarled. "And you don't tell me when to go to bed."

"Well, it's time and high time somebody did. Run along."

"I can't run. You forgot, didn't you? I'm lame."

"Limp along, then," she snapped.

He smiled triumphantly at this slight loss of control and left the room. When he had gone she leaned back and wondered if the Princes in the Tower had been at all like Albert. If so, Tyrrell or whoever it was had been perfectly justified. She chuckled a little at the thought and saw that the old-young goblin face was looking at her round the door.

"Why don't you ever get any letters?" he asked. "All the others did."

"Because I don't write any. Go to bed."

"Why don't you write any?"

"Because I spend what leisure I have answering impertinent questions from little boys," she told him patiently. "Go to bed, Albert."

"You should call me Master Albert," he told her, watching her face. "The other servants do."

"Bed," she reiterated and watched him withdraw his head from the doorway. It would be a miracle if he survived to become an adult. When her imagination presented her with the image of an adult Albert she shuddered and then laughed at herself.

Amelia was not surprised when the long awaited arrival of Master Mark Hoggett proved to be a fairly dramatic affair. Her few brief meetings with the Mistress of Blackyetts had been enough to demonstrate that Mrs Hoggett was as spoiled and pampered and self-centred a creature as Amelia had yet encountered. The first meeting had been some four days after her arrival; she had been summoned to the presence by Ellis, Mrs Hoggett's dresser, a person who considered herself infinitely superior to any governess. Ellis informed her haughtily that the Mistress found herself well enough to receive her but Miss Lester would oblige and not tire the Mistress by too much talking. As Miss Lester was doubtless aware the Mistress was in a delicate condition. Amelia seated in a darkened, stiflingly hot room, listening to a monologue from the ample recumbent form which she could just discern upon the day-bed, had thought the injunction better addressed to the invalid herself. As her eyes became accustomed to the dim light she could see that the Mistress was a woman about her own age. She had been a pretty girl but the neat features were now blurred with fat and lines of discontent ran from nose to chin. Amelia, who had expected to discuss, however briefly, the instruction of the Misses Hoggett, heard instead about the triumphs of Miss Jessamine Thwaites, who, it appeared, had been the toast of the county before she dwindled (if that was the *mot just*) into Mrs Hoggett and was forced to endure the hard lot of women. A series of complaints succeeded this recital, divided equally between the discomforts of her situation, the delicacy of her constitution, the shortcomings of Mr Hoggett who did not understand her sensitive nature and was only too ready to ride rough-shod over her feelings and inclinations.

"As, for example, in the matter of your appointment. A mother likes to have some say in the choice of the person who is going to be in charge of her little ones."

She raised herself on her elbow and gazed at Amelia who nodded politely and said nothing. She was, in fact, wondering whether Mr Hoggett didn't understand his wife much better than she imagined, or would have wished.

From the shortcomings of her husband she then embarked upon those of Amelia's predecessors. These, she was given to understand, consisted of an inability to prevent Mrs Hoggett from being worried by the children, an inability to keep them quiet when she was suffering from those headaches which were worse than she could describe and for which the only cure was rest and *absolute silence*. Finally, none of the incompetents who had taken their vast emoluments under false pretences were able to provide her daughters with those essential accomplishments which had graced Miss Thwaites and which she proceeded to describe in detail: her ability to sing in a fashion which had drawn tears from the guests at Lowcombe House, her ability to paint in water colours and produce pictures which had been admired by real artists, her ability to embroider birds so lifelike that such a one had declared that he expected them to burst into song. This list might have been extended but for the merciful intervention of Ellis who told her Mistress firmly that she must not let Miss Lester tire her and held the door open for Amelia who had departed with alacrity.

There had been another summons: this time it had been less amicable. The news that the schoolroom party had invaded the kitchen, the garden and the stables in pursuit of the elements of good housekeeping did not please Mrs Hoggett at all. As she left such mundane matters to her housekeeper she considered them thoroughly unsuitable for her children. She accused Amelia in far from wilting tones of simply not comprehending the social standing of the family with whom she was now fortunate enough to have found a place. If the news of such a procedure as instructing the children how to make bread or make up a menu were to spread among their friends it would make the Hoggetts a laughing stock. Such lessons were to cease immediately . . . upon her word there was never anything so shabby-genteel . . . and was it true that Miss Lester had actually forced those poor girls into stitching the curtains of the schoolroom? What was wrong, pray, with the curtains which were there already? When Amelia took advantage of a pause in the tirade to suggest that the education of the Royal Family included the study of Domestic Economy Mrs Hoggett sat up among her nest of cushions and observed sharply that of course the dear Queen must set an example to the Lower Orders but that need not concern such people as the Thwaites or, of course, the Hoggetts.

The lessons were discontinued to the disappointment of Louisa who had come into her own in the stables, through her knowledge of proper feeding and grooming, and Amy who had delighted in the mysteries revealed in Cook's making a summer pudding and then letting her cut out with her own hands a whole trayful of gingerbread men with currant eyes and buttons. Alice, however, was pleased. Household duties did not figure in her scheme of education. She knew her worth on the marriage mart to the last penny piece and did not expect to have to exercise economy, domestic or otherwise.

Other manifestations of displeasure had emerged from the darkened rooms across the courtyard, curt ill-written notes, or short verbal messages delivered with evident pleasure by Ellis. The children were too noisy; their singing made their mother's head ache; the children should wear hats and gloves even in the garden; Dorcas must not be allowed to sit upon the grass; Miss Alice was scamping her piano practice; and much else of the same nature. Why, she demanded in a heavily underlined note, was Miss Louisa's work so much concerned with the stables: her sums were about hay and oats and the distances run by race-horses, her poems were all about horses and her sewing seemed to concentrate upon horseshoes and such equine subjects. Amelia could have replied that unless this was the case Louisa would do no sum, write no essay, learn no poem and sew no sampler. As it was she replied in a beautiful formal hand that the matter would be attended to. For the rest, Amelia smiled and clenched her jaw and complied as far as she was able.

Coincidentally the birthday of Master Mark Hoggett was also the departure day of his two half-brothers. They piled themselves, their trunks (filled to the brim with clothes checked and named by Amelia), their battery of bats and boots and racquets and other sports equipment into the station fly because the Blackyetts' carriages were careering about the countryside conveying doctors, accoucheurs, nurses, medical supplies, anxious relatives and news. Every stage of the confinement was reported by Ellis to a somewhat irritated Mrs Thwaites who had borne it all twice before. Bethune, who found a household in which these events were taking place not to his liking, decided to escort his ex-pupils to the station and did not return until the following day so that Amelia amid all else had Albert on her hands.

By the time Bethune returned the household had spent a wakeful night. Mrs Hoggett, convinced that no one suffered as she did, was determined that she should not suffer in silence. Her screams and yells and bellows had echoed across the courtyard for most of the night. Her invalidish habit had made the birth long and protracted.

Amelia joined Mrs Sands in comforting and reassuring the children.

"If it's like that," Louisa said forcefully, "I won't have Coppertop covered."

Mrs Sands, tight-lipped, let fall the grudging information that not everyone suffered to this extent. What she meant, Amelia thought with a private smile, was that not everybody made quite such a hullabaloo.

In her pocket reposed a note sent from the boudoir some days before.

I hear from Miss Alice that you passed the remark in the schoolroom that your mother will be better after the baby comes. This is not *at all* the thing to say to children. If I am poorly they are *not* to know why. I am *most displeased*. It is *most indelicate* that they should have any notion of my condition. It is so easy to rub off the bloom.

That night, not even Dorcas could be unaware of what was happening.

In the morning the children were left to sleep late. Their introduction to the new brother would be after luncheon. Meanwhile the household was in almost as much of a bustle as on the previous day. Callers left cards and flowers and fruit, relatives arrived and left, the doctors (Mrs Hoggett had augmented local resources by calling in an accoucheur from Manchester) came and went and consulted. Between the month-nurse, the wet-nurse and Mrs Sands a state of hostilities came into existence, veiled by a terrifying politeness and stateliness of demeanour in which each took full advantage of her essential functions to frustrate and irritate the others. Amelia, slightly wan from a sleepless night, and torn between exasperation and amusement at the to-do about an event which could not be said to be unusual, marshalled a cross and yawning flock into the dining-room for luncheon where they were joined by Bethune, ushering in Albert. The meal before them bore all the signs of having been carelessly and hastily prepared in the intervals of laying trays, making beef-tea and jellies and other restoratives and catering for the multifarious needs of sickroom and nursery.

"What do you mean to do after they have been presented at the court of King Baby?" asked Bethune.

"They are to have a holiday," Amelia replied.

Bethune raised his eyebrows.

"Is this permitted?"

"It is force majeure. None of them is fit for anything and they have been in and out of the morning room since ten o'clock."

"If anyone else asks me how I shall like having a darling little baby brother," declared Louisa, "I shall say I would rather have a puppy . . . like the little boy in the story."

"I shall like it," Alice announced. "I *dote* on babies. All proper females dote on babies, don't they, Mr Bethune?"

"Doubtless they do," agreed Bethune and smiled benevolently.

"Do you think stepmama would let me hold it?" Alice asked of no one in particular with a beatific expression on her face.

"If they let *me* hold him, I shall drop him, I know I shall," Amy said anxiously. "I won't have to, will I, Miss Lester?"

"No, my lamb," Amelia assured her. "You'll just be allowed to look and maybe to touch."

"I don't want another brother," Albert said through a mouthful of tough, cold beef. "I think he should be drowned in a bucket . . . like the kitchen cat's kittens."

This pronouncement was greeted with a mixture of revulsion and horror which greeted most of Albert's utterances. In the reproachful glances cast at him was an element of speculation as to whether or not he said it to shock or whether, as was perfectly possible, he really meant it. Amelia, slightly light-headed with sleeplessness, suddenly found herself wondering if Albert was already calculating his share of the inheritance. She came out of this train of thought to find Bethune addressing her.

". . . a walk," he was saying. "It is a pleasant sunny day. An Indian Summer I declare. And it would be a pleasure to accompany all these charming young ladies."

It was a popular idea except with Albert who asked sourly if they expected him with a lame leg to keep up with all those strapping girls.

"You can ride Plod," Louisa interrupted bluntly. "If I lead him you'll be all right. And he'll walk on."

Plod was a donkey chiefly employed to pull the lawn-mower and not renowned for liveliness.

"Oh, Miss Lester . . . could we take a picnic? I love picnics," pleaded Amy. "We could have it on the field by the weir."

"So I have to share the saddle with a great heavy basket. Thank you," snarled Albert.

"I'll see," Amelia temporised. "The kitchen is all at sixes and sevens. They may not be able to put us up a basket, but we'll take some cake and some fruit and something to drink."

"I shall take my sketch-block," said Alice virtuously. "There will be some splendid subjects down by the river."

The ceremony of greeting the baby was not wholly successful. The bundle of shawls held by the month-nurse could be heard to contain an infant and on inspection there was to be found an angry, screwed-up, purple, goblinesque face

61

embedded in the lace and wool and nuns' veiling. The children looked doubtfully upon it.

Jane echoed this sentiment. Albert looked sourly outraged and the baby howled louder than ever. Alice cooed at it dutifully but without much conviction. There was no doubt that Mark did look like Albert and cooing seemed out of place.

Of Mrs Hoggett, the proud mama, only the barest glimpse was to be had through the doors of her bedroom. There, in the great bed, her blonde hair combed out over the pillows, she lay in a subdued and becoming light and raised a languid hand to greet her family. An odour of scent, beef-tea, port-wine and over-heated flesh wafted out upon them. After a very few seconds of this vision Ellis shooed them firmly away.

The picnic, by contrast, was an enormous success. Released from the constraints laid upon them at the house and the strain of waiting they romped round the meadow. Even Alice cast off her grown-up airs and played an energetic game of tag with them, quite forgetting that running made her face red. Amy and Jane rolled unrebuked in the soft grass like little fillies. Albert found a stick and urged Plod into a fast trot along the river path. He thwacked the poor beast and yelled with a quite uncharacteristic glee, or so they thought until Louisa found that the stick was armed with very large sharp thorns. She wrenched it from him and hurled it into the river and Amelia was obliged to call her to order for using unbecoming language. This cast a shadow on the proceedings because Albert limped ostentatiously to a bank where he sat like the late Lord Byron, gloomily surveying the revels. Bethune organised a game with bat and ball and bases made of their hats and Amy was in her element scudding from base to base like a rabbit, her skirts held high. Alice and Louisa then made them play Pig-in-the-middle. Albert listened to the shrieks of delight for a while and then limped away to prospect along the hedge. Amelia, repacking the basket, wondered whether he hoped to find a clump of Deadly Nightshade. She was joined by Bethune who lay on his back beside her, his straw hat tilted over his face and his arms behind his head.

"You know," he observed, "this is the very first time since you came that I've had a chance of a private word with you."

"Indeed," Amelia agreed. "It has been a very busy time."

"I am given to understand that this is your first post," he went on. "One wouldn't have thought it."

Amelia wiped a plate with a wisp of grass.

"Aren't you going to ask why?" he demanded.

"I can only presume you think that I am performing my duties adequately," she said primly. "I thank you for the compliment."

"More than adequately," he said sleepily, "admirably. What puzzles me is why you took them up in the first place."

"I have a prejudice in favour of eating," she returned.

"You haven't the air of poverty," he said. "Or the habits. Your clothes for example. They are of the very best materials and you don't wear them with the anxious consideration of those uncertain of being able to replace them."

"You are observant, sir."

"I have observed more than that. You have dealt much with servants. You are not in the least afraid of them and you exact service as if it were your due. Most governesses either conduct a running feud with the servants or walk in terror of them."

Amelia made no comment.

"And you have travelled a good deal," he mused. "Travelled in comfort too. You have first-hand acquaintance with pictures and statues which the rest of us know only by report. You have met, or claim to have met, poets and novelists and artists and so, presumably, you have moved in the same circles. You ride extremely well and you drive. In fact . . ."

He raised himself on his elbow and pushed back the hat so that he could look at her directly.

". . . you present the most intriguing mystery. Why should someone of your order take a post with this galli-maufry of nouveaux-riches?"

"I told you. I like to eat."

"I am sure you have a story to tell," he coaxed. "Won't you tell me what it is?"

"I have no story."

"Your name does not begin with a B?" he suggested.

"My name is Lester."

"You receive no letters and you send none."

"You are uncommonly well-informed," Amelia commented icily.

"Oh, that is my privilege," he admitted. "I could say, my hobby."

"Well, you will get no more information from me."

"That is to admit that there is information to be got."

"No," she insisted. "You make something out of nothing."

"I am positively consumed with curiosity about you. Are you a runaway wife, fleeing from nameless cruelties, an heiress under siege, a hapless criminal . . ."

"Oh, don't be so ridiculous," she said tartly. "My father suffered some reverses and is now dead. That is all."

"No relations?"

"None that I wish to be obliged to."

"No lovers?"

"Mr Bethune, you go too far," she said sharply.

He seized her hand and held it fast.

"Too far for you, not far enough for me," he said and looked up at her in a possessive style which made her feel hot and angry. "I would like to go much, much further."

"Well, you will not have the opportunity, Mr Bethune. I value my post here."

"And is that the only reason?"

Amelia suddenly felt irritated out of all reason by these airs of a Don Juan.

"No," she said primly, "but it would be neither kind nor polite to enumerate the others. Kindly leave go my hand."

"So, ho, she scratches!" he laughed but Amelia had seen the flash of indignation which preceded the laughter and felt a mean kind of satisfaction. She liked Bethune no better on further acquaintance than she had done on the first day. His eyes bulged, his mouth was too red and too wet and his hands were damp. He released her hand after a prolonged squeeze and she rose, brushing the grass from her skirt with unnecessary violence. He lay back and stared up at her under the brim of his hat.

"All the same," he remarked, "I think I shall make a push to pierce the mystery."

To her fury Amelia blushed from neck to brow at the tone of this declaration and Bethune smiled . . . leered . . . at the sight of the colour in her face.

"Such a delicious little mystery," he persisted.

Amelia laughed at him.

"Make a mystery if you wish," she shrugged, "but you will be disappointed."

"Never," he said fervently.

It was somewhat disconcerting to discover later that this unwelcome exchange had been witnessed.

"You were flirting with Mr Bethune," Alice accused her after prayers.

"What nonsense," Amelia said lightly.

"You held hands, I saw you. I shall tell Mama."

Amelia suddenly realised that Alice was genuinely upset. This was not a hostile gambit of the usual kind. Alice, as might have been expected, was in love with the tutor: it was a complication which Amelia should have foreseen. She laughed, partly at her own naïvety and partly at the stupidity of the situation.

"I expect Mr Bethune flirts a little with every female that comes in his way," she said indifferently. "It is his mode of being kind and polite. It is not to my taste, I admit, but he doesn't mean anything by it, you know. He wouldn't treat anyone he felt a genuine passion for in that style, depend upon it."

Alice stared at her uncertainly.

"I wouldn't advise anyone to take Mr Bethune seriously," Amelia went on.

"Oh," said Alice and for once looked very young. "Wouldn't you?"

"No, I would not," Amelia said firmly.

"Don't you like him?" Alice asked shyly.

Dangerous ground, Amelia thought grimly, there's no safe answer to that.

"I suppose one must try to like the people you have to work with," she said lightly. "It is too wearing to be involved in petty likes and dislikes when there's a job to be done."

Alice's face cleared.

5

"Adversity flattereth no one."

In the four weeks which followed the birth of Mark Hoggett
the schoolroom routine became established. Slowly Amelia
began to find her task easier as her charges began to accept,
even to enjoy, the discipline of regular hours and the challenge of work which they were expected to accomplish.
Even Mrs Sands was brought to a grudging approval and
stopped invading the schoolroom to remove the younger
occupants on various pretexts. One evening she took the
trouble to leave her domain and come to knock on Amelia's
door in order to inform her that Miss Dorcas had gone for a
full week without 'offending' or having a 'tantrum' and that
she, Mrs Sands, was convinced it was due in part to the new
régime in the schoolroom.

When she had left Amelia sat for a while looking at the
door, a half-smile on her face: how her expectations had
altered, she thought, when such news could gratify and to
such a degree. Praise grudged was praise indeed. Alice, too,
had become slightly less hostile as she realised that her governess was making no pretence to appear well-read and accomplished, that she was in fact both these things and, moreover,
was most repulsive in her manner to Mr Bethune. Louisa,
who had appeared such a problem at the beginning, was now
embarrassingly devoted, her devotion being almost as difficult to handle as her resistance. Amelia found it hard to
believe that three months earlier she had not even known that
these people existed.

However, there remained certain difficulties; one was
Albert and the other was his tutor. Albert's enmity seemed to
increase as the days passed. She could discern no reason for

it unless it was that her policy was to ignore him, to treat his rudeness with amused contempt and protect the younger children from his wasp-like, and often cruel, attentions. Even that, she thought, could not account for his implacable dislike: the word 'hatred' sprang to the mind but she refused to believe that a child of his age could harbour such destructive emotions. She tried to dismiss him from her thoughts but he was not readily dismissed. He would appear silently at unexpected times and laugh when she jumped to find him at her elbow. Out of school hours he seemed to dog her footsteps like a lover. He overheard any conversation she might have, he knew the paths she took for her solitary walks, he hid and defaced the books she read and would spoil any work she left in view. Her bedroom had to be locked, for to leave it open was to invite him to rummage destructively among her possessions and put insects and thistles in her bed. It was a constant silent persecution and the harder to bear because she could not see how she had deserved it.

One remedy might have been to complain of him to Bethune but this she was reluctant to try for the tutor's subtler pursuit of her was almost as irksome as Albert's devilries. To avoid it she kept the girls with her constantly and when they were with their mama or Mrs Sands she would lock herself in her bedroom. But a visit to the library for a book was to invite Bethune's attentions and once he had found her he was as hard to shake off as a burr. He had a command of insinuating compliment and innuendo which was hard to counter politely; he pressed constantly for an assignation and, like Albert, dogged her footsteps when she was out of the house. It was with considerable relief that she had discovered a place in the grounds where she could be alone without the danger of either discovering her. There was a small belvedere down beyond the succession houses. It was almost disused but she cleared the ground floor and in good weather the girls and she would take their work there. What no one knew but Amelia was that above the open apartment was another tiny room, lit by a cupola and reached by a flight of steps concealed in a cupboard. The key to that she found in a drift of dead leaves in the cupboard and now wore round her neck. The belvedere, she discovered, was older than the house and had been built at the same time as the little Queen

Anne manor house which had been demolished in order to build the Hoggett mansion. Up in this retreat she was secure from Albert's prying or Bethune's blatant approaches and sly fondlings, or she would be until the winter set in. There she could keep anything she did not want spoiled or broken. Above all it gave her the privacy she had missed so desperately.

After a month in her bed-chamber, where she held daily receptions from her bed, Mrs Hoggett, amid considerable ceremony, reappeared downstairs. At first it was merely to exchange the bed in her room for the day-bed in the parlour or the drawing-room, attended still by a battery of medicines, smelling bottles and restorative sweets, jellies and broths. Amelia now found herself summoned more and more frequently to the Mistress's presence to receive her instructions and remonstrances. The girls were to do this or not to do that, they were to visit here or avoid there, to wear this or not wear that, to learn this song or that poem or to learn this, that or the next piano piece. The girls were also summoned during the morning or the afternoon to appear in the drawing-room when visitors were expected. Mrs Hoggett loved to be told that it was quite impossible that she should be the mama of these great girls and that she was more like their sister and to achieve this she did not care how she disrupted the schoolroom routine. Even when there were no visitors she liked to have a daughter to run all the errands which Ellis did not. She also liked to have regular accounts of what went on in the schoolroom from one or other of the girls. Alice was particularly ready to oblige in this.

After a week or so Mrs Hoggett abandoned the day-beds and, as she put it, resumed her usual habits. There was not, at first glance, a great deal of difference to be seen. Instead of reclining she sat in an armchair, protected by screens of her own work from any possible draught, with her feet, small, plump feet of which she was rather vain, on a footstool, beadwork and also of her own design and execution. Here she was waited on hand and foot by Ellis to the constant tinkle of a little silver bell. However, during the afternoon if it were fine she would take the air in the carriage accompanied by one or more daughters, thus giving at very little

68

trouble the public appearance of being a devoted mama. Dorcas never made one of the carriage party. She would recover from this exertion by resting in her room with the blinds drawn and pastilles burning before dressing for the evening. She dined out on three or four evenings a week and increased her covers for guests on the remaining evenings. On these occasions the schoolroom party would sup early in the breakfast parlour, though Bethune was often asked to 'make up numbers' in the dining-room.

On Sundays she walked the seven hundred yards from Blackyetts to the tiny village church of Blackyetts-under-Edge surrounded by her family. Amelia, at her employer's request, walked behind with Mrs Lucas, the housekeeper, and Mrs Sands. Dorcas did not attend. Bethune did not attend either, being, as he told them, required to worship at his father's church in the neighbouring parish. His father might have been surprised to hear of this requirement.

A fortnight after this 'resumption' Amelia was a little startled when Mrs Hoggett exerted herself to walk along to the schoolroom during morning classes. She came in unheralded, stared very hard at Amelia and then pointedly asked Louisa if Mr Bethune had been in that morning. Louisa answered forcibly, as was her habit.

"He's in and out like a rabbit in a burrow. He's been twice already. Once to borrow some ink and once to ask for the dictionary."

"That was in the library all the time," Alice added.

Mrs Hoggett again stared hard at Amelia but did not see fit to address her before she left, leaving the door ajar. Amelia moved to close it and saw a small hunched figure in the corridor. He was smiling. He stuck his tongue out at Amelia and scuttled clumsily after his stepmother's purple satin flounces. Amelia closed the door, conscious of a faint unease.

The next day Albert was sent to do his lessons with his sisters, something they all disliked very heartily. Amelia had been half-expecting such an infliction since she had read in the newspaper of the nearby Autumn Race-Meeting. Bethune rarely missed any such meeting within a day's journey. A note would come from the Rectory, perfunctorily notifying some slight indisposition and consigning Albert to her care. It was a fine warm October morning and after the regular schoolroom routine was over Amelia told the party to take their preparation and come down to the belvedere. Albert thrust his Latin primer across the table at her and limped after the girls. Amelia called after him.

"Carry your own books, Albert."

"It's your place to carry them," he told her insolently.

"I have books of my own to bring," she said without heat and picked up a small notebook and a pencil before she too followed the girls. She did not look to see if he had obeyed her, though she was conscious of his eyes boring into her back. When he arrived in the belvedere he had not brought the primer and proceeded to distract them all by wandering restlessly round the little stone structure, kicking the walls and doors and nosing into all the corners.

"If you are bored why not fetch your work?" Amelia suggested.

"You fetch it," he snapped. "I'm lame. I don't carry things. You're paid to do it for me."

"Don't you talk like that to Miss Lester!" Louisa bellowed.

"Why not?" asked Albert contemptuously. "She's just another servant."

Louisa went scarlet.

"Be that as it may," Amelia interrupted, "that is not the way that gentlemen talk to servants, Albert."

"And how would you know that?" demanded Albert.

As soon as he had said it he knew he had gone too far. Louisa rose in her wrath and gave her little lame brother a box on his ear which sent him staggering to the wall where he stumbled and fell. Louisa was a strapping girl and her muscles were well-developed: it took Albert a few moments to recover his wits.

"You warty little toad!" raged Louisa standing over him. "You mind your manners or I'll give you another taste of home-brewed . . ."

The episode was so unexpected (especially by Albert) and the spectacle of the malign creature blinking uncertainly up at his Amazon sister so unusual that Amy gave vent to a high nervous giggle. Dorcas joined in with the hoarse sound which served her for laughter. Before Amelia could retrieve matters Alice began laughing as well.

"Oh, Lou!" she gasped, "if you could just see yourself! It's just like Punch and Judy! What a Punch Albert makes!"

In a second all the girls were rocking with laughter. Albert didn't laugh: he sat fingering his reddened cheek and looking, not at Louisa, but at Amelia who eventually succeeded in calling them to order and reproved Alice for her unkind remark. When he got to his feet he came to the table and glowered up into Amelia's face.

"I'll pay you out for that . . . you see if I don't," he announced softly.

"Don't be theatrical, boy," said Amelia briskly. "Run and fetch your books and I advise you from now on to take care not to provoke your sister."

For the world and all she could not prevent a quiver of amusement in her voice because of the unexpected retribution which had fallen upon him, but when she looked up at him the amusement died. There was no doubting any more that it was real hatred which glared out at her. The children were still laughing so she hushed them with a trickle of fear under her neatly fitted bodice. Absurd to be afraid of a small boy, she told herself, but the fear didn't leave her. Albert did not fetch his work but spent the remainder of the time nosing round outside the belvedere. When she dismissed the girls to eat their biscuits and drink their milk he came back in, his foot dragging over the floor.

"What's in there?" he demanded and kicked the door of the cupboard where the stairs were.

"A cupboard, I suppose."

"I asked what was in it."

"It's locked," she told him.

"Where's the key?"

"Lost, I daresay."

He looked very narrowly, first at her, then at the door, gave it a last crashing kick which brought the paint flaking off in showers and then limped off back to the house, his hands in his pockets. He looked small and slightly pathetic.

After the break he didn't come back. When they returned to the schoolroom he was seated at the table writing busily.

71

When the door opened he put his work inside a book in a decidedly furtive fashion and left the room without a word.

On the following day Bethune sought her out after Louisa and Jane and Amy had gone, rather unwillingly, to accompany Mrs Hoggett on her carriage airing, leaving Dorcas and a mutinous Alice to do afternoon lessons. Albert had spent the morning in the schoolroom because the tutor, apparently 'recovered', had spent the morning closeted with Mrs Hoggett. Albert had been quiet, possibly because of Louisa's glares, and intent not upon his lesson but upon some scheme in his mind. After luncheon he had not come back and Amelia had sighed with relief. Bethune's appearance did not surprise her. He made a habit of coming when Mrs Hoggett was safely out of the house. Amelia ignored the almost imperceptible jerk of the head which invited her to leave the room and speak to him. She turned instead to inspect Dorcas's current picture. It was, she was amused to see, a rendering of the incident in the belvedere, a very vivid rendering. Dorcas's satisfaction in the downfall of Albert was eerily clear to see in the lively drawing. It was as if all that was left of Dorcas's intelligence was in her clever hand. The child looked up and smiled vacantly at Amelia who automatically wiped the dribbling mouth.

"Lou'sa," she said.

There was no sign of Louisa in the drawing but her presence could certainly be felt. An unmistakeable and apprehensive Albert huddled against the wall looked up and out of the picture. Amelia chuckled and nodded appreciatively. Bethune came into the room and leaned over to see the drawing. His hand felt its way to her waist and she could feel his breath on her neck. She moved away pointedly and went to stand beside Alice who was watching intently.

"Very good," he said carelessly to the heavy-breathing Dorcas and moved round the table.

"I am given to understand that you had a slight contretemps yesterday," he observed in an undervoice. "Albert is far from pleased with you all."

"Louisa should not have hit him," Amelia said primly. "I have told her so. But I am bound to say he deserved it. Perhaps he will mind his manners in future."

"I doubt it. I came to say he will be with you tomorrow as well. I am to assist Mrs H send out invitations to her soirée."

"I won't be so untruthful as to say he will be welcome," Amelia said acidly. "Perhaps you would be good enough to look among his books. He has purloined a quantity of my copy sheets, some notes I was making from Macaulay and a few sheets of my own writing paper. I particularly need the notes as they were for tomorrow's lesson. However, I imagine they are now destroyed. As usual. You might also enquire," she continued coldly, "if he was responsible for the damage to the new paint on the window seat, but I don't suppose for a moment that he will admit to it."

Bethune examined the deep scratches on the seat which spelled out, 'A L IS A SLUT'. He drew in his breath between his teeth.

"Now that," he said, "is going a little too far. I'll send Edwards up with a plane."

"No, I thank you. I prefer that the servants don't make a tale of this. Perhaps as the creature purports to be a pupil of yours, you might remove it yourself."

He gave her a sharp, calculating glance and then smiled in his practised way.

"It will be a pleasure. Positively," he said mockingly. "Who could refuse?"

He bowed to them all with a flourish and left the room.

About five minutes later howls of rage and pain were to be heard and Albert was observed stumbling across the courtyard, hugging his left hand against himself. Amelia raised her eyebrows at the sight, and thought that Bethune could not have been very successful at the races.

"I think Mr Bethune's caned him," said Alice in surprise. "I didn't think papa allowed Albert to be caned."

"Your father is, of course, in America," Amelia observed very reprehensibly.

Alice giggled.

When Mrs Hoggett returned from the airing and brought the girls to the schoolroom, expecting to lodge a complaint on the score of the inkstain on Amy's finger, she found Mr Bethune there in his shirt-sleeves. Amelia was there too and her cheeks were flushed and it was plain she had not been paying a great deal of attention to replacing the notes which had been discovered in shreds on the library floor. It was unfortunate that Alice had been summoned by Mrs Sands a few minutes earlier to try on a new dress which was being made for her appearance at the soirée by a flaunting female from Manchester who styled herself Madame Mimi. Dorcas, curled up in an armchair, her thumb in her mouth, was not immediately visible. Amelia's cheeks were flushed from a distinctly disturbing encounter.

"Do you suppose that she . . ." Bethune had said just after the door closed behind Alice, "would be able to tell tales of us if I stole a kiss?"

He jerked his head at Dorcas and left the window-seat.

"You know," he continued in a kind of purring voice, "you look good enough to eat, sitting there, prim as a pie. I don't think you are prim in the least . . . Amelia."

"Dorcas is perfectly well able to draw what she sees, Mr Bethune," Amelia had returned coolly.

Bethune laughed softly.

"I'd give a year's salary to see what she'd draw if I did what I have in mind. You are really a very enticing little morsel, you know. Quite wasted on a schoolroom. I can think of a much more suitable setting."

"I don't know what I can do more," Amelia had replied bitingly, "to convince you that these advances are quite unwelcome to me."

"Holding out for marriage, are you?"

Amelia had stared angrily at this, her lips in a tight line.

"Well, I'll be plain with you. You won't get marriage from me. I can't afford a wife, especially a penniless one."

"Let me assure you, Mr Bethune, that marriage with you is *not* what I . . ."

"All these virtuous airs don't impress me," he declared and moved round so that he could put his hand under her chin. She snatched it away and glared.

"And no one you're likely to meet would want to marry a penniless female with a doubtful past . . ."

She jumped to her feet.

"My past is not doubtful!"

"Then why do you tell me nothing of it? The others were

74

ready to describe their homes and their relatives in lachrymose and never-ending detail."

"Others? Am I to understand you make a habit of trying to seduce the governesses? They are tutor's perquisites just as the kitchen dripping is the cook's? Is that it?"

He laughed again. "My word, but we are outspoken. All the same let us face facts. You are pretty and young and unlikely to marry. Ours is a very hard calling. All I'm suggesting is that we make our pleasures where they are to be found. And I could take very great pleasure in you, believe me."

He moved round the table and slipped his hand round her waist smiling complacently.

"Come, why so coy?"

Amelia lost her temper and struck at his arm with the edge of her hand.

"I assure you, Mr Bethune, that such an interlude would give *me* no pleasure. And let me also assure you that my objections to your proposal are not wholly moral! You may think yourself irresistible, but I do not. In fact I would be glad and grateful if you would keep your hands to yourself and your dubious attractions for those who appreciate them!"

The expression on his face would have been laughable at any other time. It was compounded of surprise, anger and rank incredulity. He had remained silent for a second or so, time enough had Amelia been wary, to hear Mrs Hoggett and the girls approaching.

"You would be surprised if I told you who they were . . ." he said at last.

"I doubt it," she returned, still in a fine rage. "I know just the silly kind of female who might succumb to your blandishments . . ."

It had been at this precise moment that Mrs Hoggett had come in through the door. She looked from one to the other in angry surmise.

"What are you doing here, Mr Bethune?" she demanded. "I find Albert alone in the library and the place like a paper-chase and you here, where you have no business to be!"

"I was attempting to remove some marks from the

window-seat," he said boldly and waved the plane by way of evidence.

"And why could not a servant have done that?"

He cast a malicious look at Amelia.

"Miss Lester was most insistent that I should do it, madam," he said.

"Was she indeed?"

Mrs Hoggett turned to Amelia whose face had turned from pink to white.

"Why was that, miss?"

"Because Albert had scored some unpleasant remark into the wood and I was unwilling to let the servants see it. Mr Bethune has charge of Albert so I told him."

Mrs Hoggett looked angrily incredulous.

"Let me see this unpleasant remark."

Bethune stood back to let her view the seat. The comment despite his efforts was still faintly visible. Mrs Hoggett's eyebrows were lifted almost into her hair.

"I would be very interested to know what the child has witnessed for you to merit this," she announced.

"Nothing sinister to my knowledge," Amelia said calmly.

"You cannot tell me that he would do such a thing without good reason."

"Indeed he would," Amelia said with feeling.

Mrs Hoggett stared at her with bulging blue eyes and her bosom heaved with emotion.

"I am very seriously displeased," she shrilled. "I mean to get to the bottom of this. Louisa, Jane and Amy go to your rooms. I doubt if this is fit for your ears. I will send for you later in case you have any knowledge of what has been going on. Where is Alice?"

"Madame Mimi sent for her for a fitting."

"And how have you managed to dispose with Dorcas?"

Amelia stood back to let her see Dorcas curled up on the armchair, her eyes staring under the half-closed lids, her thumb, slimed with saliva, half in and half out of her mouth.

"Ugh!" said Dorcas's stepmother and looked away.

Schoolroom supper that night was a silent and uncomfortable meal. Amelia, uneasily conscious that to be guiltless was not necessarily to escape blame, tried to appear as usual, but

76

Alice was red-eyed and resentful and refused to look at her or speak to her. Louisa looked bewildered and sullen, while Albert, his left hand in a large bandage, gobbled his food unpleasingly, his eyes fixed on Amelia with a curiously greedy triumphant expression which did nothing to allay her feeling of disquiet. Mr Bethune was not there: presumably he was supping tête-à-tête with Mrs Hoggett, another circumstance which was the reverse of reassuring.

When the meal was over Alice rushed away and locked herself in her room. Louisa excused herself to go and have the fitting that she had missed that afternoon. Albert left the table after her but Amelia was conscious of his presence in the hall when she fetched her cloak. It was a damp evening but she needed to spend a little time alone. She also wanted to write a letter and did not want Albert to appear suddenly at her elbow while she was doing it. There was a little garden door in the west wing and she slipped silently through that with a candle in her pocket. She didn't see a face at the window of the sewing room regarding her with intent interest.

Once safe in her retreat she lit her candle and got out paper and pen. She started a letter to Mr Hoggett in America. However, she got no further than 'Dear Mr Hoggett . . .' before she realised that it was quite impossible to describe her predicament, especially as she could not be sure that there was as yet any predicament to describe.

She sat there staring at the candle, hoping against hope that Bethune would give the true version of what had happened and knowing all too well that he was too vain and too self-seeking to do it. She wondered bleakly what she would do and where she would go if the worst happened and she was dismissed. She had never felt quite so alone or so helpless. She had only a few coppers left and the salary due would not take her very far. Without a good reference, and it was unlikely that Mrs Hoggett would wish to give her one, her chance of obtaining another post was non-existent. There were far more governesses than there were posts. She had a mental picture of Cousin Emily's face, should she turn up at Wheatley, penniless and in disgrace, and her back stiffened. Surely anything would be better than that. She could find work as a servant, perhaps? She could be a housekeeper, surely, she had run her father's household since she was sixteen. But . . . who would take her without references?

She had reached the gloomy conclusion that Wheatley was her only refuge when she heard the footsteps. They came across the wooden floor of the room below. Amelia held her breath and blew out the candle. She had closed the cupboard door but it was not possible to lock it from the inside. The sounds ceased momentarily and then to her dismay she heard the cupboard door creak and the steps trod up the staircase. In the gloom of the recess where it emerged she saw the figure of Bethune. Even in the twilight she could see that he was smiling.

"So, Miss Amelia . . . you need my help. I quite agree. You need it very much. You are to be dismissed without a character. However, I didn't expect you to come begging for it quite so soon."

There was a gloating note in his voice which gave her a sick feeling.

"I did not ask for your help. You're the last person I would ask."

He waved a piece of paper at her.

"But this tells a very different story. 'I need help desperately' you say here, 'please come to the belvedere after supper. I am in the upper room. The staircase is in the cupboard. I'll be there just as it gets dark. Please come. We must talk.' There! Very affecting, I must say."

"I did not write that. I wouldn't be so . . . so abject."

"Who else would?" he said disbelievingly and put the note back in his pocket.

"Let me see it."

"Why? I've come after all. And you do need help. And I am very willing to lend you my aid."

"After lying your own way out of trouble, I don't doubt!"

"Now, wouldn't you lie a little in such a case?" he asked sarcastically. "I had to protect my own interests, after all. They are quite considerable, believe me, and my circumstances are not so comfortable that I would wish to relinquish them for the sake of a prim little prude."

He moved slowly into the room which at once seemed to Amelia to become stiflingly small.

"Of course, I might be persuaded to use my . . . dubious

78

attractions, wasn't it? to see that you are dismissed with more decorum. I might even supply a character. My father would doubtless oblige if I asked him. He has a heart as soft as butter."

She turned away in disgust.

"Of course," he continued after a tiny pause and to her dismay she found he was at her shoulders, "I would expect some return for such assistance. Nothing for nothing in this world of woe. I suppose you understand me. I have never found you slow of understanding though you are decidedly backward in other respects."

"Oh, I understand you," she returned bitterly.

"Good. I think I will collect a little payment on account tonight," he added and reached out to grab her round the waist. "It's an uncommonly good opportunity you have provided and such opportunities are likely to be limited in the future. You won't be here for much longer . . ."

He was stronger than she expected for she found it impossible to break his hold however hard she struggled and she struggled as hard as she knew how, hitting out frantically in a panic of distaste. He caught her hands and held them both in a crushing grip in one of his, grinning with enjoyment at her breathless striving to wrench them away.

"Oh, but I am going to enjoy this little interlude," he said softly.

He pulled viciously at her gown with his free hand and ripped her bodice open to the waist. She kicked out at him, hampered by her skirts and he grabbed at her leg through the folds of material, overbalancing her so that she fell to the ground where, with an obscene little grunt of satisfaction, he pinned her under his weight. Amelia wrenched a hand free and clawed at his face. He swore and slapped her face so brutally she was partly stunned and saw stars.

"Lie still, you little whore," he panted. "Lie still and pay your debts or I'll show you who's master. I'll choke you if I have to . . ."

The blood thundered in her ears and she tore frantically at the hand squeezing her throat. She thought she heard a scream and wondered if it came from her. The grip on her throat eased. The crushing weight was lifted and she was free, sobbing with fright and gasping for breath. When her eyes cleared she saw a purple silk skirt by her and above it, hideously foreshortened, the face of Mrs Hoggett, scarlet with outrage, her mouth screaming incoherent abuse. As Amelia raised herself on one elbow, feeling her throat tenderly, her eye fell on another face just appearing above the topmost step of the staircase. It was Albert and he was laughing.

6

"Better to be Alone than be in Bad Company."

The Parliamentary train from Manchester to Euston paused briefly at Bindleton, discharged a few passengers, mostly new-come Irish, hopeful of employment, and uplifted Amelia, pale and neat, at half past five in the morning. Jem Matthews saw her trunks bestowed on the roof, abjured the large lady with her bundles spread all over the wooden bench to, "Leave the lass sit down, missus,' and handed Amelia into the stuffy compartment with more ceremony than if she had been a countess entering the Royal Train. Amelia turned and leaned through the window to thank him, an exercise he brushed aside as unnecessary. He wished her good fortune in London and expressed a desire to see her in better stirrups next time around. He then stood waving his livery hat until the train and Amelia were quite out of sight.

"There goes the best on 'em yet," he muttered regretfully.

Amelia squeezed between the large lady and a sleeping gentleman in a peaked cap and shabby ulster who smelled of liquor, found a space for her feet between her dressing case and the large lady's bundles and leaned back against the unyielding wooden partition. A movement above her head made her turn and look up. A small girl was peering over and down at her with a solemn unwinking stare. Amelia smiled faintly at her which caused the child to vanish immediately with a stifled giggle. Further along the bench opposite a soldier in red regimentals, his round cap at a jaunty angle, looked at her in a friendly approving style. Amelia looked down at her hands hastily. The large lady was less friendly.

"Mind me bundle," she warned, "there's a chiny teapot in it."

81

It was not quite light enough to read. Amelia leaned her head back and closed her eyes, wincing slightly as her bonnet strings pressed on to her bruised neck. She opened her eyes and encountered at close quarters the curious gaze of the large lady fixed upon the bruise which she knew was beginning to show redly on her jaw. The train gathered speed and the other occupants of the benches lost interest in the newcomer. Amelia fell to wondering what Louisa and Dorcas would do when they found she had gone. They would not be awake yet, not for an hour or so. They would miss her . . . for a time. Amelia sighed and wondered who would be chosen to take her place. A slight smile twitched at her lips at the thought of Mrs Hoggett exerting herself to this extent. Doubtless she would choose the oldest and ugliest available. She was sure that Bethune would be able to explain himself satisfactorily to willing ears. He had departed the previous evening without apology or explanation leaving Amelia to stand the shock. It had been a hideous noisy scene which she would not be able to forget for a long time . . . a very long time.

Mrs Hoggett once she had become coherent had instructed her to be gone as soon as she could pack her trunk, told her that she never wanted to set eyes on her again and called her a number of very unpleasant names of which 'trollop' was the least offensive. She had then adamantly refused to pay either her wages or any journey money saying that both these were forfeit on account of her scandalous behaviour. As far as she was concerned, she screeched, she did not care whether Amelia ended in the river or the gutter. Amelia, half-stunned by Bethune's blow, was at first only conscious of relief that rescue should have arrived, even in such an improbable guise. Then, as she gathered her wits and the ringing in her ears dwindled, relief was overtaken by a sick tide of humiliation and anger. She had tried in despair to describe Bethune's pursuit and his attack on her, but Mrs Hoggett had shouted her down, waving a scrap of paper in the air and bellowing that she wasn't going to listen to any lying tales, that she knew what to believe and whom to believe and it wasn't any lying mim-mouthed little street-walker. Amelia gave up the attempt to defend herself. It wasn't until afterwards, lying waiting for the morning, that she had been struck by the theatricality of the scene. It did not ring true. It was the sheerest melodrama. It had been followed by sheer farce when Mrs Hoggett flouncing out in a lather of outrage had fallen headlong over the eavesdropping Albert, much to the entertainment of the servants who had gathered to find out what all the shouting was about.

The servants it had been who had come to her rescue. Tears squeezed themselves from under her eyelids when she thought of them. Baxter had come into the belvedere and supported her back to the house, brought water and lint and arnica for her bruises and then helped her pack, bursting every few minutes into a tirade of indignation against 'that Bethune'. Later, when the household was quiet she had come again to Amelia's door bearing a message.

"Beggin' your pardon, miss, but Mrs Lucas's compliments and would you oblige by stepping over to the Room."

Amelia had looked her astonishment.

"You'd best come over, miss," Baxter advised, abandoning the formal for the motherly. "They're that put-about in the Hall. When they heard the news Mrs Lucas was fit to bust her stay-laces and Mr Booth had to stop Jem Matthews going straight and handing that Bethune a few for himself. And Mrs Sands," she ended respectfully, "says as how summat must be done. So they wants to see you."

In the Housekeeper's Room Mrs Lucas, Mrs Sands and Cook were seated round a table on which stood a bottle of port and four glasses. When Baxter ushered Amelia in they all rose in a surge of skirts and aprons and begged her loftily to be seated. Baxter, who knew her place, curtsied and retired. For a few moments there was an oppressive silence broken at last by Cook who lifted the bottle and filled the glasses.

"Port wine," she said. "Wouldn't harm a babby and you needs a drop, miss, I wouldn't wonder."

The others appeared to need a drop also. They tasted solemnly with expressions intended to indicate that the flavour was strange to them.

"Go on, Mrs Lucas," Cook urged, smacking her lips and topping up the glasses, "You say your piece."

Mrs Lucas looked about her and the other two nodded encouragingly, the frills on their caps flapping up and down.

83

"In the Hall," she began majestically, "we feel that this . . . this unpleasantness is none of your seeking . . ."

"We all know that Bethune," interrupted Cook, "randy as a goat and sly as a cartload of monkeys . . ."

"If you please, Cook! You must understand, Miss Lester, we know . . . that is we have our suspicions, well, more than suspicions . . . we are tolerably certain . . ."

Mrs Lucas seemed to be bogged down in uncertainties.

"It's happened before," stated Cook coming to her rescue and draining her glass. "Poor critter."

"The circumstances," said Mrs Lucas in protest, "were not at all similar."

"Pooh," said Cook. "The only differ is that last time he lifted her skirts."

"Cook!" Mrs Lucas was purple with embarrassment. "Your unfortunate predecessor was dismissed in . . ."

"*That* one," said Mrs Sands speaking for the first time, "deserved all she got. Silly little slut, making sheep's eyes . . ."

"Point is, as I sees it," Cook put in, "you didn't make no sheep's eyes . . ."

Mrs Lucas's lips thinned with impatience.

"Cook, if you please . . . permit us to explain. It was agreed, was it not, that I should try to make our feelings on this matter plain." She cleared her throat. "Mrs Sands tells us that you have no family, Miss Lester. Is this the case?"

"Some cousins only," Amelia said.

"Are you able to go to them?"

"When they hear about this they'll most likely disown me."

"We have also come to hear," Mrs Lucas said delicately, "that the Mistress has declined to pay you what is owed."

"Mean as a Cardiff collier, that one," declared Mrs Sands who hailed from the north-west.

"Less'n it's her own back or her own belly," Cook commented.

"I have been in service in this family," Mrs Lucas said patiently, "since the time of the first Mrs Hoggett . . ."

"Now, she was a proper lady," Mrs Sands interrupted. "A good kind soul and not above her company like some I could name . . ."

84

". . . and I feel that I could *not* face the Master when he comes back and hears the tale unless I could say that someone here had had an eye to you. He'll be fit to tie when he hears . . ."

"And hear he will," said Mrs Sands. "I've wrote him. Four page . . . and crossin's. Told him everything."

The other two stared at her in dismay.

"*Everything*, Mrs Sands?"

"What I ain't said, he can work out for hisself," Mrs Sands retracted. "There's some things ain't nobody's business but his. Save as it touches the babby, bless 'im."

The others looked at one another and shook their heads mournfully: then they came back to the matter in hand.

"There's a question of a situation," Mrs Lucas said delicately. "No character."

She shook her head again and drew in her breath between her teeth.

"I thought I might try for a position as housekeeper," suggested Amelia, and looked to see how this was received. "I know no one would have me as a governess. But I have kept house for my father for years. Or I might be a dresser?"

The atmosphere cleared as if by magic: smiles blossomed and the three ladies leaned forward.

"We were not sure how to suggest it," Mrs Lucas said with evident relief. "But it is a position, a decent respectable position. *As* I know."

"Ah," said Cook. "I says as how she had her head screwed on."

"A decent respectable position . . ."

"And one as you can help her to, eh, Mrs Lucas?" Cook declared and leaned forward to refill the glasses. "Come, miss, drink up. It'll put heart into you."

But Amelia was looking eagerly at Mrs Lucas.

"Can you? Can you really?"

"A sorry thing if I can't when my own brother's wife manages a High Class Agency for Domestic Employment in London. Supplies all the best houses, she does. Now, I have taken the liberty to write her a letter which you can take along to Southampton Row. She'll find you a suitable place. You can depend upon it."

"And I've a brother too," said Mrs Sands. "He's a baker in

85

Holborn. And his wife owes me a favour ever since their last was born."

"London?" Amelia said and her face fell. "But I can't . . . I haven't . . ."

"Now hush," Mrs Sands commanded her. "We're none of us what you might call plump in the purse and we've our old age to consider but we reckoned it up that we could put down five pound between us. Thirty shilling from Mrs Lucas and me and forty shilling from Cook here . . ."

"I has me perks," said Cook and winked over her port.

"But I couldn't . . ." Amelia had gasped.

"You can and you must," Mrs Sands stated and no nursery would have defied her, "London ain't no place to land penniless and friendless, and it'll be nineteen and three train fare by the Parly. We have it arranged that Jem'll take you in to catch it and confound them all. He don't care whether he has this place or another and it'll make up to him for not being able to give that Bethune what he deserved."

At this point Amelia who had endured all that the evening had brought forth without shedding a tear broke down and was comforted with cold compresses and nursery endearments by the redoubtable Mrs Sands.

When she returned to her room just before midnight, much cheered by such practical kindness, she found an envelop thrust under her locked door. To her astonishment it contained ten sovereigns. There was nothing else: no note and no superscription. Amelia frowned over the coins and decided that Mrs Hoggett must have had second thoughts – it was more likely that she wanted Amelia to leave the district after all – and decided to pay her at least some of her quarter's salary. Amelia wondered whether she should give back the five pounds at once but came to the conclusion that it would be churlish: in any event even fifteen pounds was none too much if a situation was not to be had immediately. She decided she would keep it as a reserve and send it back as soon as she had secured a place.

The train rocked and rattled south, stopping and starting and dawdling on its way and the temperature in the crowded carriage rose. Amelia who had spent a sleepless night fell sound asleep and her head fell sideways on to the large lady's plump shoulder. That worthy sighed but accepted the

86

burden philosophically. As she said gruffly when Amelia apologised for the liberty, she had girls of her own and would miss care for a piece of pie. Amelia, whose breakfast had been a glass of milk and a crust of bread at four in the morning, would.

Some three days later Amelia, a list of names and addresses in her gloved hand, approached a tall house in Chelsea. It was the last house on the list and she looked at it without a great deal of optimism. At each of the others her application for the post of housekeeper had been turned down. She had been turned down at every interview since her arrival in London so that her early buoyancy had dissipated completely. The truth was, as she had come to realise, she did not look or sound in the least like a housekeeper. She was too young for one thing: the elderly preferred staid grey hairs. She was too pretty for another; mothers with young sons or wives with susceptible husbands rejected her out of hand as an unnecessary hazard to domestic harmony. The only household which had not conformed to one or another of these patterns was that of a youngish widow with a sour mouth and a down-trodden parlour-maid. There, Amelia had heard with guilty relief that the post was filled.

She felt guilty because Mrs Lucas's sister-in-law had been very kind and very patient but it was patent that she was fast running out of suitable possibilities. Moreover, Mrs Sands' brother, the Holborn baker, while he had taken her in was expecting their regular lodger to return in two days' time. Amelia looked up at the Chelsea house and fought down her sense of hopelessness and fear. Her feet hurt after three endless days of London pavements. She climbed the steps slowly and stood outside the door while she consulted the list to make sure of the name: Mr and Mrs Quentin Cartaret. There it was, engraved above the brass bell-pull.

She paused before pulling it and looked about her: first, she wanted to see whether there was a servants' or a tradesmen's bell. She had found out painfully that to ring the other when such a bell existed was to invite rebuke. Second, she had also found out that it was possible to discern a good deal about a household from the outside of the house. This house was tall and beautifully proportioned, four storeys high with large windows. Many of them were open, she noticed, in this unseasonable October sunshine, showing big rooms rather sparsely furnished. There were no layers of lace and net and blinds at the windows, just a hint of richly coloured brocades at either side. The paintwork was not the customary green or chocolate brown but a gleaming white defying the London soot. Only the front door made a splash of rich scarlet among all the white and grey. Below her on the area steps were pots of late-blooming flowers, dahlias and chrysanthemums. The whole gave a cheerful and generous impression. She gave one last look round before raising her hand to the bell and saw with a start that among the flowers was standing a small man in a green livery glaring at her from one small bright brown eye: over the other was a black patch.

"Are you a-going to ring, miss, or are you a-going to take yourself off?"

Amelia stared in astonishment.

"You been a-standin' there five minute by the kitchen clock," he accused. "You mistook us for the tooth-drawers or summink of that?"

She recovered and moved a little way down the front steps to lean over the balusters and speak to him. He was small and skinny and had the most bandy legs that she had ever seen.

"I've come to apply for the post of housekeeper," she told him diffidently. "They sent me from Southampton Row."

"Gor!" he said in patent disbelief. "You don't mean it? Things ain't 'arf lookin' up. Last two they sent was a couple of proper ol' tabbies. Not wot they was used to, sez they. They'd allus been in *good* service, they sez, where there was three kep', three at least . . . not jus' me an' women comin' in by the day. So off they both went wiv' their noses in the air an' a good riddance, sez I. What you been used to? If'n it ain't a rude question?"

Amelia chuckled.

"I'm not used to anything. This is the first time for me."

"Well, now . . . is that so?"

He peered up at her inquisitively.

"There's jus' me," he warned. "I'm cook, parlymaid, chambermaid, scullerymaid, 'tweenmaid, gardener, groom and valet, I am. Nursemaid too when 'Im-up-there's in his

88

altitoods. But I won't wash nor iron. There's a coupla wimmen comes in for washin's and scrubbin's."

Amelia sighed.

"You don't seem to need a housekeeper," she said regretfully. "Should I go away?"

"No. You come in and see if you takes to us. I don't 'old wiv old tabbies tellin' me wot's wot in me own kitchen, but you looks a bit of all right you do. 'Im-up-there, he likes a pretty face about 'im but no dah-de-dah if you takes me meanin', nuffink o' that, I *will* say. D'ye want I should open the front door or will you come in froo me kitchen?"

Amelia came down the steps at once, past the plants and down into the area. The green-clad figure flung open a tiny door under the front steps and she stepped unexpectedly into a bright sunny kitchen with light streaming in through the window at the other end. It winked off copper pans and gleaming plates and the polished satiny black range. It was like a fairytale where a hole in the ground led to a palace.

"Me kingdom," he said proudly, "and don't you forget it. Pantry . . . scullery . . ."

He opened and shut doors revealing glimpses of neat shelves and gleaming paintwork, rows of glass and china, orderly as soldiers on parade.

"Me garding . . . Polly's pride and joy, that is. Ain't a better garding in Lunnon."

It was indeed a beautiful sight. Row upon row of late vegetables, parsnips, leeks and cabbages; clumps of parsley and mint, carpets of thyme and deep green broccoli flourishing in a young forest.

"Don't need no greengrocer's rubbidge in this 'ouse," he said proudly. "Sparrow-grass there, see . . . raspberries, strawberries and I dunno what all. 'Im-up-there, 'e swears by me gardining. Brought up in the country I was. Me pa were a gardiner. What's bred in the bone they say . . ."

At the very bottom of the garden two horses looked mildly over a stable door.

"Lannie and Mac," he said. "Couple o' nice ol' gents. 'Im-up-there named them after a brace o' painter coves. The roan's Landseer and the bay's Maclise or summink o' that."

He drew her out on to the brick path which led up to the stable and turned her about to look up at the back of the house: a huge wall of glass, sloping very slightly inward, had replaced the whole of the back roof.

"'Im-up-there's studio. He's a painter cove an' all. I don't care for 'is picters but there's plenty do. You seen 'em? Quentin Cartaret RA an' all that. Paints females mostly. Very fashionable 'e is since some duchess or other had 'er likeness took."

Amelia searched her memory of the Academy exhibitions of once upon a time but like so many she had not attended in order to view the paintings. The name was not familiar.

"I don't think I know of him."

"Can't all be alike," he shrugged. "Come on."

He led the way back into the house. Amelia lingered briefly to look up at the great glass wall glittering gold in the westering sun. A shadow moved behind the panes and a face appeared, peering down. Amelia fled to follow her guide, feeling as if she had stepped into a story or a dream and would soon waken up.

He gave her a lightning tour of the house, flinging open doors to give her glimpses of high beautiful rooms with shining floors, sparsely furnished with pieces which fitted their surroundings perfectly.

"Dining-room, drawing-room, parlour . . . none of 'em ain't been used for a month 'o Sundays. 'Im-up-there don't 'ave no notion of poodle-faking. Sitting-room . . . but nobody don't sit much around 'ere, especially me. Lib'ry. 'E's in 'ere when 'e ain't up there . . ."

Amelia had a brief glimpse of books and leather chairs and richly coloured rugs before her guide flitted on.

"Morning room . . . study. Up 'ere's the bedrooms. That's 'is . . . that's mine. The rest's never used. You could 'ave yer pick."

He pattered up the next flight.

"Bedrooms up 'ere too. 'Ers. She 'ad the barfroom put in. Got a gas geyser and a patent douche an' all . . . brrr . . . everyone to 'is own taste, sez I, an' gimme a warm fire an' a nice sitz . . ."

The uppermost flight was narrow, bare and ill-lit by a grimy skylight and there was a low board-door at the head of it. Her guide paused with his hand on the latch, looked back at her and winked.

90

" 'E's in 'ere. Want to see 'im or would you rarver cut an' run now you seen it?"

"Shouldn't I rather see Mrs Cartaret?" she asked.

"Best go to Spain, then. Gone 'ome, she 'as, and she ain't a-comin' back and good riddance, I sez, with her tantrums and her garlic and her danged dogs scrattin' in my garding."

Without waiting for her reaction to this somewhat important statement he opened the door and led the way into a studio.

It was like swimming in light. Light poured in through the huge wall of glass and flashed and glittered and glowed on every surface. Amelia blinked, dazzled and delighted. The scent of oil and turpentine and size came to her nostrils. Canvases were stacked against the walls and on racks; piles of vividly coloured materials were heaped and draped over every item of furniture. On one heap was a lay-figure in an attitude of complete abandon. Oddments, musical instruments, a butterchurn, an oar, an earthenware pitcher and a hundred other curiously assorted items lay around.

"Proper Paddy's Market, innit?" said the manservant under his breath. "Props he calls them . . . litter sez I . . ."

In the middle of all this stood a large easel and in front of the easel a huge figure outlined against the light which turned his wildly untidy red hair into a halo.

"What is it, Polly?"

"New 'ousekeeper, sir . . ."

Polly paused uncharacteristically at a loss.

"Wot's yer name?" he hissed at Amelia.

"Lester. Miss Lester," she hissed back.

"What?" asked Cartaret absently without looking at them.

"She's a Miss Lester, sir. Come about the advert."

Cartaret glanced at them casually and then his gaze sharpened like sunshine concentrated in a lens.

"Yes," he said, "yes, by all means. I thought the name was something like Burrowes, though. Got a memory like a sieve. Show her where to undress, Polly and then put a match to the stove. There's still time to make a few sketches."

Amelia looked at Polly in surprise. He cast his eyes up despairingly.

"It ain't the model, sir. She ain't come. It's the new 'ousekeeper. *'Ousekeeper.*"

"What's that?" Cartaret was staring at his canvas. "Doesn't matter, she'll do."

"But she don't want to, sir. She come to keep 'ouse, not pose in 'er buff."

Cartaret applied a swirl of yellow with enormous concentration, stepped back, nodded and laid aside his palette.

"Now what's all this? I distinctly specified someone ready to pose in the nude. You're no use to me if you don't."

Polly sighed ostentatiously.

"This is Miss Lester, the new 'ousekeeper, sir. She don't want to pose. 'Ousekeepers don't pose."

Cartaret advanced upon them. He was an impressive figure, more than six feet tall with a bony, ugly face dominated by a great high-bridged nose. He might have been any age from thirty to forty. His eyes were a blue-grey and brightly intent. He wore a paint-stained workman's shirt and a pair of trousers so stained and filthy that the original material was hardly to be seen. His bare feet were thrust into Turkish slippers. He examined Amelia minutely.

"This one could," he said. "I'd be happy to have her pose. Interesting face, not vapid, good colouring. Good figure too, though she could do with a few pounds extra."

Amelia was uncertain whether to laugh or to flee in dismay. She was conscious that she liked this rather antic figure.

"I can't believe you've ever kept any house unless it was a doll's house."

His gaze sharpened suddenly and he took her chin in his hand. His fingers smelled of turpentine. He ran a forefinger of his other hand gently down her cheek.

"Who gave you that bruise?"

Amelia blushed scarlet and jerked her chin away.

"It was an accident," she mumbled.

"If you mean it's none of my business, say so."

"Then, it's none of your business . . . sir," she added hastily.

He chuckled.

"So you want to keep house? Are you sure you wouldn't rather pose for me? I pay well, you know."

"No thank you."

"No family to support?" he enquired.

"I'm not married."

"That is not always a concomitant to dependents. That . . ." he pointed at the bruise on her cheek, "has a domestic touch about it."

Amelia blushed again and covered it with her hand.

"No family at all," she affirmed. "No dependents."

"Hmmm . . ."

He looked at her minutely and seemed to like what he saw. Amelia was conscious that she wanted this post very much indeed.

"You'll keep us in order?" he enquired. "See us warm and clean and well-fed?"

"It seems that . . . er . . ."

She looked at Polly who grinned gappily at her.

"Me moniker's 'Enry but 'im-there calls me Polly . . . because o' me eye."

"Polyphemus," murmured Mr Cartaret. "It was charmingly inappropriate. He doesn't answer to anything else now. You will find he is indispensable."

"I can see that."

Polly jerked his head at her in a gesture of approval and appreciation.

"I think he could do with help," Cartaret said. "And we lack the feminine touch. Do you think you can bear with him . . . and me, of course?"

"I would be pleased to . . . sir."

"Then you shall come and try it. Fifty pounds a year and all found, whatever that means. Your own room and sitting-room and a voyage to Italy every winter. Could you keep house in Italy?"

"Italy?" she cried in delight. "Oh, indeed I could. I can speak Italian."

"Do you indeed? It seems that you're a housekeeper in a thousand. My last one departed in tears from Gemignano because she could not obtain what she wanted from the market and she was convinced the maids were laughing at her . . . which, of course, they were. So that is settled."

He looked back at his easel.

"I must make use of the light while it lasts. Harness up Landseer, Polly and take her to fetch her traps. Put her in the

93

rooms below here. She can have the little sitting room for her own."

"In the missus's rooms, sir?"

"Why not?" Cartaret had wandered away and was beginning to mix colour on the palette. "My wife won't be needing them. Ah . . . now there's a snag. No chaperone. Unless you count Polly, here. No other female. It'll burst the bubble reputation with a bang. Perhaps you'd better think twice before you accept. You're no withered choppy-chapped ancient, after all."

"It doesn't signify," Amelia murmured uncomfortably, "if you have no objection. It will reflect on you just as much."

Polly gave her a sharp glance. Cartaret frowned at his canvas.

"Artist's licence," he said vaguely and smiled. "Settle her in, Polly. I've work to do."

"If you want references," she began, "I've got a . . ."

"No," he said. "They don't mean much, I find. I've written glowing references for people I was glad to be quit of. Try it for a month. Then we'll talk again."

Down again in Polly's kitchen kingdom, drinking coffee in the golden evening sunshine, Amelia could scarcely believe her good fortune: it seemed she had found a post where she might even be happy as well as fed and sheltered. Polly and his master were people she could like. To look after them would be no hardship.

"It's a beautiful house," she remarked dreamily.

"I think it's a bit bare-like meself," Polly said. "But there's no denying it's easy to keep."

"You'll tell me how to go on?" Amelia asked. "What's to be done and when, and what he likes . . ."

"Ain't you kept house, then, miss?"

"Oh, yes . . . ever since I was sixteen, but it was not . . . I was not . . ."

"Ah," he said. "Your own house like?"

"In a sense," she agreed.

"Don't you worrit," Polly said paternally. "I'll see you right, never fear."

That night, lying in a prettily draped bed, her clothes stowed in the ample drawers and cupboards, Amelia stretched like a cat. For the first time since that hot June night when she had been brought downstairs in the London house by the sound of Mrs Grey's hysterics Amelia felt secure, even content. Life had put on a visage less grim and fearful. She could look forward to the new day . . . even the day after that.

7

*"Those who have no shame
have no conscience."*

It was as well for her new-found content that Amelia, learning her duties, was quite unaware of what was happening at
Blackyetts. There her departure had marked a number of
changes. Dorcas, blubbering with distress, hunted all morning for her governess and when she was not to be found had a
frightening 'tantrum'. From that day on she 'offended' constantly and her 'tantrums' became worse and more frequent.
Mrs Hoggett, with a convincing display of grief and regret,
sent to the establishment of Scarborough which advertised
discreetly that it cared for 'unfortunate members of good
families unable to remain within the confines of the family
circle'. This was in grim fact a small lunatic asylum run
economically and at a considerable profit by a retired medical
man and his wife with the invaluable aid of a midwife and
an ex-prizefighter. Mrs Hoggett declined to inspect the
premises. The journey would have been long and tedious
and the experience distressing to one of her sensibilities:
moreover, she was convinced that Dr and Mrs Postlethwaite
were good Christian people and would treat her little Dorcas
with kindness. And doubtless they would have done had
they had much to do with the inmates. As it was the midwife
and the ex-prizefighter had it pretty much their own way and
their ways were not always kind. Letters were exchanged
and the midwife came to fetch Dorcas away. The last the
tight-lipped and tearless Mrs Sands saw of her nursling she
was screaming with terror and bewilderment behind the
closed window of the station fly.

Louisa whose mind, though limited in scope, was

96

markedly tenacious, disgraced herself by a vehement (if rather incoherent) defence of her beloved Miss Lester in the drawing-room where her stepmama was regaling avid morning-callers with a sensational account of the events leading to the governess's dismissal. It was a phenomenon as entertaining as the account had been and Mrs Hoggett felt it deeply. For this offence Louisa was confined to her room on bread-and-water for a week, a punishment she endured stoically, feeling in some obscure fashion that she was helping to establish Miss Lester's innocence. She had a good deal of sympathy in the household. Baxter contrived to smuggle in certain delicacies and Jem offended against standing orders by exercising Coppertop daily over the newly raked gravel of the front drive under the windows of her room. Amy and Jane risked punishment by creeping to the door and whispering their sympathy and support through the keyhole.

Mr Bethune was, as Amelia had anticipated, quickly re-established. He absented himself for a day or two at the end of which he returned as if nothing untoward had happened. 'Bold as bleeding brass,' was Cook's comment and it was echoed by the rest of the Hall. He resumed charge of Albert, if that was the word to describe his casual supervision of Albert's studies, and gave his support to the banishment of Dorcas. Mrs Hoggett passed on to her acquaintance his description of 'that Miss Lester's' unremitting pursuit of him and was at some pains to make it plain that these disgraceful events were in no respect Mr Bethune's fault, that he had behaved himself, in trying circumstances, in a most gentlemanly way. She would follow up these assertions with the intelligence that she had given him charge of the schoolroom and would she, she asked with sweet reasonableness, have done such a thing if Mr Bethune had been in the slightest to blame for Miss Lester's downfall?

The truth was that having got her own way and rid herself of Amelia she was unwilling (on more than one count) to give herself the trouble of finding another governess. As she told anyone patient enough to listen the whole race was thoroughly unreliable. Baxter became chaperone. Alice was delighted with this arrangement and worked as she had never worked for Miss Lester, overwhelming the bored tutor with essays and extracts and poems. Amy and Jane followed her example, though they had wept for a day and a night when they heard Miss Lester had gone. Louisa, however, refused to have anything to do with him and declared that her education was at an end, a pronouncement which Bethune was content to leave uncontradicted. He found her sullen, suspicious hatred disconcerting. Louisa returned to haunt the stables and lay plans for her stud farm. For this establishment she engaged in advance the services of Jem who was willing enough to sympathise with her, even if he had reservations about the likelihood of her succeeding in her plans.

The Room and the Hall observed these developments with hostile disapproval. Bethune was studiously ignored and persecuted as only the Room and the Hall knew how: he contrived not to notice, or, at all events, not to comment upon the unanswered bells, the disregarded orders, the ill-served food and the other slights laid upon him. Blackyetts settled down to await the return of its Master in the spring of the year in much the same mood as England under John awaited the return of Richard the Lionheart. At the end of four weeks, however, there arose another major crisis.

Mrs Hoggett announced at the dinner table in front of Booth and the tablemaid that she would need Mr Bethune's assistance in settling the quarterly accounts and paying the household wages. When, next morning, in his presence and that of Ellis, she went to the bureau to take out the money she found the drawer empty. Mr Hoggett who had had, not unjustified, doubts about the Bindleton Bank had left more than a thousand sovereigns in that drawer which was 'secret' insofar as it did not immediately announce its presence. These had gone together with a leather case of jewellery once the property of the first Mrs Hoggett and now held in trust for Louisa and Alice. These jewels were the source of a certain amount of chagrin to the second Mrs Hoggett for there were amongst them some very valuable and pleasing pieces; pieces which, she felt, had not been matched by Mr Hoggett's offerings to herself. Ellis, emitting little squeaks of horror and dismay, ran to the drawer where the other jewels were kept and found them untouched.

The discovery of her loss was signified by Mrs Hoggett with a shriek which rattled the windows of her boudoir and brought every member of the household within earshot eagerly running to discover who was murdering the Mistress.

During the hours which followed Blackyetts hummed and scurried like a disturbed hive. The Mistress, fainting and distraught was revived with burnt feathers and sal volatile, only to lie tearfully lamenting her loss, while the servants talked uneasily of what must follow. Lamentation was followed by wild and extravagant speculation upon how such a robbery could have been contrived. It took very little time to settle who must have been the culprit.

"Depend upon it," she wailed, "it must have been that nasty, wicked, loose, *thieving* creature. She had the run of the house. She knew where it was. She saw me work the drawer. Who else could have done such a thing!"

"Send for the police and tell them," Alice suggested, rejoicing unkindly in this revelation about Louisa's fallen idol. "She ought to be put in jail."

Bethune did not oppose this suggestion; obviously the theft would have to be investigated. It was, there could be no doubt, a considerable sum. Mr Hoggett would have to be informed without delay and perhaps they should wait upon his instructions before proceeding in the matter. It was possible that he had thought better of leaving all that gold in a wooden bureau and had banked it elsewhere before he left. After all, he had mentioned that he might be home sooner than he expected. His palterings exasperated Mrs Hoggett.

"Of course he left it! You saw it yourself, Telemachus . . . you saw it when I took the Sunday sixpences from the drawer . . ."

He agreed reluctantly and with more than a hint of irritation in his voice that he had.

"And what would Mr Hoggett say to me if I did nothing in the matter?" she demanded dramatically. "And then there are the jewels . . . all those poor dear lambs have left of their beloved mama. They were in the drawer, I know they were. Did you not look at them with me, Alice, my love?"

"Yes, Mama," Alice agreed. "And don't you recall . . . when I tried on the garnets Miss Lester laughed and said I should not make such a guy of myself. So she knew they were there as well."

"It must be she!" Mrs Hoggett exclaimed dramatically, "It can be no other! We must report that matter without delay."

Bethune agreed petulantly that he supposed there could be no other course and pulled the bell.

Jem was sent to Bindleton to return with a uniformed sergeant and a constable. Both were somewhat overawed by the surroundings and the style of the bereft victim who interviewed them from a day-bed with two daughters and a maid in support and ordered them very much as if they had been part of her domestic staff to find, arrest and imprison one Miss Amelia Lester, present whereabouts unknown. In these somewhat difficult circumstances the policeman made a few enquiries which Mrs Hoggett answered impatiently, assuring them that she was right and they would find she was right without all these tiresome questions. To their credit they persisted. Why, they asked, if Miss Lester was to blame and she had left some four weeks earlier had the theft not been discovered sooner?

"Because I had no occasion to need money," she answered impatiently. "I only settle the household accounts once a quarter and Mr Hoggett had done it up to the end of the month before he left."

When the sergeant suggested tactfully that she must have had occasion to need money during that time she was indignant.

"This sum was quite apart from my own pin-money."

What she did not say was that she was expected to account for every penny of the housekeeping fund, a task she found difficult.

"When did you last see the money, madam?"

She shilly-shallied and could not be sure but thought that it was a few days before her confinement. Bethune agreed. A few outstanding accounts had been settled at that time. Receipts were produced. Mrs Hoggett lost her patience and demanded that they go straightway and arrest the thief. The force said stolidly that they needed a little solid evidence before their superiors would agree to the investigation of Miss Lester's possible complicity. Alice, in support of her stepmama and revelling in the drama, remembered that she had heard Miss Lester leave her room very late on the night

100

that she was dismissed and it was more than an hour before she came back.

"If I had but thought!" mourned Mrs Hoggett. "I am too trusting. Out of the goodness of my heart I permitted her to stay one more night under my roof. I did not do as I should have done, thrust her out of the gates that very instant and sent her possessions after her. No, I must lay the household open to danger and let her stay . . ."

"How might she have found the key, ma'am?" asked the sergeant, examining the empty drawer. "The lock has not been picked or broken."

"What? But it must have been!"

"No, ma'am."

She flung herself back on her cushions.

"Where do you keep your keys?" asked the sergeant.

"In my reticule. They are always near me."

"Did you leave them anywhere, that night?"

"I cannot recall . . . I was distraught . . . distressed beyond measure . . ."

"But Mama, don't you remember?" Alice broke in, delighted to be able to supply yet another piece of information. "Albert found your reticule in the belvedere. He brought it to you in the morning and you gave him a sixpence."

"Of course . . . I had quite forgotten. She could have found it easily," Mrs Hoggett said eagerly. "I left her there . . . I could not bear to look at the nasty creature another moment."

Albert when summoned from the library confirmed this.

"I found it in the morning," he said. "Mr Bethune wasn't there for lessons so I went for a walk. I wanted to look at the little room above the summer-house . . ."

"The place of assignation," said Mrs Hoggett with a shudder. "That such things should happen in a respectable household . . ."

"It was lying on the stairs, just inside the door," Albert said.

Later he added another item.

"Stepmother didn't pay Miss Lester her wages," he told them. "She said they were forfeit because Miss Lester had done something disgraceful . . ."

101

Ingenuousness sat uneasily upon Albert but the sergeant did not know him. He looked meaningly over the boy's head at his assistant.

"No money, I'll lay . . . and a motive, if she needed one. Looks bad for the girl."

The constable looked doubtful.

"*They* say she isn't the thief," he announced, jerking his head in the direction of the kitchen. "They're all for the girl. They want to pin it on the tutor. Say he's a rum 'un!"

The sergeant looked shocked.

"The tutor! But he's Canon Bethune's son and third cousin to Lord Billington. A most respectable family."

"He don't act very respectable by their account," said the constable but was very properly reproved by his superior for setting himself up against his elders and betters and listening to Servants' Hall gossip.

"Bethune's been here a matter of three year," he said. "Which would you choose for the job? A little fly-by-night what no one don't know nothing about or a decent respectable parson's son."

On the sergeant's report the decision was taken at a higher level to trace the whereabouts of Miss Amelia Lester and see whether she could throw light upon this theft. The wheels of the law creaked majestically into motion, grinding exceeding slow but advancing inexorably nevertheless.

After some six weeks in the Chelsea house Cartaret had persuaded Amelia to sit for him . . . clothed. She wore a blue silk gown abandoned by the departed Mrs Cartaret pinned clumsily behind her and her head was bent over some white needlework which reflected light on to her face. A length of crimson velvet was draped over the chair on which she sat. She made a pleasing study.

Cartaret, mute and intent, worked swiftly with charcoal, sketching directly on to the canvas till he had blocked out the framework for his painting: he stood back after about twenty minutes and looked minutely at what he had done.

"Caught it!" he muttered nodding with satisfaction and began to tap the stretchers with his maulstick to shake out the surplus charcoal dust. "Take a rest, Amelia. You're a good sitter."

She stretched, cautiously because of the pins, and tossed her head up and down to ease her neck muscles.

"It's hard work," she announced in a surprised tone.

"It is," he agreed. "Harder than housekeeping?"

"In a way," she admitted.

"You've been here more than a month," Cartaret remarked suddenly. "Have you decided to stay with us? Or is the household too unconventional for you?"

"It suits me very well," she said quietly. "I was hoping you would keep me on."

"No question about that. Polly's devoted. Bit of all right, he says."

One of Cartaret's attributes was an ability to mimic. Amelia smiled to hear Polly's pert cockney voice emerge from his employer's mouth.

"And I've no complaints," he added. "Save one, of course."

Amelia's refusal to sit for him in the nude had become a bone of contention between them, in a good-humoured teasing style.

"My respected lady sitters and their chaperones are prone to remark how comfortably I'm placed, these days," he remarked, busily mixing colours, "when they are not trying to elicit, oh, so delicately, when dearest Constantia is coming back. I think they expected me to be living like the minotaur in its lair, surrounded by gnawed bones. Take the pose again, please."

He began to block in the figure with a pleasing sureness of touch.

"They are also very curious about you," he said suddenly. "And who, pray, is that *pretty* creature who admitted us, they ask archly. And what would dear Constantia say if she knew. I'll wager she knows. She'll have had a shoal of letters by this time."

"Will she object?"

"She has no right to object. Her present lover is a coachman, I believe. I am afraid Constantia did not care for London. The men were cold, she said, and the climate shocking."

Amelia knew a curiosity to discover why he had married her but quelled it. It was, she reminded herself, no concern of hers. It was a little disconcerting when Cartaret with a half-smile on his mouth observed, "She was quite beautiful, you know. Spanish girls are. Like a ripe plum with the bloom on it. Irresistible. And guarded, my God. Veils and brothers and mamas and aunts and duennas. I accepted the challenge and found myself walking up the aisle."

Amelia smiled at the tone of his voice.

"She had a *succès fou* when I brought her home," he went on. "All that black hair and creamy skin and the Spanish accent. Quite delicious. But she liked attention. She was accustomed to being treated like a goddess, with regular sessions of worship. She objected to my painting other women and sulked . . . my God, how she could sulk. And she liked dogs. There were five of the little brutes. They drove poor Polly wild."

"Did she like Polly?"

"No. She wanted me to exchange him for a nice smart butler with a good set of calves and a dignified manner."

"He would have hated that."

"Yes. She gave me a choice, she said. It was Polly or her . . . so, I decided that Polly was a lot more important to my comfort and chose him."

Amelia stared, torn between amusement and dismay.

"You don't mean it?"

"Oh, indeed I do."

Cartaret glanced up from the picture.

"I was bored beyond belief. You know, it isn't infidelity which destroys marriage. I was quite prepared to put up with her affairs. At least they took her off my hands. But boredom . . . it is destructive. And she was as bored as I. So I handed her back her settlement, which was considerable, kissed her on both cheeks in the Spanish style and saw her off thankfully by the boat-train at Victoria."

He began to lay down a thick ground of ultramarine.

"Are you shocked?"

"No, I don't think so," she answered thoughtfully. "I think you've told me the truth and that's always gratifying."

"Yes," he agreed. "The best of compliments, I think."

For about five minutes he painted in silence.

"Do they interrogate you?" he asked suddenly.

Amelia looked at him blankly.

104

"Mind the pose!" he said sharply. "I mean the ladies who come to the house."

"Oh, yes," she admitted.

"Are they any more successful?"

"I usually answer in Italian," she told him and enjoyed his startled look. "It is really quite effective. They are taken aback and I can bring them up before they decide how to continue."

"Masterly," he commented, obviously entertained. "Unless your interrogator also speaks Italian. Mrs Drummond does for one."

Mrs Drummond's portrait was looking at them with an intent pale-eyed stare from the corner where current work was put to dry.

"Oh, she is delighted to show how good is her Italian," Amelia said. "And I am admiring. We exchange compliments all the way upstairs."

He laughed outright.

"And when they pin you down? For I suppose they do. London Society contains more vulgar curiosity than any other. And they are adept at eliciting information."

"Then I say modestly that they cannot possibly be interested in me and show them upstairs rather quickly. At the top of the second flight they are so blown they can't pursue the matter any further."

Cartaret laughed without restraint.

"I had no notion you could be so devious," he declared delightedly. He stood back from the canvas, screwing up his eyes to check the colour of the ground against the blue of the gown. "Of course you realise they are quite convinced that you are my mistress," he added abruptly.

"I realise that."

"I don't suppose your unwillingness to reveal anything about yourself does anything to disabuse them of the idea. Not that anything would. In your place that is what they would be. Do you mind?"

She didn't answer right away.

"It was inevitable, I suppose. You did warn me."

His next comment was indistinguishable because he had a brush between his teeth.

"I beg your pardon?"

105

"It was an impertinent and unimportant observation."

He was laughing again. As he worked, looking at her with that curiously hard impersonal painter's gaze, she wondered if he had heard some of the barbed comments of the sitters; if he had heard about the family next door. There was a little girl in the house next door, a child of about ten, a lonely, rather neglected little girl. Her parents went very much about and entertained a great deal and Patty was in the care of the servants who left her to her own devices. She and Amelia had met in – of all places – an apple tree. It grew in the Cartaret garden but in the manner of apple trees did lean down low over the garden next door. Amelia, on a ladder gathering some especially desirable russets, discovered one hoary fork occupied by Patty and a book. Their acquaintance ripened speedily. Patty made frequent use of this informal way into the garden and would invade the kitchen where she devoured biscuits and discussed poetry (she had determined upon becoming a poet, not a poetess; that was, she thought, an ugly word). She was there one afternoon when the front door bell rang lustily and because Polly was in the garden snugging down the asparagus for the winter Amelia had gone to answer it.

The scene which followed she would find hard to forget. Patty's mother with an angry guilty nursemaid in support demanded the return of their precious charge and abused Amelia for enticing an innocent child into a den of vice. Everyone, they said in chorus, knew what went on in this house. She was never to speak to the child again or the police would be informed and she would be given in charge. Patty was whisked away in tears and the only memento of the brief friendship was a grubby piece of paper which had been wrapped round an apple and thrown into the garden.

'You are a good true friend,' it declared in a shaky copy-plate,

'And I am yours for aye.
My love for you will never bend,
No mater what they say.'

Underneath this poem in a much less elegant hand she had scrawled,

'Mama says you are a loos woman and I must not speak to

106

you ever agane. I said you werent loos and I liked you and they whipt me and said I would com to a bad end like you. What badend. When Im grownup well be frends. Lottie in the kitchen said about scarlet women but you wear grey. I wish people would tell people things.'

It had been a hurtful incident and it had underlined for Amelia what it meant to abandon the appearance of virtue. It seemed that events had her in a grip which not all her struggles would serve to break. It was not enough to be virtuous, it seemed, it was necessary to appear so. She felt a coldness at the pit of her stomach. Only last spring she had been happy, she had had an assured future, a family, friends. It was just turned winter and she had lost all of these and her reputation as well. If Cartaret sent her away she might yet end on the streets.

"Don't look so desperate," he said suddenly. "You need not regard what people think."

You need not, she thought bitterly, you are a man, wealthy, talented, master of your own fate. I am not in the same situation. For a moment she knew a surge of bitter acrid resentment at what had happened to her and none of it her fault. To be helpless was not something she could expect Cartaret to understand.

"Now you are formally installed," he said suddenly, "not just as a member of the household but also as my maîtresse – en titre – if not in fact – I don't suppose you could be induced to confide in me?"

Amelia did not reply but her hands clenched suddenly on her sewing.

"Relax . . . that's better. I don't suppose there is anything very dreadful to tell. And I did give you refuge, after all."

"Refuge," Amelia repeated. "I was under the impression that you gave me a job."

"Refuge," he insisted. "I employed not a genteel little nobody but a gently bred girl with traces in her habits and her wardrobe of a wealthy past. I find out that she has an excellent education – you are really very well-read, you know, Amelia – and she has many accomplishments which suggest she ought to be a governess rather than a house-keeper. Intriguing. And you are really very good to look at . . . almost a beauty. Not usual in mousy housekeepers, I promise you."

Amelia's heart beat hard.

"There was that bruise," he went on, "and a general air of being at the end of your tether. Dammit girl, don't look so startled. My job is to *see*. If I don't see more than appears on the surface I wouldn't be a good painter. And I am a good painter."

He laid down his palette and began to mix up a wash of scarlet.

"Take a rest. At first I thought you must be a runaway wife and for the first few days while you were with us I was expecting an irate husband to appear on my doorstep and demand your return. But I don't think you have ever been married, have you?"

Amelia shook her head.

"No, you don't have the air of it."

"What air is that?" she enquired.

"A subtle change occurs, I find, not one I can describe. Lester is not your name, is it?"

Amelia jumped and looked as confused as she felt.

"Why should you think that?"

"You are sometimes slow to answer to it," he observed and picked up his palette. "Take the pose please."

He began to paint again, frowning.

"Don't you trust me?"

She did not answer. Trust was something she was wary of giving. To trust was to lay yourself open to betrayal. She had trusted her father and he had left her to bear the consequences of what he had done: she had trusted Mr Hoggett and he had abandoned her to cope alone with a situation which was quite beyond her. She would have liked to trust Cartaret but if he turned on her or did not believe her she could end on the streets. All the same, the temptation to lay her burden on his shoulders was very strong.

"I think my feelings are hurt," he said and it was not wholly a jest.

Amelia remained silent but he looked up from the canvas and saw the distress and confusion in her face.

"Hell and damnation!" he ejaculated. "Don't look at me like that. Forget what I said. You'll tell me some day in your own good time. It was just . . ." he added awkwardly, "I thought we had become friends. I can't imagine the place without you . . . oh, Hell . . ."

Amelia made her decision and opened her mouth to speak and explain why she had hesitated but just then the door creaked open and Polly appeared.

"The food's on the table," he announced peevishly, "and it has been this arf hour. Didn't neither on you 'ear the gong? And miss 'as got the up'olsterers comin' this arternoon, along o' the dining-room chairs."

"The devil fly away with the dining-room chairs," Cartaret said irritably, for he had seen Amelia's decision in her face. "What's up with them?"

"The velvet is worn. We agreed they needed reseating," Amelia explained.

"And your luncheon's on the table," insisted Polly.

"I need five minutes . . . just five minutes."

"I knows you, guv. That'll stretch to an hour before you knows it."

He waited, adamant, in the doorway with a silver turnip of a watch in his hand and the moment passed. Cartaret was not sure enough of Amelia's feelings to insist that he went and reflected that even if he had been, the interruption had somehow broken the rapport which would have made the confession (if that was what it was going to be) bearable.

Later, Amelia, clad again in her neat grey gown, braiding her hair before her looking glass, regretted that the moment had passed.

"I'll be sitting again tomorrow," she reminded her reflection.

But, if she told him would he be able to understand just what had happened to her? Her descent from wealth and what she had thought to be security to a precarious, almost disreputable, existence might seem incredible to him, a romance. Her mouth twisted at the prospect of being disbelieved. It was not that she minded being a housekeeper. It was not especially onerous, not nearly so onerous as being a governess. Polly did some of the cooking while she prepared the menus and the shopping lists and took care of the accounts. In any other establishment there would have been a kitchen-maid; as it was Amelia lent Polly a hand, prepared vegetables, helped him wash dishes. She would have served the food but that he preferred to do this himself and Cartaret liked her to eat with him. The polishing and the cleaning of the house and the laundry was done by two daily women, red-faced, ginny cronies who had favoured her with lewd, avid, all-too-audible speculation. "Some folk knows what's good for them," she had heard, and, "Housekeeper's one word for her, eh?" Polly had put a stop to that. At least, he had silenced the remarks: she suspected that under their, "Yes'm, right away mum," their opinion of her was very much what it had ever been and she could not persuade herself she did not care, because she did. It was humiliating to be thought a trollop.

In some ways it would have been easier to bear if it had been true. The injustice galled unbearably. She looked at herself in the mirror and realised that the past six months had left their mark on her; Cartaret liked to paint her face now but in six years would he feel the same way? If he asked her to be his mistress, as she thought he might, would she agree? She liked him, she liked him better than any man she had ever met and she had done since the day she came into the house. Where Bethune's sly fondlings had roused in her nothing but a sick disgust, Cartaret's occasional impersonal touch as he moved a hand or adjusted the angle of her head made her feel as she had never felt, even when she believed herself in love with Oliver. She would find 'that side of things', as she phrased it to herself, no hardship. In any case she admired his forthrightness, his impatience with folly and humbug, his humour; his view of things echoed her own opinions, rarely voiced except to Ailey. He made Oliver pale into a rather callow, conventional young man for whom she had entertained a tepid affection not to be compared with the sense of fellowship she enjoyed with Cartaret. Illogically, considering the pains she had been at to prevent Oliver's finding her, she felt that Cartaret would have raised heaven and earth to find her given the same circumstances, and, she smiled, would certainly have succeeded.

Staring at her face in the mirror she put the last few pins into her braid and admitted to herself that she had been

110

within an ace of telling Cartaret her whole story. She knew instinctively, also, that he had been just as close to asking her to be his mistress. She wondered what she would have said if he had come to it and knew with a jerk of surprise that she would almost certainly have agreed. She could justify such a decision perfectly cold-bloodedly if she wished. If she were asked and refused she could not stay, and there was nowhere else she could go. Her virtue seemed a small price to pay for security, especially when she had already lost the major benefit of that evanescent possession. She could not expect to marry now. When the time came . . . she shivered a little at the thought . . . when Cartaret tired of her she could trust him not to fling her penniless into the street. The shiver of dismay she experienced at the prospect of losing Cartaret told her that she could rationalise her wish to become his mistress all she liked but had the circumstances been different, had she met him on much more level terms, her wishes would have been just the same. She had, in every sense that mattered, met her match.

Had she but known it Cartaret was a floor below her scrubbing paint out of his nails and cursing Polly for his untimely arrival. Cartaret was not a man to indulge in heart-searchings. He had no doubts and if he had scruples they were not the same as those which others might have entertained. He liked Amelia and wanted to take her to bed: he liked her enough to want the decision to be hers and he had enough experience in such matters to know. But, first, she would have to tell him whatever it was she was hiding. Cartaret did not imagine that it was anything very terrible, she seemed more of a refugee than a fugitive. Nor was he beset by any moral scruples about taking a gently bred virtuous girl for his mistress. He intended to treat her as his wife and that intention weighed more heavily in the scales than the fact that she could not be his wife in law. He was more concerned by the timing of his approach: he must not drive her into leaving. If she did she would be unlikely to find a post and if she did a similar situation was almost certain to arise. The thrust of anger he endured at such an idea surprised him. He had an impulse to hit any such lecherous swine who would try to take advantage of her hard on his slavering mouth! Dumbfounded by such a reaction, it came to him that his emotions were much more involved with Amelia than he had realised.

It was a silent meal. Both Cartaret and Amelia would have been hard put to it to say what Polly put in front of them. Amelia was trying to come to terms with her situation where she was being forced into doing something she very much wanted to do in any event and Cartaret was bitterly regretting that he had not encountered Amelia before he went to Spain and was caught in the parson's mousetrap. He forgot she would still have been in the schoolroom. The account of his marriage which he had given her was perfectly accurate. Cartaret habitually told the truth, not so much because he believed in the truth for its own sake but because he considered that few things were worth the effort of lying. He had described the collapse of an ill-founded relationship without sugaring over his feelings or his wife's: but he had omitted a good deal which he did not think to be important. Constantia had been discreet in her affairs and the story to which Society had attributed her departure was of Cartaret's own unfaithfulness. He had been unfaithful, he would never have denied it, but he did not consider his lapses in the slightest degree important; they were impulsive, never compulsive. Handed a peach on a platter, he ate it, but, to the annoyance of more than one peach-profferer, he did not feel compelled to seek out the tree on which they grew. His own view of the matter was that he was a man cut out for marriage . . . not a view shared by all his acquaintance . . . and he had married a woman cut out for the demi-monde. Cartaret liked to have a woman about the place but he could not be bothered with what he termed the flummery and poodle-faking which Constantia demanded. It came to him that Amelia might share his views on flummery and poodle-faking: she would not inflict dreadful dinner-parties on him when the light was right and he wanted to paint on into the evening. To do him credit he did not reflect that her opportunities to attend such dinner-parties would be few even if she wanted them, her value to him lay in that he did not believe she would want them at all, they would bore her as they bored him. He bit noisily into an apple and considered the future. Dammit, he'd got uncommonly fond of her: it wouldn't be just the comfort and convenience of having his own woman instead of having to make do with other men's, he would enjoy making her happy and secure, chasing that unhappy, wary look from her face, buying her clothes . . . she could do with a good fur for the winter . . . she would pay for dressing, he thought . . . and undressing, he added happily and bit off another chunk of apple. He wanted to give her presents and watch her face when she opened them. And if there were children, so much the better. He liked children. He was godfather to a score of them, the little blighters: it would be pleasant to have a few of his own. The house was large enough for a round half-dozen.

After lunch he ran upstairs to the studio, smiling. Once there he pinned up all the sketches he had made of Amelia and stood looking from one to another, savouring the future. He would make haste slowly, he decided, let things take their course. There was no need to rush.

Amelia, three floors below, being decisive with the upholsterer about the superiority of leather over haircloth, was conscious of being like a child confronted by a birthday or the prospect of Christmas and chid herself.

Next morning she went shopping early. This was unusual, for Polly did most of the shopping, but he was engaged upon the brewing of beer. He distrusted all commercial brews and the racking of the liquor from brewtub to barrel was a long business. She went early because sitting was to start at ten o'clock and she wanted to have all her work finished before it began. Cartaret took little account of the need to scrape carrots or polish silver. Soon after eight she emerged from the scarlet front door and ran down the steps. It was a dull, chilly, misty November morning; the plane trees which lined the streets were golden and red and russet and great drifts of their leaves choked the gutter. Amelia pulled her grey serge cloak about her; it had a soft rabbit-fur collar and she snuggled her chin gratefully into it. Behind the elegant Regency terrace where the house stood ran a narrow mews lane and at the far end of that was a cluster of small shops and stalls. Here she could obtain all the odds and ends she had on the list in her pocket; a card of shoe buttons, a length of velvet ribbon, a box of Albatum for the silver and, if it was to be had, a copy of the *Quarterly Review*. She checked the list as she turned into the lane. Already the shops were opening, the shopkeepers shouting comments on the weather at one another as they took down the shutters. It was not a place to which Amelia came very often since Polly enjoyed shopping and was on intimate terms with most of the tradesmen for a long way around. This included the stallholder who had the pitch outside the little draper's to which Amelia was bound. On his stall she found some splendid apples and a basket of cobnuts. She bought some of these and was putting them in her basket when a polite voice spoke from behind her.

"Miss Belchamber?"

"Why, yes?" she said unthinkingly.

"Miss Amelia Belchamber?" the voice insisted.

Her heart jerked in her breast as she realised what he had said. She turned and saw two policemen, immeasurably tall and imposing in their top hats, looking down at her with a kind of impersonal curiosity. One of them had a paper in his hand which he consulted carefully before folding it and putting it deliberately away in an inner pocket. She felt cold with apprehension.

"Yes . . ." she faltered.

"Then I must ask you to come with us to the police-station."

"To the . . . whatever for?"

"If you comes quiet, miss," he told her, "we won't need to put these on . . ."

He made a foray into the pocket of his greatcoat and Amelia to her horror glimpsed a pair of handcuffs.

"Are you arresting me?" she asked incredulously.

"Yes miss."

"But why? What am I supposed to have done?"

"Larceny, miss. And other charges pending."

She stared at him, her mouth dry.

"I don't believe it . . . I don't believe it . . ."

He gave her a rather weary cynical look as if to say, 'Go on, they all say that.'

"Best come along quiet, miss. It'll be explained at the station."

The other policeman who had had the piece of paper took

114

her by the arm, not ungently but with a comprehensive grip which suggested that she would find it hard to shake off. Bewildered and frightened she went with them meekly. The stallholder, who had been straining in vain to hear what was said, stared after the trio as they turned the corner.

"Well, I'll be betwattled," he exclaimed. "The likes of 'er!"

He beckoned at an urchin, hanging round in the hope of carrying a heavy basket or finding a discarded piece of fruit. He was sent scurrying to the house in Middleton Row with a message which brought Polly bursting into Cartaret's bedroom, his face screwed up in distress.

"She's been took up," he said breathlessly. "She's been took away by the blue-boys."

Cartaret turned round from the looking-glass.

"Who has?"

"Miss has."

Cartaret stared at Polly for a long moment and then wiped his razor clean of the lather. He turned back to the glass and carefully shaved his upper lip.

"So that was it," he said more to himself than to Polly.

"What was what?" demanded Polly almost dancing about in his distress.

"Never mind."

Cartaret pulled on his dressing gown and went down to the morning room where his breakfast was laid ready. Polly followed him, almost in tears.

"Aincher going to do summink?" he demanded angrily.

"Nothing much we can do at this stage," Cartaret told him. "You can pack a bag with some night clothes and washing things, I suppose. She'll need those."

"Wotcher mean?" Polly shouted angrily. "She never did nuffink, I'll lay me life she never! She'll need lawyers and such!"

"Run along, Polly," Cartaret snapped.

Polly retreated sullenly to the door.

"And while you're at it, best send to the agent's. I expect we'll be needing another housekeeper."

The little manservant went scarlet in the face and the tears ran down.

"She never done nuffink wrong, I'll take me oath . . .

115

strike me blind if she did! And you sits there and orders anuvver like she was a pounder tea . . ."

"Oh, hold your tongue, man," Cartaret said wearily.

Polly flounced out of the room and slammed the door behind him.

"Bleedin' *fish!*" he ground out and ran sobbing up to Amelia's room where he packed a small bag with everything he thought she might need, his neat-handedness at variance with his distorted face and his virulent mutterings. Downstairs Cartaret sat heedless of the cooling coffee staring grimly at nothing in particular.

Polly left the house with the bag and was gone nearly all day. He came into the library which was almost in darkness except for the flickering of the fire. He was obviously tired out and his face was white.

"I can't find 'er, guv," he said hoarsely. "I been to arf a dozen stations and none of 'em never 'eard of 'er. She just vanished. It ain't right."

There was no reply from the figure slumped in the chair.

"'As there been a message, guv?"

"No. Didn't 'spec' one," came from the depths of the chair.

Polly's eye lighted on the decanter and widened slightly at the reduced level of the brandy in it.

"Wot they done wiv 'er, guv?"

"What name did you ask for?"

Polly stared.

"Miss Lester, out o' course!"

"Tisn' her name . . ." Cartaret said muzzily. "Sure'v it."

"Then wot is 'er name?"

"Don' know . . ."

"You mean we won't never be able to find 'er?"

"Have to wash . . . watch papers . . ."

Cartaret's voice faded away. Polly moved round the table and considered his unconscious employer.

"*Not* such a bleedin' fish!" he muttered with some satisfaction.

116

8

"Facts spread like ripples on water."

Cartaret's injunction to 'watch the papers' was good advice: the trial of Amelia Belchamber for larceny at the winter assizes was featured more widely than it might otherwise have been because the scandal caused by the death of her father had barely died down. Moreover, the charge included, for good measure, the conversion to her own use of certain valuable articles from her father's estate which should have been sold for the benefit of the creditors. Her abstraction of these was held to account for her assumption of a different name and her secret removal to a distant county, both suspicious circumstances. The London papers gave the trial a headline on an inner page and summarised the proceedings into half a column. The provincial papers were more generous, they featured the trial on the front page and gave verbatim the speeches for the Crown and for the defence as well as the judge's summing up. In the *Northern Echo* there was an editorial, advising fathers of families to take extreme care in their selection of private governesses and tutors 'the number of which is now so great,' it warned, 'that it cannot but happen that some doubtful characters may insinuate themselves into positions of trust.'

Amelia, penniless and friendless, had had little chance of establishing her innocence: all circumstances seemed to be against her. Counsel for the Crown was an ambitious man who saw in this case a chance of coming at last to public notice and was determined to win at all costs and by any means. The witnesses brought against her were, as the papers stressed, all 'persons of consideration', whereas the few who were prepared to speak in her defence were servants and

117

other persons of small account. No character witnesses were called: Amelia had refused to reveal her whereabouts during the six weeks since she had left Blackyetts. Her negotiations with the agency in Southampton Row, as it chanced, had not passed through the company's books. Mrs Lucas, under considerable pressure had passed on the name of the agency but by that time her sister-in-law had been dismissed, had departed elsewhere, rumour suggested to her husband's brother in Canada, and was not to be found. Amelia's fee had not been the only one to drop straight into her own pocket. All the new manager at the agency could suggest was that if she had obtained a post through the agency it would most likely have been in Chelsea if only because it was from that borough that most of their customers came. Amelia refused either to deny or confirm this assumption.

The magistrate who committed her congratulated the Constabulary on its sharp eyes. It was a remarkable feat, he opined, first to connect this young woman wanted for the misappropriation of articles from her father's estate with another young woman under suspicion of larceny in quite another part of the country. It was fortuitous that those officers investigating Miss Belchamber's disappearance had encountered others from the north who were following up a suggestion (following a casual conversation with the groom) that the missing governess had come to London. Mr Bethune's observation that her hand-luggage was marked AB and not AL had also contributed to this identification. How fortunate also that the late lamented Mr Belchamber had had the happy notion of having his daughter sit for her photograph. This portrait, found amongst the Belchamber effects had made possible the recognition of the accused in Chelsea as well as making certain that Miss Lester of Bindleton was also and indubitably the Miss Belchamber of Aspel Square. He went on to make a few appropriate comments on the wonders and achievements of the age before he observed that Miss Belchamber's refusal to indicate where she had spent the past weeks was very suggestive and that in his opinion she had been somewhere spending her ill-gotten gains for, he stressed, none of the purloined items, or the stolen gems, nor the very large sum of money had been recovered.

Mrs Hoggett had been called early in the trial; she was

118

sombrely dressed and veiled from public gaze. She answered questions in a soft, almost inaudible voice. She was persuaded to describe her kindness to this young person, so hastily and so rashly appointed by her absent husband; she mentioned how this Christian kindness had been repaid by unseemly, nay, immoral behaviour which had forced her into dismissing her. She adopted an air of 'more in sorrow than in anger' which impressed the jury, at least four of whom regarded her as a valued customer. Her evidence concerning the money in the bureau and Mr Hoggett's dislike of banks they greeted with wise nods: her husband's opinion of the Bindleton Bank was shared by more than one. The story of the lost reticule they accepted; females, so their expressions suggested, were prone to such vagaries. Mr Bethune had made an equally favourable impression. He appeared most serious and sober, his air one of mature responsibility and he won public approbation by his gallant refusal to enlarge upon the events which had led to the accused's dismissal. He even turned in anger upon Counsel for the Crown who pressed him eagerly for details, hoping for lurid items which might sway the jury. He thought that his greatest difficulty was going to be the accused herself whose youth and good looks and quiet composure were likely to make a favourable impression. He very much wished the jury to glimpse depths of depravity below this seemingly attractive exterior.

"Miss Lester . . . Belchamber is not on trial for what happened that night," Bethune told him in icy rebuke. The judge nodded agreement and everyone clearly thought, 'what a decent young man . . .' except for someone in the public gallery who made a very vulgar noise indeed, strongly indicating disbelief. In the horrified silence which followed this Amelia could be seen to be smiling. She was brought to a proper seriousness by the judge.

"This is no smiling matter for you, young woman," he reproved her.

"No, my Lord," Amelia agreed. "But I find excess of anything is frequently ludicrous – even hypocrisy."

"I do not take your meaning," spluttered the judge.

"No . . . but I imagine Bethune may."

The contempt in her voice bit. Bethune flushed and the jury looked at one another in wild surmise.

119

"Hell hath no fury . . ." mouthed the foreman to his neighbour and looked very knowing.

Alice, shy and uncomfortable, described almost inaudibly how she had heard the defendant leave her room on the night in question and return some time later.

"Return furtively?" suggested Counsel for the Crown.

"Well," Alice hesitated very conscious of gorgon looks from Louisa sitting in the front row of public seats. "It was very late."

"Come," coaxed the lawyer, smiling like a crocodile, "Miss Belchamber had no reason to be considerate of anybody that night. Was it not a furtive return?"

Alice agreed unhappily. She did not look at Amelia.

Albert was next called and came to the stand limping ostentatiously so that the public cooed under their breaths with pity. He described how he had found his stepmother's reticule containing her keys in the summer-house on the morning after the defendant's dismissal.

"She could have found it easily on her way down the staircase?"

"Probably trod on it," Albert said.

It also emerged that he had seen a figure come out of the garden door in the west wing on the night in question and go into the turret where his mother slept.

"This was after the scene in the belvedere?"

"A long time after," said Albert. "It was nearly dawn."

"And what was a little boy like you doing, awake at that hour?" asked Counsel archly.

"I don't sleep well," Albert returned. "My back hurts me."

Another murmur of pity traversed the court. Counsel wanted to know if he could identify the figure that he saw. Did Master Albert know who it was?

"Miss Lester," said Albert.

"How did you know that?" asked Counsel.

"It was getting light. I saw someone who wasn't very tall wearing a long cloak with a hood."

The defendant's grey cloak was produced. Could it have been a cloak like that?

"Yes," Albert said.

"And you are sure the person you saw was Miss Lester . . . er . . . Belchamber?"

"I suppose so," Albert answered indifferently. "She often used that door when she sneaked off to the belvedere. I've seen her often."

Amelia's defence was being conducted *in forma pauperis* by a very young barrister who went in mortal awe not only of the judge but also of his distinguished opponent. However, even he could not let this pass.

"It might also be anyone of the same height," he suggested, "you did not see her face?"

"No," agreed Albert.

"In fact it could have been someone of a similar height wearing a similar cloak. She was not the only one in the household to wear a cloak, I imagine?"

Albert did not answer right away and when he did he licked his lips in a way Amelia remembered well.

"Far as I know, she was the only one with a cloak," he said.

"And you say you saw this figure, not at midnight, but much later . . . when it was nearly light, you said."

"That's right," agreed Albert.

Counsel for the prosecution jumped up.

"Is it not the case that the night seems endless to those who cannot sleep?" he enquired. "Doubtless the poor lad confused moonrise with the dawn."

"Did you?" the young man asked obligingly.

"Might have done."

"And you saw her go in . . . that is you saw this person go into the turret where your mother slept? But you cannot identify the figure you saw positively?"

"What do you mean?" asked Albert.

"I mean you can't be absolutely sure it was Miss Belchamber."

"Don't know who else it could have been," Albert returned surlily.

Counsel for the defence gave up.

Later he called for Mrs Lucas, the housekeeper, to witness to the summons she had sent to Amelia on the 'fateful night'. Mrs Lucas answered audibly and composedly. Counsel for the Crown rose to cross-examine.

"Was this not an unusual summons?" he asked in puzzlement.

121

Mrs Lucas agreed that perhaps it was but the circumstances, she averred, were unusual.

"Why did you wish to interview this disgraced employee? I have to suggest that it is a wish that smacks somewhat of disloyalty to your employers, does it not?"

"She was a nice young lady and we thought she had been hard done by," said Mrs Lucas sturdily.

"A nice young lady?" he asked incredulously, "you thought she was a nice young lady . . . the daughter of a criminal masquerading under a false name . . . a nice young lady?"

Amelia's counsel jumped up to protest, rather ill-advisedly.

"Is my description of your client true or false?"

"It gives a mistaken . . ."

"True or false?"

"True," admitted the young man wretchedly and sat down.

"Evidence of identity has been given," Counsel for the Crown persisted. "I suggest that my description is factually correct."

He gave the young man a look of tolerant contempt and turned back to Mrs Lucas who was looking decidedly put-about.

"Tell me, Mrs Lucas, why did you and the others wish to see this 'nice young lady'?"

"She had no family, as far as we knew. We wanted to make sure she would be all right. Life isn't easy for a girl on her own without a character. The master . . ." she stared defiantly at Mrs Hoggett, "would have wanted it, I'm sure."

"Very laudable, Mrs Lucas, very laudable, I'm sure. Do I understand that she persuaded you to give her some money?"

"That she didn't. She didn't say a word about money. We had it all collected before she came over. We knew she didn't have much."

"How did you know? Did she tell you?"

"No," Mrs Lucas said sturdily, "she did not. But the Master had sent her a five pound note for journey-money and she hadn't been in the house much more than a couple of months and even if the Mistress had paid her, which she said she wouldn't do, it wouldn't have been much."

"And how did you know she had been sent journey-money?"

"We knew. The Master's clerk mentioned it to Mr Booth."

"I put it to you that she pleaded poverty and asked for money."

"That she did not," Mrs Lucas declared.

"In other words, she was not penniless. She knew she would not need money?"

"She did not ask for any. We collected it and gave it to her."

"And how much did she take from you?"

"Five pound. And we gave it willing. And . . ." a gleam of triumph came into her eye, "we got it back. Every penny. Within the fortnight."

"In a letter?"

"No. In a little packet with presents. Silk handkerchiefs for all of us. Very handsome, we thought it. And there was a little note saying she had got a good situation and thanking us for our kindness."

"Was there an address on that note?"

"Not as I recall. Just London."

"Ah," he breathed significantly, "so she did not mean to keep in touch with you. Tell me, this sum of money that she returned. How was it made up? Coins?"

"Five gold sovereigns," said Mrs Lucas.

"Five gold sovereigns. And these came less than a fortnight after she had left?"

"Yes."

"Did it not occur to you to wonder how she had earned five gold sovereigns in that short period?"

"No," said Mrs Lucas. "It did not."

"Thank you," said Counsel for the Crown.

Amelia's counsel questioned Mrs Lucas but did not succeed in eliciting anything useful from her except her unshakeable goodwill. Mrs Lucas left the box and was followed by Ellis, Mrs Hoggett's dresser. She had been called to give evidence that Miss Belchamber had access to the boudoir and must have known where the money was kept.

"Madam had her into the boudoir, time and again," Ellis said.

"Why was this?"

123

"Because madam wasn't satisfied."

"Oh," said Counsel with a great appearance of interest, "why not?"

"Miss Alice wouldn't pay no heed to her and spent her time reading and ruining her eyesight instead of practising her music and Miss Louisa just ran wild in and out of the stables, she said, and the little ones never knew any pretty poetry to recite when there was visitors and they was left on their own half the time while Miss Les – Belchamber was down in the library making eyes at the tutor. And she wasted time with that Dorrie."

"Dear me. It would appear she was not the paragon that the other servants seemed to think. How did she take these criticisms?"

"Stood there," said Ellis. "Just stood there."

"She made no protest? No attempts to excuse this conduct?"

"No."

"You did not hear any argument? No 'words' as you might say?"

"No," said Ellis.

"I expect Miss Belchamber complained to you and the other servants."

"No," said Ellis. "Leastways not to me. Miss Lester wouldn't pass the time of day with *me*. Much too uppish was our Miss Lester. She'd stand there and look at madam as if she was an . . . an objeck. Dirt under her feet. I seen her. But she never said a word, barring yes and no and the like."

"Am I to understand that she did not show proper respect for your mistress?"

Ellis hesitated.

"She'd say yes ma'am and certainly ma'am . . . but it didn't sound respectful. More like talking to a child, like."

"Insolent?"

"No . . ." Ellis admitted reluctantly. "But not just respectful either."

"Mmmm . . ." said Counsel who had hoped for something more damning. "But you say she was quite familiar with the boudoir?"

"Oh, yes," Ellis agreed. "She was up in there to get her

124

fortune told every other day. Sometimes Miss Alice would be there. Miss Alice took against her."

"And Miss Belchamber would know where the money was kept?"

"The young ladies and gentlemen all went in there Saturday evenings. Madam went to the escritoire and took out the platemoney for church and gave it to them. Miss brought them up. Even that Dorrie," Ellis added with great distaste, "even after madam had asked her to leave her with Nurse."

"So she knew there was a considerable sum in the escritoire?"

"Must of done," Ellis said.

"And on the night of the theft . . ."

"With respect, m'lud . . ." faltered Amelia's counsel, "there is no evidence . . ."

"Speak up," growled the judge.

". . . no evidence that the theft was committed that night," bellowed Counsel for the defence.

"True," agreed the judge, "and you may moderate your voice, Mr er . . ."

"Very well," said Counsel for the Crown looking tolerantly superior," on the night Miss Belchamber was dismissed did you hear someone moving in the boudoir?"

Ellis agreed.

"Stealthily?"

"Sort of."

"Did you go and investigate?"

Ellis went red and her mouth opened and shut.

"I thought it might be madam . . . madam didn't like for me to . . ."

"Oh, we understand perfectly," said Counsel for the Crown hastily. "Few of the ladies care to be seen in déshabillé, so to speak. But you did see something suspicious?"

"I wasn't in bed. I was mending. Madam ripped her gown that night. On a nail. In that summer-house place. I was at a table in the window with a candle. I heard the garden door open downstairs. I blew out the candle so I could see and looked out the window."

"Was there a moon?"

"Bright as day."

"What did you see?"

"Someone in a long grey cloak. She was walking across the grass to the schoolroom door."

"Does your mistress have a long grey cloak?"

"No," said Ellis. "Madam likes a bit of colour. She don't wear grey or the like."

All eyes turned on the sombrely clad, black-veiled figure of Mrs Hoggett.

"Unless occasion calls for it," Ellis added hastily.

Counsel for the defence rose.

"Miss Ellis," he enquired diffidently. "How could you tell it was a she? The cloak was long, was it not? And if you saw the same figure as Master Albert Hoggett it had a hood and the hood was up."

Ellis hesitated.

"It didn't walk like a man," she said at last. "Short steps like."

"But you cannot be sure it was a woman?"

"It wasn't a man," she persisted.

"And you certainly can't be sure it was Miss Belchamber."

"I thought it was at the time. Still do."

"Why?" demanded the defence counsel.

"Because I knew she'd been to the Room."

"The Room? What Room?" asked the judge.

"The Housekeeper's Room," explained Amelia's counsel.

"They'd been talking in the Hall," Ellis went on, "saying she'd been hard done by and that . . ."

"And you did not agree?"

"Not me," Ellis said scornfully, "I said she was a ladedah piece and she got her comeuppance and if they gave her any money they'd never see a penny piece of it again."

"It appears you were wrong. The other servants in the house seem to have approved of Miss Belchamber, even to have liked her. At least one of her pupils might be said to have been devoted to her. Why did you not approve of her Miss Ellis?"

"Because she didn't act right with madam," Ellis said, "she behaved like my lady wasn't anybody special. She listened to her talking like it was a raree-show. I could see it if madam didn't. And she made her sheep's eyes at Mr Bethune. I seen her. Holding hands and that."

126

She ended on a note of spiteful triumph. If looks from some of the earlier witnesses could have killed she would have been stretched out on the spot.

"The other servants insist it was Mr Bethune who made the advances."

"Oh, she'd got around the lot of them with her mimsy ways and her please this and if you would be so kind that. They thought she was a proper lady. Them! They don't know what a proper lady is. They knowed *Mr* Hoggett brought her into the house and it didn't make no neverminds with them that my lady didn't like her. They was all against her. They was all at Blackyetts when the first Mrs Hoggett was alive."

This glimpse of the Blackyetts below stairs seemed to embarrass Counsel who hurried on.

"You knew she would be out of her room at that time?"

"Oh, I knew. For all they talk behind my back there isn't much I don't know. I know what they say about my lady. They was going to send for her to come over after *we* was in bed."

"Did you tell Mrs Hoggett of this plan?"

"I wouldn't soil my lady's ears with such stuff," Ellis said loftily, "she was overset enough with what had happened anyway. I'd to use the smelling bottle with her."

"So your mistress did not know the servants intended to give Miss Belchamber some money?"

"No," Ellis said. "I didn't want her in another rage."

"I really cannot understand my learned friend's insistence on this trivial point," interrupted Counsel for the Crown. "It seems irrelevant."

"If Mrs Hoggett had had second thoughts about turning my client out of doors with neither money nor a character," observed Counsel for the defence, "she would then have known that there was no need for her to make sure that my client had enough at least to take her out of the district."

"Mrs Hoggett," said Counsel for the Crown, "has told the court . . . on oath . . . that she did not send your client any money that night."

"I gather from that," returned Amelia's counsel, greatly daring, "she was prepared to let a gently bred girl starve on her doorstep."

"Sir!" thundered his opponent, "that is a very ungentlemanly thing you have said."

"Sir," quavered Amelia's counsel gamely, "it was a very unchristian act."

"The offence," retorted Counsel for the Crown, "was rank . . . it smelled to heaven."

"Sir, we have, as yet, been given no proof that it was committed."

"The word on oath of a gentlewoman . . . and her son . . ."

"Is hearsay only!"

They glared at one another.

"Gentlemen," said the judge irritably. "We are here to try a case of larceny. Mrs Hoggett is not on trial. I would be obliged if you would both of you keep to the point."

The court next heard from a representative of the lawyers for the creditors of the Belchamber estate concerning the missing bibelots, then the ticket clerk at Bindleton station, a reluctant and obstructive witness who expected to encounter Jem later on in the Horse and Groom and account for every word he spoke about her proffer of a sovereign to pay for her ticket.

The defence counsel put Amelia in the box and took her rather hesitantly through her own version of events. She answered his questions quietly and without emphasis. It was beginning to come home to her that to be innocent might not be enough. When he had finished the jury looked stony-faced and unimpressed. Counsel for the Crown rose to cross-examine.

"You ask us to believe that you took this extraordinary course of running away and changing your name in order to get away from your fiancé. Why?"

"Because in the circumstances it would not have been a good thing for him to marry me."

"But surely, all you had to do was to write and release him from the engagement."

"I was not at all sure that he would accept this. He was . . . is an honourable man and might have felt it ungentlemanly to leave me in such a predicament."

As she spoke she wondered whether he would have married her in the teeth of his parents' disapproval and let his career go hang. She doubted it. Perhaps this action was merely protecting my own amour-propre, not his prospects. Somehow, I would have expected him to come to my aid in this particular fix. If his parents would permit it. Counsel for the Crown was speaking again.

"I put it to you that all this farradiddle of false names had quite another motive."

"My father's suicide was not a tale I wanted hanging round my neck in my new situation," Amelia agreed.

"In fact, had they known your real name they might not have employed you?"

"Mr Hoggett did know," she said. "I told him at my interview."

"You have no proof of that. The letter you produced was addressed to Miss Lester."

"It was the name we had agreed upon."

"Indeed?" Counsel sneered. "Unfortunately . . . or perhaps fortunately for you he is not here to deny or confirm this assertion. His wife . . . his own wife had no notion of it. Would he not have told her of this . . . philanthropic impulse of his?"

"He might not have thought her capable of keeping the secret," returned Amelia drily.

"Your assumption of a false name had nothing to do with your illegal retention of certain very valuable ornaments belonging to your father's creditors? You were quite happy for them not to be able to trace you?"

"They were not in my possession. If you had cared to find out you would have discovered them listed on the inventory which I prepared for the lawyers. If I had wished to take them I would have hidden them before the inventory was made."

"You accuse the lawyers? The servants? Who?"

"No. I suspect they are to be found at Wheatley Hall."

This answer caused a sensation.

"You accuse Lord Wheatley of theft?" The outrage in Counsel's voice was electrifying. "The representative of Her Majesty's Government on the present Committee enquiring into Trade with France?"

"No. I think my cousin, his wife, may have taken them as . . . keepsakes."

"Keepsakes! Their value is more than a thousand pounds!" he exclaimed. "Miss Belchamber you are quite shameless."

Amelia's counsel rose to protest at this comment and for once was sustained.

"Now let us leave these keepsakes and consider the interesting matter of the five sovereigns. You were given five pounds by your . . . er . . . friends in the Servants' Hall?" Counsel for the Crown went on.

"They were extremely kind," said Amelia and her voice shook a little, "when I was in very great straits."

"How was this five pounds made up? Five sovereigns?"

"No. Smaller coins. Half sovereigns, half-crowns, florins, shillings. It came from their savings."

"No sovereigns at all?"

"No."

"Yet you paid for your railway ticket next morning with a sovereign. How was this?"

The court stirred with interest. The foreman of the jury mouthed, 'Oho!' at his neighbour. Amelia took a deep breath.

"Because when I got back to my room that night I found an envelop with ten sovereigns thrust under my door."

"You did? And which benefactor had done this?"

"There was no note and no mark on the envelop."

"Just the ten gold coins?"

"Yes."

"So, what did you think?"

"I thought the children's stepmother . . ."

"Do you mean Mrs Hoggett?"

"Yes."

"Why call her by that curious circumlocution?"

It was a question Amelia could not answer. Perhaps something of the old superstition lingered in her, that to call a thing by its name was to call it to you. The Greeks, she remembered, called the Furies, the Friendly Ones. She hesitated.

"I suppose that is how I thought of her."

"Interesting." Counsel for the Crown turned to the jury. "Not as a wronged female, a person with feelings to be wounded, just the children's stepmother. Tell me, Miss Belchamber, what did you think about the ill-used Mrs Hoggett?"

130

"I thought she had changed her mind about not paying me. I thought she had chosen this way so as not to look foolish or have to face me again."

"You really believe that we . . ." he glanced at the jury ". . . will credit this?"

"It is what I thought at the time. The envelope was from her writing table."

"And how could you know that?"

"It was scented. Mrs Hoggett always used scented paper."

"Ten sovereigns was a curious sum for you to receive, surely," Counsel suggested, "you had been working there for three months according to my information?"

"Yes."

"And your salary . . . a generous one, if I may say so . . . was in the order of eighty pounds a year?"

"Yes."

"So you should have been entitled to double the sum in the envelope?"

"Yes," Amelia agreed, "but, I had been told that I was to be dismissed without a penny so I was relieved to see even half the sum which was owed me. I was not in a position at that time to complain."

"That, at least, is the truth. Why, do you think, did your employer relent in this curious way?"

"I thought it must be conscience money . . ."

"Conscience money!"

The court buzzed with excitement and glances were directed at Mrs Hoggett sitting with her veiled head bowed.

"You continually astonish me, Miss Belchamber, indeed you do. Why should a decent respectable person of irreproachable character like your employer be constrained to pay you 'conscience money'?"

"Because she knew perfectly well I was innocent of the fault for which she had dismissed me."

"Did she? Did she indeed? Why then had she dismissed you?"

Amelia's heart was beating hard and she swallowed before she answered.

"Bethune knows," she said and looked across the courtroom at him. "Why not ask him?"

"You are on the stand, not Bethune. I am asking you."

There was complete silence as the court waited for her answer. Amelia looked around at the jury avid for scandal, the judge unready to hear, the greedy faces in the public gallery. She saw Louisa and Alice. The idea of describing the obscene struggle in the belvedere before these people made her gorge rise. Nor would it be the slightest use. No one would believe her for she had no witness . . . except Albert.

"No," she said hopelessly. "Bethune lied then. He'll lie now."

"I am glad to see that there are some depths to which you are not prepared to sink, Miss Belchamber. May I remind you that in similar circumstances, Mr Bethune defended *you*."

Amelia stared contemptuously at him.

"How gullible you are," she observed. "A child could have seen that he was unwilling to describe his part in the evening's events. Not surprisingly."

A titter trickled round the court and Counsel for the Crown went scarlet.

"Be that as it may," he said spitefully, "I am not gullible enough to believe your fairytale of the gold sovereigns pushed under your door. I put it to you that they were a figment of your imagination."

"I cannot prove their existence, but they were there when I returned to my room."

"If they were, why did not you immediately repay the pitiful hard-earned handful of coins you had extracted from your fellow servants?"

"It was late. They would have gone to bed. In any event I thought it would be a churlish thing to do. Besides, I did not know how long it would be before I found a situation and I was sure they would not object if I kept it in reserve. How would you care to arrive in London with less than ten pounds in your pocket?"

"I am not on the stand, Miss Belchamber."

"I sent it back to them as soon as I had secured a post."

"Ah, yes . . . this mythical London position. You have consistently refused to name this family with whom you spent the intervening weeks between your departure and your arrest."

"I do not wish that they should be involved in this. It is no fault of theirs."

"I put it to you you were in clover somewhere, spending your ill-gotten gains."

It would be so easy to name Cartaret. If this part of her story was shown to be true perhaps the jury might listen to the rest. She shaped the name in her mouth and then failed to articulate it: the situation was too damning. It could make things look worse for her, not better. She remembered not Cartaret's friendly interest but the prurient curiosity of the sitters who coveted her chances, Patty's outraged mama.

"I was keeping house," she repeated, "but I do not wish to name them."

The counsel for the prosecution swept a speaking look at the jury and sat down.

His speech for the Crown took the line that she was a doubtful character who had entered into a mean deception. The gullibility of Mr Hoggett was delicately touched on in this connection and his susceptibility to a pretty face. She had been caught out in a sordid attempt to debauch a young man of good character and thus had a double motive for her theft: the wish to revenge herself upon the good lady who had caught her *in flagrante delicto* and the wish to cast suspicion upon the upright young man who had spurned her advances. He made much of the sovereign spent at the station and the five returned from London and rather more of the opportunity presented by the lost reticule and the figure in grey which had emerged from the garden room at dead of night.

Counsel for the defence ambled uncomfortably and unconvincingly through Amelia's version of events and succeeded only in making the explanations sound more unbelievable than had Counsel for the Crown. He did not have the gift of narrative. However, he did stress, as well he might, the circumstantial nature of the evidence against his client.

"The only substantial evidence the prosecution have shown you is her possession of a sovereign the morning after her dismissal and to any reasonable person her explanation of this seems not impossible. Mrs Hoggett after her anger had cooled might well have thought better of an impulsive and cruel action and left some money for her. No one would have thought the worse of her had she done so. However . . ."

He looked across at Mrs Hoggett who was being sustained by Ellis with a smelling bottle and Alice, wielding an officious fan.

". . . she has assured us on oath that she did not, in fact, repent of this uncharitable action. We are forced to assume in this situation that someone else put the money under the door. My view of the matter is that this was the real thief who wished to cast suspicion on my client."

The jury remained unimpressed.

"Whom better?" he asked them. "A friendless girl dismissed under a cloud. May I remind you that Miss Belchamber was not the only person who knew where the money was kept . . ."

He swung round and pointed at Ellis.

"Her maid knew . . ."

Ellis's mouth dropped open.

"All the children knew and children talk. Anyone in the household could have known the secret of the hidden drawer. Is it not a suspicious circumstance that the theft did not come to light until nearly a month after Miss Belchamber's departure? And may I point out that the prosecution's case rests heavily on statements from partial and prejudiced persons. We have evidence that the child Albert, 'detested Miss Lester and wanted her gone'. Miss Ellis resented her because she thought that she slighted her mistress. Mrs Hoggett disliked her because she had had a governess foisted on her without consultation by her husband and because that governess, as Mrs Sands the nurse has told us, resisted her wish to consign her feeble-minded stepdaughter Dorcas to the care of an institution. It would seem to me, m'lud, that many of the sources of evidence against my client are too tainted to credit."

There was a subdued murmur in the court as if the truth of this was being absorbed. Encouraged, Amelia's counsel continued.

"Moreover, there appears to be a discrepancy between the maid Ellis's description of Miss Belchamber returning to her room from the servants' quarters soon after midnight and Master Albert's allegation that he saw a figure in a grey cloak entering the turret where his mother's rooms were very late . . . nearly dawn. In Ellis's story the grey cloaked figure crosses the courtyard in the opposite direction. I put it to you that both stories cannot be correct. Either it was a grey cloaked figure entering the door nearest to the room where the money was kept very late at night or it was Miss Belchamber returning from the Servants' Hall and going to her own rooms. If both stories are true it would indicate that there were two cloaked figures . . ."

Another implication of his peroration struck him forcibly and he stumbled to a halt.

"However, I will leave you to draw your own conclusions on that matter . . ."

Plainly the most popular conclusion was that the second cloaked figure had been his client also. Miserably he realised too late the damage he had done. He stammered through the rest of his speech, had to be instructed sharply not to mumble, and ended, ominously, with a reference to his client's youth and sex as grounds for clemency.

The judge summed up briefly and it was plain that he had no doubts whatsoever about her guilt. The jury was out for less than ten minutes and when they came back returned a verdict of guilty on all counts. Amelia was instructed to rise and did, numb with disbelief, to hear her sentence. The judge mumbled about modern criminal tendencies and the recent reduction in the penalties of which it was plain he disapproved. He reminded Amelia that not so long ago she would have been hanged for such an offence and that she could still be transported. Amelia went sheet-white at this threat and the wardress beside her frowned and caught her arm. The judge wandered on about the responsibilities of servants to their masters, betrayal of trust, intentional deception, money not recovered and doubtless squandered, so many young women in similar positions of trust, necessary to make an example . . . fourteen years' penal servitude to be served . . .

From the back of the public gallery came a bellow of outrage and all eyes turned upwards to see Cook standing on the bench in a panoply of green bombazine trimmed with yellow satin, her huge bonnet astir with copper-green cocks' feathers. Her face was flushed a dark red and she brandished an umbrella in one hand and a large bag in the other.

"It's a bloody shame!" she bellowed. "If I'd thought they . . . it's one law for them and another for us right enough! That for your bloody justice!"

She made a gesture at the judge which the reporters were later forced to describe in a restrained fashion as one of 'extreme vulgarity'.

"She never done nothing!" Cook yelled. "Why weren't I asked to speak? I'd tell a thing or two about Mr Slimy Bethune, that I would. It's a bleedin' shame! And her sitting there in her silks like a cat at the cream . . . I'll give her Christian kindness! Christian kindness my arse," yelled Cook at the pitch of her lungs. "What you done to Miss Dorcas, then, you she-cat you?"

The rest of this forceful speech was drowned in the hubbub which it stirred up. The last thing Amelia heard as she was being hustled down the steps was the crash of glass as Cook hurled her bag at the two ushers deputed to eject her.

The long black van with its bony horses was waiting below, for hers had been the only case that day. The wardress bundled her in before the crowd could gather. The doors were slammed. The wardress sat down opposite her charge in one of the tiny compartments in which prisoners travelled to and from the prison. She did not close the door as regulations demanded.

"Got a friend there, eh?"

"She's the cook at Blackyetts."

"*Was* the cook, more like."

The van rattled and bumped over the cobbles. Amelia began to recover from the shock.

"Where are they taking me?"

"County jail. Just outside Bindleton. There's a Female Wing there. Built two year ago. You're to serve your sentence there."

The woman looked curiously at Amelia. She wasn't screaming and crying and cursing and protesting her innocence as 'they' usually did. It was as if she was walking in her sleep. The wardress wondered whether she was innocent like the woman in the gallery had said. She'd put her job on it which said a lot. Jobs weren't all that easy come by these days. Not in good service.

"Who done it, then?" she asked with a sarcastic smile.

"I don't know for sure," Amelia said wearily. "I have my suspicions but no way to prove them. No one will listen anyway."

The wardress frowned and fell silent. There were rules about chatting to prisoners. Felons, they called them after they were sentenced. This one was a felon, for all her soft voice and pretty face, and she'd better not forget it.

The following morning the papers printed their various accounts of the trial. The house in Chelsea took *The Times* and the *Morning Post*. Polly never touched *The Times*, that was sacrosanct, but he had got into the habit of peeping into the *Morning Post*. He saw the report at once.

EDWIN BELCHAMBER'S DAUGHTER TRIED FOR THEFT. GUILTY VERDICT

He read the account below and learned that Miss Belchamber had gone under the name of Lester.

"It's 'er . . ."

He grabbed *The Times* and searched it in a fashion Cartaret would not have liked. *The Times* had a longer account and a réchauffé of the Belchamber suicide. The account of the trial was more detailed and there was a vivid description of the accused.

"It's 'er. Fourteen year! Oh, the poor little critter!"

He ran up to the morning room trailing a double handful of newspaper.

"Belchamber," he announced without ceremony, "that's the moniker. Got a fourteen stretch. Look."

Cartaret heard Polly's excited version of what he had read and felt sick. Amelia a thief. Was that what she had been hiding? He grabbed the paper and read it for himself. Polly stood by, shifting impatiently from one foot to the other, waiting to hear what Cartaret meant to do. When he had read every syllable he looked up at Polly frowning in bewilderment.

"Polly, if she had a thousand in gold tucked away and another thousand in assorted bibelots, that would have kept her in comfort for years. She could have gone to France or

Italy. No one would have found her. What the blazes was she doing carrying trays and darning sheets for us with all that stowed away. It doesn't make sense."

"But it is 'er. Look at the description. And it says . . . wait . . . 'ere, look, 'believed to have obtained employment in London' . . . see?"

"No," said Cartaret energetically. "I don't see at all. I thought she might have run away, been involved with a husband or a son . . . but not this. It's just not in character. It doesn't ring true. I'd trust her with my last penny."

"Never done nuffink o' that," Polly agreed emphatically, "take me oath she never . . ."

Cartaret reread the accounts and was sensible, once again, of that hot desire to punch some person or persons unknown hard upon the nose.

"Polly, out you go and get me the northern papers. You'll get them at the railway stations. If they haven't any get them to telegraph for them. I want every rag which saw the light up there last week while the trial was going on."

As he spoke he was scribbling frantically.

"And on your way take this note to Edward Gardiner in Doctors' Commons. If he asks why I want to see him in such a bang tell him I mean to take out my fee in legal advice."

Polly departed, his bandy legs twinkling with eagerness.

Cartaret read the accounts for the third time.

"Even if she had done it . . . even if . . . dammit," he ended his sentence aloud, almost shouting, "she couldn't have. Something's wrong . . ."

After that he paced up and down the length of the library swearing under his breath until he heard a cab stop at the door and ran downstairs to admit his old friend, Edward Gardiner QC. Mr Gardiner was a dapper, desiccated young man who disguised his cleverness under a fussy old-maidish manner. Cartaret shook his hand painfully and then took his cloak and hat and flung them on to the settle in the hall. Gardiner made an agonised sound, retrieved them and hung them neatly on the hall-stand. He stretched the fingers of his kid gloves and laid them tenderly on the settle.

"For God's sake, Ned, this is serious . . . never mind your damned cloak," Cartaret said irritably.

"I'll listen better if I don't have to think of it lying in a

138

crumpled heap," Gardiner said mildly. "What have you been up to? Crim. con.?"

In the library he listened to Cartaret's tale without interruption; looking the while at the sketches scattered on the table showing Amelia in various moods and aspects. Cartaret had brought them down as a way – the only way open to him – of explaining how he saw her. Gardiner settled on one of her polishing silver and smiled approval.

"Looks a conversable female," he commented, "doesn't smirk. Not a fool. But not open, I shouldn't think. She gave you no hint of this business, I suppose?"

Cartaret paused in his restless prowling.

"I guessed there was something up," he admitted.

"She didn't tell you what it was, though?"

"No, dammit. No. We were interrupted."

Gardiner looked up at that but didn't comment.

"You have no evidence of any kind that she is innocent but you insist that she must be. After, what? Six weeks? You feel you know her well enough to be certain?"

His voice was flat and uninflected.

"Yes."

"You're in love with her," Gardiner accused.

"If you mean, is she my mistress, no, she isn't. If you mean would I like her to be, yes, I would. But that's got nothing to do with it – or not all that much," he added frowning.

Gardiner went back to the papers and Cartaret prowled restlessly to and fro. In the middle of this Polly arrived with an armful of northern papers, all of which contained very much fuller accounts and the two men scanned every one.

"Mm," said Gardiner at last.

"Well?"

"It smells. Is my considered opinion, it smells."

Cartaret's face lit up.

"What can we do?" he demanded fiercely. "You really think she is innocent?"

"Don't you?"

"Of course I do," Cartaret said impatiently, "but I know her and you don't. I was more than a little surprised you agreed with me, that's all."

Gardiner waved his hand over the mass of the papers round his feet.

"The evidence was mostly circumstantial. Her own story was lame but not unbelievable and she weakened it by not bringing you into it. She had a young fool for a counsel and the Crown had a wily aging fox, overdue for the bench. There are a good many pointers."

"Then what do we do?" Cartaret repeated.

"Ferret. If she didn't do it, someone else did. She has a good idea who it was . . . so have I. Other people knowing more about it may have come to the same conclusion."

"Can't we appeal . . . get her out of that damned place? I'll stand bail if I have to paint vapid dignitaries for the rest of my life."

"No," Gardiner shook his head. "That could be dangerous. We need some solid evidence before we approach anyone on her behalf. Go to the Appeal Court without it and she could have her sentence revised. She could have been transported, you know; in fact in view of the amount involved she was uncommonly lucky not to be."

"Transported!" Cartaret went white.

"It was that stuff which vanished from her father's house. That really swayed the judge. If she could do one, she could do the other . . . that was how he argued. Interesting what she had to say about it, don't you think?"

"If the blighter is her cousin he might have come forward to give her a hand," Cartaret suggested.

"He's in France. Heading the Trade Commission," Gardiner said. "Won't be home for months."

"How do we set about things?"

Gardiner didn't answer at once.

"You do realise," he said gently, "that in spite of everything there may be nothing to ferret out? You must face that possibility."

"I don't accept that," Cartaret said. "I won't."

Next morning shortly after six o'clock Cartaret descended upon Polly in his kitchen.

"Pack, Polly! Pack at once. Pack enough for a month. We're going north."

"Both on us?"

"Both of us," Cartaret agreed. "And we are going in disguise."

Polly gaped.

"I mean to sink Quentin Cartaret RA in Peter Quentin, Lightning Likenesses a speciality. Pencil fifteen shillings. Pen and ink twenty shillings. Oils by arrangement. Immortalise your nearest and dearest."

Cartaret thrust a card with these enticing words neatly laid out upon it into Polly's hand.

"Find a jobbing printer and tell him I want fifty of these by this afternoon."

Polly looked doubtfully at it.

"There's nothing more convincing than a business card."

"But I don't see . . ."

"It will give me the entrée into the respectable houses in Bindleton. They'll be just as happy to have their fat phizzes immortalised as my more fashionable customers. If I went up there as me I'd be suspect . . . a wicked Bohemian . . . and my prices would scare them off. No one would nibble. But as a cheap-jack likeness-taker, especially if they think they are getting a bargain, I should be invited all over the place."

"You mean . . . you're going to nose about a bit?" Polly grinned his delight.

"Exactly. Sitters talk. My God, how they talk. The only person who hears more secrets than a painter is a doctor. I am replete with scandal. Half of it is so dull that I forget it as soon as I hear it and get the name of being discreet, but with the other half I could blackmail most of the people I meet. It'll be just the same at . . . what's its name?"

"Bindleton, guv."

"You'll see. So, two tickets, second class, I think, for Bindleton, on the first train."

"The lawyer what came don't think she done it, guv?"

"Not only that but he thinks he knows who did! Come on, shake your shanks. The sooner we start the sooner we'll have her out of that blasted jail."

Gardiner saw them off at the station.

"It isn't just love," Cartaret told him indignantly. "I'm no Sir Blasted Galahad. I'd be just as upset and determined to do something if she were plain and old and I knew as surely as I do that she couldn't do such a thing."

141

"Just like Sir Galahad," grinned Gardiner and Cartaret hauled up the carriage window with a bang.

Mr Hoggett read the accounts of the trial in a large bundle of newspapers which arrived in the SS *King Cotton* fifteen days out of Liverpool. The news struck him in much the same way it had struck Cartaret, more indeed, for he was much better informed on the matter. A four page, much-crossed epistle from Mrs Sands arrived at the same time as the newspapers and another shorter one lamenting the departure of her Dorcas and setting forth her doubts about the place she had been sent. Hoggett first thought of the telegraph but instead decided it was a matter not to be settled through such a medium. Within an hour he was to be found at the shipping office of the National Steamship Company in Hoboken, demanding immediate passage to England, any class, any accommodation, as long as it was on the next available steamer. The clerk displayed a commendable amount of Yankee hustle, applied himself to the telegraph and in a very short time had provided him with a berth on the SS *Liverpool* sailing at midnight. Hoggett paid in cash and retired to a table to put the documents safely away and make room for the person who had been shuffling impatiently behind him. He looked up in stunned surprise when he heard a cultivated English voice demand immediate passage to England, any class, any accommodation as long as it was on the next available steamer. Under his expensively clad arm was a copy of *The Times*.

The clerk looked suspicious.

"You two gents on the square?" he demanded. "You ain't tryin' to make a monkey out of me?"

"I certainly am not," said the elegant young man with *The Times* under his arm. "It is imperative I return to England as soon as possible."

"Then you can room with him," said the clerk, jerking his head at Hoggett. "There jest ain't another cabin left. You can swap yarns on the way over. Guess you've got a lot in common."

142

9

*"It is allowable to derive instruction
from an enemy."*

Bindleton greeted 'Peter Quentin' with suspicion. Artists
were not thick on the ground in the industrial north. His
cards were regarded with distrust and his advertisement in
the paper brought no response. However, he had a letter
from a friend to one Mrs Underwood. She was new to the
district but she was third cousin to a lord and thus very
highly regarded. She was quite ecstatic about her portrait (as
well she might have been for in the normal way it would
have cost her some two hundred guineas) and she hung it in
her drawing-room where it attracted a great deal of attention.
To everyone who commented on it she recommended 'Mr
Quentin' highly with the whispered rider that, 'he was really
very gentlemanly', so that before long the initial suspicion
gave way to enthusiasm and he found himself besieged with
requests to reproduce the faces of consideration throughout
the district.

It was not at all difficult to persuade sitters to talk about the
Belchamber trial. It had been the most notable event in the
neighbourhood since the riots which followed the introduction of spinning frames. 'Mr Quentin' heard any number
of versions. He found they tended to fall into a pattern:
those who had encountered Amelia during her brief stay at
Blackyetts were usually puzzled and bewildered. They
would say that she had not seemed at all 'that sort' and they
could not understand why Mrs Hoggett had thought fit to
dismiss her. However, these were few. Mrs Hoggett had
not encouraged the governess to accompany her pupils into
the drawing-room: the charitable, a minority, said this

was because the one who was, you know, a trifle lacking, needed constant supervision if she was not to attack her sisters and this was certainly true because as soon as Miss Belchamber left the child had had to be sent to a place where she could be kept under restraint.

However, those who had never met Amelia were, as a rule, markedly hostile. They were ready to point out that she was, after all was said and done, the daughter of a criminal and that Hoggett should have made much more careful enquiries before he employed her. As for his being 'in the know', as the creature had claimed at the trial, that was all so much eyewash. He was prone to be impulsive, they said, and to stick to his opinion buckle and thong. Not a few went on to point at his marriage to the beautiful Miss Thwaites, a girl less than half his age and as vain and silly as she could stare. There were not lacking those who hinted that the marriage was not as successful as one might have hoped. Mrs Hoggett, they suggested, was not altogether contented with her lot. There were some who pooh-poohed the notion of Mr Hoggett's being taken in by a pretty face: it was a marriage of mills, they declared, Hoggett's Canvas and Thwaites' Cottons. Some thought Hoggett had paid dear for his side of the bargain and hinted that he might pay more dearly yet.

Among these last was one Mrs Howard, a lively matron whose husband was a well-to-do farmer, not ashamed to muddy his boots with his men for all he was a warm man and rode to hounds as often as he could. Mrs Howard had been a rival of the handsome Miss Thwaites when they were both young and attended the Bindleton Assemblies. There were some, she did not blush to say it, who had thought that of the two she, Miss Allan, had borne off the palm . . . but those days were long gone and it did not do to be thinking of such ancient triumphs: it was just that dressing with such care for her likeness to be taken she had been put in mind of those days.

"And are you still rivals?" Cartaret enquired, thinking that he might have admired the erstwhile Miss Allan; she had traces of beauty still. It was no hardship to draw her. It seemed that Mrs Howard was not upon the Blackyetts visiting list.

"She said to Lucy Mellow that a line had to be drawn

144

somewhere, and at clodhopping farmers and their dowdy wives she drew it. Of course Lucy told me."

Of course, thought Cartaret, much amused. Mrs Howard laughed gaily to show Mr Quentin how little she cared.

"And dear Lucy was so unkind, I declare. She insisted that it was because Jessamine Thwaites cannot bear to invite comparisons and she has put on so much flesh since her marriage."

The suggestion invited him to compare and it was true that Mrs Howard had kept her figure.

"I'm sure I have no wish to dine at Blackyetts but there was a time when the first Mrs Hoggett was alive . . . she was the dearest creature, you know and a friend of my mama, and we were all thunderstruck when we heard she had been killed. Mr Howard was used to dine there often and often because his father was at school with Mr Hoggett and Hoggett was never one to forget his obligations. But he doesn't go now, oh, dear me, no. The line has been drawn."

She went on at some length about how those whose own origins were not above reproach (she hinted that Mrs Hoggett's grandmother was an innkeeper's widow) were always the greatest sticklers. It was real ladies and gentlemen who had no need to keep themselves on a very high form.

"Are the Bethunes high sticklers?" enquired Cartaret. "I have heard that they are very well-connected . . ."

Canon Bethune, he was promptly given to understand, was a gentleman and his like was not to be found anywhere in the north and he thought nothing of dismounting and passing the time of day with a roadmender.

"And his son?" Cartaret asked gently.

Mrs Howard gave him a speaking look.

"Mr Howard said to me when he heard they had taken him on as a tutor that he'd as soon let the bull . . ." she swallowed and censored what she had been about to say. "That is to say that Mr Howard did not think Mr Bethune was a suitable person to employ in a household where there were young girls."

Excitement swelled inside Cartaret. He felt like a hound on the scent.

"Mr Howard told me that there is a young woman up at the Roman Gate who wishes she'd never clapped eyes on

Bethune. And I daresay she isn't the only one from what Mr Howard says."

"Did you ever meet this Miss Lester or Belchamber or whatever who's said to have been so enamoured of him?"

Mrs Howard looked at him roguishly.

"I declare, Mr Quentin, you have forgotten the line which must be drawn. But my friend, Miss Enderby, is on the far side of this line and she tells me that Miss was a very pleasant quiet ladylike girl and the younger girls minded her very well."

It appeared that Miss Enderby was to visit in the afternoon because Mrs Howard was quite sure she would be anxious to have her head done in chalks too and if Mr Quentin felt inclined . . . Mr Quentin did. However Miss Enderby proved a disappointment. What she remembered about people was not what they did or said but what they wore and she remembered this in precise and wearisome detail. It did emerge that she had no liking for the lady-killing Bethune. Mr Quentin thought he detected a touch of the woman scorned.

"There's one who thinks himself above his company. A parson's son, when all's said, in spite of all his grand relations, and not a penny to bless himself. And whatever he earns at the Hoggetts he spends on his back. Nothing but the latest and best for Mr Bethune and what he owes at his tailors would buy an abbey – or so my brother says."

She professed herself delighted with the portrayal of her second-best tabby-silk gown and admired the way in which he had drawn the lace at her neck and while both ladies were gloating over their likenesses tea was brought in. It was not a dainty four o'clock tea, but a substantial meal, laid out upon a table. The company was invited to draw up their chairs to home-made ham-and-veal pie, home-cured ham, a bowl of cold potatoes dressed with vinegar in the French style and any amount of new-baked scones and cakes and biscuits furnished forth with crystal dishes of jam. As they discussed this spread Mr Howard came in. He came in like a north-east wind, smelling of the stables, his face wind-stung. Mrs Howard he kissed smackingly, nodded to Miss Enderby and shook Mr Quentin by the hand. Given a cup of tea he downed it as if it were medicine, carved and ate a vast slice of pie, picked up and pocketed a handful of macaroons and invited Mr Quentin to view the stables. Mr Howard, it appeared, was not only a farmer, he was a considerable horse-coper. Mr Quentin agreed with alacrity. The ladies had no more to tell him and he wished to hear more of the unfortunate girl at Roman Gate.

The stables were large and airy and filled with splendid creatures, healthy and shining. Mr Howard 'liked nowt better than a good horse' so he said and he had to live with his neighbours so he couldn't unload wrong 'uns.

"If you find yourself with a wrong 'un?" Cartaret asked.

"I send it off to an auction. I reckon anyone who buys a horse at auction not knowing owt about him deserves what he gets."

He indicated a large black mare with four white socks, a vast rump and a thin rat-like tail.

"This 'un, she's a tartar. I keep her because she throws good colts, good as gold they are. But her fillies, you'd think the devil sired them. Nor it doesn't matter where I get her covered. Ugly and sour as a lemon all of them. The last one I sent to the auction and back she came to the place like a bad penny. Parson's son bought her. Needed her to ride between Bindlewick and Blackyetts. He's tutor there."

He added a thoroughly actionable speculation concerning Mr Bethune's real job in Blackyetts which suggested that the mother had more to teach the tutor than he had to teach the children. This suggestion was not new. It had been hinted at before but this was the first time when someone had come out into the open and told it to him as a fact. If it were a fact it put a very different interpretation on the events which had sent poor Amelia to jail.

"That would be the end of October or thereabout," Mr Howard began to chuckle. "He rode her over to Blackyetts and she decanted him into a blackthorn hedge on the way, then she got away with him on the high road when she was frighted by a carrier wagon and didn't stop till she was winded. After that she went quiet enough till he got to Blackyetts and she unloaded him in the lilypond in front of the steps. Miss Louisa was laughing fit to bust her stay-laces. She knew, she knows horses, Miss Lou. Next day he turned up here with a bit that would have held a runaway railway engine and tried to sell her to me. It would have made a cat laugh. I could have her cheap, he says, only seventy guineas. She'd cost him a hundred, he said. Quiet to ride and drive, carry a lady, he said."

"What did you do?"

"Sent him packing. I didn't want her. Lying son-of-a . . . parson. He paid forty pounds for her and paid twice what she was worth. I had the money in my desk while he was telling me. He took her over to Manchester and sold her to some poor deluded critter there for twenty. Then he bought a nice little colt off me. Now he was a real bargain. That's his full brother over there and as like him as he can spit."

"How much did he pay?" asked Cartaret stroking the colt's nose.

"Thirty-five guineas. You can have this one for thirty. Things is slow this time o' the year but the tits don't stop eating."

"Did Bethune pay cash?"

"He did. Thirty-five jimmie o'goblins. His credit ain't good for much in these parts . . . though I do hear he's paid off the worst of his debts . . . or someone has. Anyone's guess who, I reckon."

Ideas were burgeoning in Cartaret's mind. He held out his hand.

"I'll take him. I'm going to be needing a horse, I expect."

Mr Howard beamed and wrung his hand.

"You won't regret it. And when you leave the district I'll buy him back off you if you haven't broke his knees."

Because of his sober demeanour and gloomy expression the colt was named 'Shaftesbury' and a shabby gig was bought for him. Mr Howard had given Cartaret a lead to follow and he hunted through his letters to find an establishment near Roman Gate. He found one: it belonged to one Mrs Jane Thackry who was the relict of Joshua Thackry, once Staneley Hoggett's partner which seemed an added bonus. Polly was sent on a number of errands in Bindleton itself while Cartaret and Shaftesbury took the road into the hills.

While Mr Quentin was immortalising the plump and pleasant features of widow Thackry, Polly went in search of

148

the best bootmaker in Bindleton. He had in a brown paper parcel a pair of Mr Cartaret's boots which required soling and heeling. While this was being done Polly passed the time of day with the clerk who spent his days imprisoned in a box no bigger than a sentry shelter which held him, a high desk, a stool and a pile of ledgers. Polly soon discovered that the clerk longed to visit London. It was for him a sort of Eldorado. Polly's familiarity with the capital was a passport to confidences and admission to the box. There he was permitted a glance at the ledgers, just to see if they kept them the same way as they did in London. Polly turned the pages admiring the neatness and scrupulous legibility and saw that one T. Beth had run up a debt of seventeen pounds eleven shillings and fourpence three farthings. It had run for nearly a year and had been paid off on the twentieth of October. The elaborated Paid was followed by an equally elegant Cash, the long 's' expressing, or so the fanciful might suppose, a certain relief and surprise. Polly collected the boots, accepted the cobbler's compliments on his master's choice of bootmaker, paid the fee to his friend in the box and saw it entered. He then bade them both farewell and crossed the street.

Here he was confronted by an imposing emporium, the most significant shop in the town of Bindleton. Clearly it had at one time been several establishments but by this time bright purple paint had lent them homogenity and large gilt letters all along the front above the windows declared them to be the domain of one Ernest Ellershaw, Draper and Outfitter. Each window declared in its turn one aspect of Ernest Ellershaw's stock; haberdashery, linens, drapery, millinery, gloves, woollens, and the last window where a single dummy stood in a nonchalant attitude in full evening dress had written in gold letters across the glass, Bespoke Tailoring. Polly made for the last. Over his arm he was carrying a long black cloak which Cartaret described as his artist-kit and wore with a soft black wideawake hat. It had been much worn and the hem was disintegrating and the blue silk lining needed considerable mending.

The Bespoke Tailor was small and wizened and looked as if one more task would involve his immediate retirement but he agreed with a weary sigh to reline and refurbish the cloak within the next three days. He held the garment to the light and admired it. It had been, he guessed, made in London.

"Messrs Hamilton and Kimpton, I reckon," he opined. "This is very much in their style and they have a way with the collar which I recognise. A fine piece of work but much mishandled if I may say so. Your gentleman doesn't take the care he should of his clothes."

Polly agreed meekly.

"You make many of them cloaks round here?" he asked.

The Bespoke Tailor shook his scanty locks.

"Not here. They have come back into the mode in the south I believe but here gentlemen prefer the ulster or a caped coat. I made one last year, I recall, but that was the only one. Mohair suiting, lined throughout in pale grey silk to tone. I remember the young gentleman wished for a hood. Unusual. I told him so, but he insisted that it kept his hats dry. Very humorous."

"I don't care for cloaks," Polly said. "Haven't the height for them. My gentleman looks a treat in his, very tall he is."

"My customer was too small to wear one," agreed the Bespoke Tailor. "I took the liberty of telling him so but he paid no heed. Nor anything else," he added feelingly.

"Bad debts?"

"I would say so," the Bespoke Tailor said emphatically. "Our trade is the worst there is for debts. The clothes is wore out before they pay for them."

He shook his head gloomily.

"And the gentry is the worst. You ask in the counting-house. Bills running for over a year. The gaffer don't care for it but what can you do? If you don't sell he'll want to know why and if the customers don't pay it's your fault. That cloak was on the books near a twelvemonth, and the gaffer nagging about every settling day. And when it was paid you'd have thought he was doing us a favour."

The conversation was resumed later in the day over mugs of beer in a small dark taproom, evidently the haunt of the drapery trade, for the counting-house clerk arrived there too. Polly bought the beer and listened. Later he went back to the inn where they were staying with two pieces of paper, two

150

signatures and a view of Mr Bethune very different from that entertained by Bindleton Society.

Cartaret's sitter near Roman Gate was comfortable, plump and deadly, quite deadly. She had donned her best plum-coloured velvet gown, placed herself on a bright blue velvet upholstered sofa and beside her on a table was a great spiky monster of a potplant. Her face was pink, her eyes still blue and her hair softly white under its black lace cap. She was everyone's idea of a beloved grandmother. Her tongue, however, was a weapon unmatched in the whole county. Kindly, sweetly, without haste and without mercy she demolished every claim to virtue, every pretension to gentility put forward by anyone in the neighbourhood. Cartaret listened in horrified amazement as he laid down the outlines on his canvas. She had requested a head and shoulders in oils and had beaten him down to a mere fifteen guineas. She intended, she said, to leave it to her nephew instead of the fortune he expected.

"He thinks I don't know he has a trollop in keeping in Manchester."

Her daughter had married to disoblige her mama and was now living in want with four children.

"An usher," Mrs Thackry smiled, "a penniless usher. She shall not have a stiver."

Cartaret felt slightly sick at the venom in the soft voice.

"I understand there are a great many who wish to have their likenesses taken," she observed after a short silence. "And doubtless Mrs Hoggett will be one of them. She would never pass up an opportunity to indulge her vanity. She was a silly girl and if I mistake not she is a wanton and stupid woman. Hoggett should never have married her. But men cannot see beyond a pretty face."

Thackry, Cartaret thought, must once have thought this monster pretty: she would have been fair and plump and pink and white with wide blue eyes. She still wore the smug expression to be found in those who have been pretty in their youth.

"If Mr Hoggett made a few enquiries at Lowick Waters," Mrs Thackry said with a soft chuckle which chilled her hearer to the spine, "he might have occasion to examine this latest

151

child's features very closely. Not that I imagine he is blameless himself. It is hard to suppose that he travels alone. Not that I have any certain information on that point. However, I cannot but wonder whether Mrs Hoggett will have any inclination to inspect the school in this village. The mill supplies Hoggett's, you know . . ."

She chuckled again.

"One dislikes being taken for a fool, Mr Quentin, and if that young woman they have foisted upon the governors is a widow you may call me a fool . . ."

She gave him a speaking look.

"Very close she is. Very close. I could discover nothing of her origins."

Cartaret had a nightmarish vision of an inquisition.

"Not from the young woman herself . . ." Mrs Thackry said, "but as you may suppose I am not dependent upon such enquiries alone. I would depend on Mrs Hoggett being able to recognise her. Oh, yes."

Somewhat to Cartaret's disappointment he heard that the school was closed so that the pupils might pick potatoes and would not take up for another day or two.

". . . and our young widow has gone to visit relations . . . or so she has given out, and taken her young Posthumus with her. I take it you know your Shakespeare, Mr Quentin?"

About Amelia she had no hesitation in asserting her belief that she was a trollop.

"People cannot be too careful whom they admit to their homes. Governesses are all the same. I never employed one. People should teach their own children. It is so much easier to keep an eye on them if you do."

Cartaret returned to Bindleton wishing very much for a bath. He felt that he had bathed over his head in venom. While he had learned much about the Hoggetts which could be useful he could not but wonder whether the source were too tainted to be reliable. In the meantime, until Roman Gate School took up again he would follow such leads as he had. However, if he were to sustain his character of itinerant portraitist he would have to accept a sitter or two. And somehow he would have to contrive a meeting with Mrs Hoggett and Bethune in order to sketch their likenesses. Not all his sitters were as 'useful' as Mrs Thackry (for which he could not but be grateful) but once he had agreed to draw them he earned his fee. One widow wanted a pencil drawing to send to her married daughter in India. As she sat resplendent in her lace-trimmed Sunday cap she responded to his well-worn opening on the subject of the Belchamber case by agreeing that you could not be too careful whom you took into your home; she had, she told him, journeyed as far as Norwich in order to interview personally the previous employer of a governess to whom she had proposed to confide her one chick.

"Wasn't worth the trouble," her companion-chaperone interjected, "she still took to the bottle."

The widow cast a pained look at her companion and smiled at Mr Quentin.

"She was, however, perfectly *honest*," she declared.

"And so she might be," the companion observed, "with every drawer and cupboard locked fast. All the same, it didn't stop her picking the lock of the cellar and drinking your poor husband's port."

After this revealing item the sitter had fallen sulkily silent for a while until she decided that she would not be browbeaten in her own parlour and observed that in spite of her little weakness Miss Spottiswoode had known her work thoroughly and had even been able to teach dear Maria a little Italian.

"A little Hindostanee would have been more useful," said the companion, "and the Blackyetts girl knew Italian as well . . . and Latin to boot," she added triumphantly, "in spite of *her* little weakness."

Cartaret, who had become an expert in provoking and prolonging these revealing exchanges, murmured:

"And what was her weakness?"

"Mr Bethune, if Mrs Hoggett is to be believed," said his subject irritably.

"Mr Bethune seems to be a universal weakness," the companion declared, crocheting frantically, "by what *I* hear."

"It is quite dreadful how people will gossip," the sitter interrupted angrily, "I am perfectly convinced it is not true. Dear Canon Bethune would be so distressed if it came to his ears that someone in *my* household was repeating such things."

153

Later on by means of ruthless blandishments he persuaded the companion to sit for him. Her face, she told him gruffly, would interest no one but herself. Mr Quentin made a polite comment about good bones and it was true that the companion had bone in plenty. The widow, evidently disgusted at such eccentricity on the artist's part, retired to write to her daughter and to pack up her picture. The companion was easily persuaded to talk and from her ramblings Mr Quentin derived two interesting tales which corroborated the evidence that Bethune had had a sudden windfall at an interesting point. The widow had a brother in a good way of business in Manchester and Bethune had been able to pay a long bill of his in cash, late in October. Also she had a garbled tale about a schoolmistress up in the dales which made Cartaret remember Mrs Thackry's unfortunate widow. All in all the picture of Bethune which was beginning to emerge was not in the least like the picture of Bethune presented to the court at Amelia's trial. The companion recounted in detail her one encounter with him when, so she had reason to think, he had made fun of her behind her back.

"If the clergy's families go to the bad," said the companion sitting as rigidly as if he proposed to draw her teeth rather than her face, "they go right to the bad. I recall that when I was with a very nice family near Keighley in Yorkshire I heard that . . ."

She retailed the sad history of one young man, Brunty or some such name, who had taken to drink and to opium and then died of a decline some fifteen years earlier and all because of a woman . . . his employer's wife, no less. It had been hushed up but was pretty common knowledge in the district, she said and went on to detail his sad decline and death and that of his three sisters . . .

". . . they were a very strange family. They wrote, you know, all of them . . ."

Cartaret was putting the finishing touches to his sketch.

"Books," she added, lest there should be any mistake. "I believe they were even published though none of them has ever come in my way."

Cartaret passed her the finished drawing and she regarded it without noticeable enthusiasm.

"Sometimes I think I could write a book. I have been companion in six households. Six. You wouldn't believe what can go on behind the most respectable façades. It gives one an odd idea of humanity. The thing is," she went on resignedly, "there is so little that a gentlewoman can do if she finds herself without support. My dear papa was never able to save. His stipend was small and he was never of a saving disposition. I would have preferred to teach but I did not have the benefit of a good education. I try not to repine but it would have been of such advantage to have been able to teach, even young children."

She looked at her portrait.

"And, as you have seen, I am getting no younger. Sometimes I wonder where it will all end . . ."

She sighed.

"The temptation . . ." she murmured more to herself than to him, "the temptation must have been very strong. The poor girl . . ."

Cartaret felt a surge of liking for her and when she began to scrabble in her net-purse for the five shillings he had suggested, he took back the drawing. It was good, he thought with some surprise. He could make something of it. A cameo kind of painting of a poor gentlewoman.

"Do you want it?" he asked abruptly. "I really wanted to draw you for my own sake . . ."

She looked up at him in astonishment, the coins in her hand.

"If you don't want it I would like to use it for some work I have in mind."

She blushed patchily.

"Why ever should you want a drawing of me?" she asked gruffly.

"Because I do. And what is more," he added, "I often use interesting models and when I do I pay them."

He laid down three sovereigns on the table and packed the sketch away. The companion gasped and was, for once, left speechless.

Two days after this Polly and Cartaret drove back to Roman Gate. While Cartaret completed Mrs Thackry's portrait Polly went to interview the harassed young woman in widows' weeds who was teaching the alphabet to a class of sullen sleepy girls in a converted weaving shed. She was somewhat distracted by a noisy infant in a crib by the teacher's desk. She admitted Polly unwillingly but later, so her pupils reported, she waved him goodbye amicably enough and came back to the class in a 'rare good humour'.

They drove back to Bindleton in the fading light in a mood which was a mixture of disgust and satisfaction.

"Arsk me," remarked Polly, "I'd call him downright dog'smeat, I would."

Back at the Lowcombe Arms they ate a large plain dinner and examined the notes which had been left for them, requesting their services. Two turned out to be of peculiar interest: one was from Alderman Ernest Ellershaw, JP, who, he insisted, had been under great pressure from his fellow councillors to donate his likeness to the Town Hall where he had served faithfully for many years. He would like a portrait, in oils, three-quarter length for a moderate fee. The other was written very largely on expensive hot-pressed letter-paper and enclosed in an envelope of a delicate lilac shade which drew attention to itself by a strong savour of patchouli. It was headed 'Blackyetts Hall' and ordered his immediate attendance so that he might paint a group portrait of Mrs Hoggett and her family. It would be seven feet by five in order to fit the space available to hang it in the small saloon. He would be expected at ten o'clock a.m. the following day and thereafter at that time for a week or as long as the portrait took to complete though the writer did not wish for too many sittings as they would interfere with her social engagements of which she had a great many.

Cartaret grimaced at this and gave it to Polly.

"There . . . no need to tout for business. We have been invited into the enemy stronghold . . . commanded, rather . . ."

But Polly was hunting back through the newspaper cuttings which were in the front of the bulging notebooks.

"This chap Hellershaw," he pointed out. "'E's the bloke wot committed 'er. 'E sent 'er for trial . . ."

After supper Mr Quentin and his servant called upon Alderman Ernest Ellershaw JP in his imposing suburban house. The Alderman was none too pleased to hear that the Town Hall must wait upon the convenience of the Hoggetts.

156

"I would have thought," he said huffily, "that a civic dignatory, if I may so term myself, and one, moreover, of some standing, might take precedence over . . ."

Cartaret waited with interest to hear in what terms he would describe Mrs Hoggett but was disappointed. The Alderman coughed and swallowed his resentment.

"However, Hoggett is a man of considerable importance in the town, very considerable . . . I suppose if you received his lady wife's request before mine I must . . ."

"I could recommend my colleague in Manchester," Cartaret said modestly and mentioned a painter who specialised in civic dignitaries and was especially skilled in the representation of furred robes and gold chains. "He is much more renowned than I am, a very talented man . . ."

Alderman Ernest looked interested.

". . . and I believe he intends to submit work to the Academy next year . . ."

Alderman Ernest's eyes popped a little at the idea of his portrait appearing in such august company.

". . . I feel sure he would be delighted to have such a commission . . ."

The Alderman's mouth opened to countermand his commission to Mr Quentin.

"His fees," Cartaret went on, "are comparatively modest still. A mere hundred guineas for a head and two hundred for a full-length."

Alderman Ernest's mouth remained open but no sound emerged.

"If you would be good enough to wait a week, on the other hand, my own fees are not so . . ."

"So I should hope!" exploded the Alderman.

"For a three quarter length, in oils, four feet by four . . . in the region of thirty guineas."

Cartaret permitted himself to be beaten down to twenty-five and returned to his rooms feeling rather pleased with himself. Polly, who had spent this visit below stairs, was equally pleased with himself for he had discovered something of interest.

"Hellershaw's missus," he informed Cartaret, "is Methody. Primitive. Very religious they says. An' not just family prayers and that. She does like the Good Book says.

'Er old man 'e puts 'em in the pokey an' she visits 'em wiv tracts and reads to them.''

"Does she indeed? Now, I wonder if she would care to have her portrait painted?"

"Not 'er," said Polly. "She's all agin vanity and picters. She give 'im wot for about you bein' axed in, the parlour-maid says. Artists is loose-livin' and sinful, she says."

10

*"That which is bitter to endure
may be sweet to remember."*

The Female Wing in the County Jail was, mercifully, new: it had been built by subscriptions collected by the Bindleton Ladies' Society for the Welfare and Reform of Female Felons only a year or two earlier and in the eating hall above the serving counter was a handsome tablet which boasted this fact and listed below the names of those who had subscribed for the project. They included, to Amelia's wry amusement, those of Staneley Hoggett and the Reverend Ulysses Bethune. The cells were stark but clean as whitewash and daily scrubbing could make them; the beds were hard and the blankets scanty but they were unshared and vermin-free. The jail had adopted, as far as it could be applied, the American idea of non-association. Each prisoner had a solitary cell with a high barred window in which was a shelf-bed, a stool and a chamberpot; in this cell each prisoner spent twelve hours of the twenty-four. Work was supposed to be accomplished in silence, meals eaten in silence and the hour's exercise in the yard taken in silence. They were moved about the prison in single file with each prisoner at a set distance from those in front and behind. In chapel each prisoner had her own little compartment, shut off from the rest by varnished boards. Talking was an offence severely punished.

Amelia, once the first black numbing despair had lifted a little, found that she could endure the life, living from day to day not thinking of the terrifying gulf of years which stretched before her, the further shore invisible and awful in its uncertainty. The grim-faced wardresses became individuals, varying in their attitudes to their charges, some

159

indifferent and uncaring, some vindictive, a few roughly tolerant. Her fellow prisoners were coarse, sullen and suspicious. For the most part they were thieves and prostitutes or both, though there was one who had escaped the rope by a hair's-breadth because she had killed her husband in a brawl; she was a vast brawny creature who walked dumbly through her days like an overburdened cart-horse. At first the inmates taunted Amelia, when they had the chance, with thinking herself a lady and being above them, but these chances were mercifully few.

The work was mostly sewing: they made army uniforms and prison clothes and coarse shrouds which were used for pauper burials. Amelia sewed her portion uncomplainingly and once or twice found time to help another, less skilled, to finish her allotment. Failure to finish was punished. For this she found a hunk of stale cake thrust into her hand one day. The female prisoners cooked, not only for themselves but for the male prisoners and for the warders and they stole whatever they could. At the time Amelia was on hands and knees scrubbing the flagged floor of the eating hall, one of eight women scrubbing in echelon

"Dahn yer front . . . 'urry!" hissed the donor and Amelia obediently opened the bodice of the coarse grey cotton gown under the sacking apron and thrust the gift out of sight, conscious of the approach of a wardress. She ate it that night in her cell, after dark, for fear of being seen through the judas in the door. She ate it slowly, crumb by crumb, savouring the sweetness and the fruit. Prisoners' fare was porridge, barley broth and bread.

It was the lack of books which she found hardest to bear. Not to read was a deprivation which irked her more than the constant scrubbing or the perpetual cold. She was never quite warm and as the winter cold increased she was tormented by chilblains. But she craved for books until she cried in bed at night as she did not for the cold or the coarse work or the harsh discipline. Without distraction her mind ran constantly round her situation like a mouse in a cage until she wondered if she might go mad and turned to reciting all the verses she could recall.

One day in mid-January when there was snow on the ground outside she had been locked in her cell after exercise

160

and was sitting on the stool, trying to rub some feeling into her feet and wondering whether it was worth the torment of the chilblains to have them warm again. She heard the clump of the wardress' boots on the stone floor outside and the door of her cell was unlocked. The wardress thrust it open and stood back to admit a small, dowdy, nervous figure, clutching a parcel.

"Visitor, 421," said the wardress, "Half an hour and I'll have me eye on you."

Whether this statement was to overawe Amelia or reassure her visitor there was no way of knowing for she locked the door again and clumped away. The visitor seemed stricken dumb and looked at Amelia like a rabbit shut into a ferret's cage. She began fumbling with the parcel. She was young, much younger than Amelia, no more than seventeen or eighteen and dressed in a gown economically 'cut down' from a much larger size. She was scarlet and trembling with embarrassment. Amelia swallowed her astonishment and smiled encouragingly. She had had no visitors since the start of her sentence, and was uncertain how to treat this one.

"Won't you sit down," she invited. "I can let down the bed, I should think."

"Thank you," gulped the visitor and perched on the very edge clutching the parcel.

"How very pleasant to have a visitor," Amelia observed after a long silence and subduing a desire to laugh at the tone of her voice which was that of a hostess. "Do you visit here a great deal?"

The girl shook her head.

"This is the first time," she blurted out. "The very first . . ."

"No need to be so nervous," Amelia assured her, smiling, "I won't do you any harm."

The girl gave her a long look as if she were seeing her for the first time and then sighed.

"No, of course not. It's just . . . I didn't know what to expect and Aunt said that I . . ."

She faltered into silence.

"What did Aunt say?"

"She said I was not to be repelled by evidence of depravity

". . . and I wasn't sure what she meant even . . . and I was looking . . ."

Amelia giggled and then laughed and the visitor relaxed slightly.

"Oh, you don't mind . . . I couldn't think what I was going to say to you. Half an hour seemed like an eternity."

Amelia rocked with laughter on her stool and the girl joined in, giggling with relief.

"Well, begin by telling me your name," suggested Amelia.

"Lucilla Ellershaw. My aunt is the Mrs Ellershaw who . . ."

"The Ellershaw Wing," Amelia nodded. "She is named as President of the Society."

"Yes. She takes a great interest in prisons and things," said Lucilla. "She wants me to be a phil . . . philth . . ."

"Philanthropist?" suggested Amelia.

"Yes. Just like she is," agreed Miss Ellershaw without venturing upon the word. "So she has decided that I must start visiting with her. I've seen a few . . . people in here, but they aren't a bit like you and Aunt did all the talking."

"So I am your first solo venture?"

"Yes. The very first. Aunt says I must attempt to bring you to a sense of your sin and then point out the path of repentance and invite you to pray with me for God's forgiveness for your transgression."

"An admirable programme," said Amelia, stifling a smile.

"Yes, but I don't know where to begin," admitted Miss Ellershaw. "Aunt does it so well but I can't remember the words she uses."

"She must have had a great deal of practice," Amelia consoled her, "I am sure the words will come easily to you in time."

Miss Ellershaw seemed doubtful.

"I may read the Bible too and leave one of these with you if you can read . . . you can read?"

"Oh, yes," said Amelia. "I can read quite well."

'These' were tracts, smudgily printed on cheap paper, describing in uncompromising terms the punishment meted out in the next world to unrepentant sinners and abjuring the reader to come without delay before the mercy-seat.

162

"I think I would prefer the Bible," said Amelia after a glance at one of them. "The English is so much better."

Miss Ellershaw looked vaguely shocked.

"Aunt wrote these."

"I rather thought she had. Tell me," invited Amelia, "why does your aunt wish you to follow in her footsteps? Has she no daughters of her own?"

"Oh, yes. She has three. But they won't come," Miss Ellershaw confided naïvely. "They say prisons are dull work . . ."

"I won't deny that," said Amelia.

The remainder of the half hour was spent in regrettably frivolous chatter in which Miss Ellershaw described her cousins and her own orphaned state. She was quite dependent upon Aunt, she said, and of course, Uncle because Papa hadn't left a penny. For the sake of the eye at the judas some Bible reading was crammed into the last few minutes, Miss Ellershaw plunging incontinently into a hideously genealogical portion of Kings which she read at irreverent speed with Amelia gently correcting her pronunciation of names such as Jotham, Remaliah and Abeldeth-maachah. When the key grated in the lock Miss Ellershaw said impulsively, "What is your name? Mine's Lucilla. I can't call you Four Two One."

"Amelia."

"Can I come again? Please Amelia, I would like to."

"Please do," said Amelia, not caring to remind her that she was in no position to refuse.

"Can I bring you anything? If it's allowed," she added hastily.

"Books," begged Amelia, "books . . . anything to read. The longer the better."

Miss Ellershaw nodded vigorously and then dipped her face to kiss Amelia's cheek, a gesture which surprised her as much as it surprised Amelia and which astounded the thin earnest female in the plain bonnet who stood in the doorway beside the wardress.

"Lucilla!" shrilled her aunt. "How very unbecoming!"

Her niece, with unexpected presence of mind said, rather breathlessly, "Salute one another with an holy kiss. Romans sixteen verse sixteen."

And thus rose considerably in Amelia's estimation.

163

This contact with the outside world had warmed Amelia but it also ended the numbness which had allowed her to accept what had happened to her. Now she understood completely what a hideous injustice had been done to her and her mind turned for the first time to trying to think how she might extricate herself. Shut in her cell the following day she was revolving in her thoughts whether there could be any use in appealing for help to Lord Wheatley. If he could at least remove from her charge those missing bibelots perhaps a way might be found to persuade authority to let her write to Mr Hoggett and implore his assistance. Suddenly the door opened and she was summoned to the Governor's Office. All she could think of was that the real thief had been found, that she was going to be released and her heart beat like a drum. However, the Governor's glum countenance dashed these hopes once and for all. He informed her in an expressionless voice that her case was coming up for review.

She knew another wild surge of hope but it was quenched rapidly.

"Questions have been asked," the Governor informed her, "about the clemency of your sentence."

"Clemency!" gasped Amelia and the accompanying wardress hushed her sternly.

"Taking into consideration the large sum involved in your crime and the fact that none of the money or the articles have been recovered," the Governor continued, referring to the letter in front of him, "there are those who consider that your sentence should have been transportation . . ."

Amelia went cold and the wardress officiously grasped her by the arm. The Governor looked up and frowned.

"I need hardly say that if you were to supply information which would lead to the recovery of the proceeds of your thefts this review need not necessarily increase the severity of your sentence . . ."

"How can I," Amelia demanded shrilly, "when I never had them in the first place?"

The wardress demanded silence and the Governor sighed.

"Take her away," he instructed. "You will be informed of the outcome of the review."

"When is it to be?"

"Within a month."

164

As they traversed the gloomy passages back to the Female Wing the wardress cleared her throat.

"No picnic, Botany Bay," she muttered. "Not much chance to get back, neither. Hadn't you best tell 'em where you got the doin's hid?"

"I can't!" Amelia said in a strangled voice for despair had her by the throat and she was close to tears. "I never had anything to hide. I never took them in the first place."

"They all says that," said the wardress scornfully. "You think about the Bay long enough, you'll change your tune."

That night Amelia cried, hitting out at the mattress and the thin pillow in a frenzy of useless anger and misery. Next morning she plodded sullenly through her tasks, scamping what she could and hating the coarse women who shouted orders and abuse at her. She felt like a mouse at the bottom of a barrel, trapped beyond hope of escape and helpless.

The following Sunday Mrs Ellershaw in full black Sabbath panoply bearing hymnbooks and large Bibles walked two miles from 'Siloam' which was the name of the Ellershaw villa to the Methodist chapel, Galaad, which stood in solid red brick on the outskirts of Bindleton. She was followed by a train of three daughters, one son-in-law, one orphaned niece, three maidservants, two manservants and her husband who would secretly have preferred to attend the service at St Stephen's Parish Church which he thought more consonant with his civic dignities, but dared not call down the vials of non-conformist wrath upon his head. This impressive pewful arrived exactly four minutes before the service was due to begin and filed into its accustomed place. Mrs Ellershaw bowed her head to tell the Deity that she had arrived and then looked about her to take note of those who had not. She felt a decided responsibility for the congregation of the Galaad Chapel. Her eyes, moving along the rows, approving a returned lamb here and condemning a frivolous bonnet bow there, were suddenly halted by the presence of two strangers, one tall, rawboned and red-headed, the other thin, small and one-eyed. They were dressed in sober suits of solemn black.

"See those two!" her husband hissed in her ear with understandable triumph. "That's Quentin the artist and his servant."

At that point the Minister came in and invited the assembly to praise the Lord by singing psalm number seventy-three, 'Truly God is good to Israel' which Alderman Ellershaw sang with greater than usual fervour. Comments about vanity and the sinfulness of chancecome artists would have at least to be tempered from now on. His wife did not respond to his information by so much as a flicker of an eyelid but after the last hymn was sung and the congregation began to stream out into the cobbled road, talking in subdued tones as befitted their surroundings, she did not refuse his introduction.

Mr Quentin, feeling as if he had been admitted to a Royal Levée, bowed to Mrs Ellershaw who was attended by the hungry-looking Minister as if she had been the Countess of Huntingdon herself. Thereafter he submitted cheerfully to a polite but thorough catechism in which he revealed that he had been brought up in the island of Guernsey where (the company were surprised to learn) Methodism flourished. A few further questions delicately elicited the whereabouts of Guernsey. A few more persuaded Mr Quentin to reveal that the great Wesley himself had been storm-stayed on a visit to the islands and his preaching had brought forth abundant witness to his doctrines. Mrs Ellershaw, somewhat to the relief of her family who were becoming exceedingly chilly in the north wind, expressed a wish to hear more of this outpost of the true faith, and, to the astonishment of all, invited him to break bread with them.

The party turned for home, walking swiftly, and Mr Quentin paced gravely at Mrs Ellershaw's side. Polly chose the most approachable of the manservants and walked with him.

"And bread's about all you'll get," said the worthy out of the corner of his mouth. "There ain't no hot vittles in our house of a Sunday. Cold commons is all you get, cold commons and good works."

Which prophecy proved true. Mrs Ellershaw was a strict Sabbatarian and no work of any kind was done in 'Siloam' on the Sabbath.

"Though," Cook said later in the kitchen, as they discussed cold beef, sliced cold potato, bread and butter washed down with cold water, "it don't stop her keeping us at work till midnight Saturday. Half eleven it was when I took them potatoes off the fire. And we're up by four, Monday mornings, to wash up the crocks by the light o' one candle."

Abovestairs the same fare was laid out in the dining parlour and Mr Quentin as the stranger within the gates was invited to ask a blessing on it. He responded to this by a long grace in a curious tongue. Mrs Ellershaw who had sat down doubtfully, uncertain of the effect of such a departure from custom upon the food and strongly suspicious that it might be in the language of Rome, enquired stiffly what tongue it was and learned with some relief that in Guernsey they spoke a patois of French.

"I found the hymns familiar," said Mr Quentin, blessing his old nurse who had sung them to him, "but not the words. In the island we sing them in French."

Such a circumstance was not wholly acceptable to Mrs Ellershaw who considered that the Deity should properly be addressed in English and connected the French with adherence to the Scarlet Woman and other similar abominations. When her guest mentioned that he came of an old Huguenot family she could be seen visibly regretting her invitation and wondering what emissary of Satan she had brought within the gates; however, the situation was saved by the orphaned niece.

"They were the French Protestants, Aunt. Cardinal Richelieu killed them all." She saw Mr Quentin's lips twitch slightly and added hastily, "I suppose some of them must have got away . . ."

Mr Quentin agreed gravely that this was so and adroitly turned the conversation from his own doubtful origins to the Methodist Mission in Bindleton.

"There has been a sad falling-off, Mr Quentin," declared his hostess mournfully. "There was a time when all the best families in the district came to Galaad but now they have left us and attend, when they do attend, the other church. They say that the congregation there is more fashionable."

"And I suppose they also cease in well-doing?" Mr Quentin sympathised.

Money was still to be had, Mrs Ellershaw admitted grudgingly, but in other respects there were many shortcomings which she was content to describe until the end of the meal.

Mrs Hoggett, he noticed, came in for a good deal of veiled abuse as a bad influence. Plainly there was discord between the households. Mrs Ellershaw was scathing about those who forgot their origins and aspired to ape the worthless so-called superior classes. She contrasted their idle useless lives with her own which was spent in sick-visiting, prayer-meetings, Bible classes, mother's meetings, sewing and knitting bees, mission collecting, tract distribution, prison-visiting . . .

"Oh, Uncle," the orphaned niece exclaimed suddenly, interrupting this virtuous catalogue, "can you spare me some books? Aunt asked me to visit a girl in the jail and she asked me if I could find her some books . . ."

This interruption drew the attention of the whole family upon her.

"Books!" exclaimed her uncle, startled out of his sullen application to cold stewed apple and cold custard, "what does a convict want with books?"

"She wants to read them," said the orphaned niece, reasonably enough, but was reproved by her aunt for pertness.

"I have no books to spare for such a purpose," grumbled Alderman Ernest Ellershaw, JP, "and of all the misplaced, nonsensical ideas. People are not sent to prison to laze away their time reading."

"I will supply you with a Bible," declared Mrs Ellershaw, overriding the Alderman effortlessly, "and I have besides some very improving magazines."

Later, in the drawing-room where drawn blinds kept the impious and frivolous December day at bay, Mrs Ellershaw whiled away the time before the afternoon service by reading from a book of sermons. After this expedition, stale bread and butter decidedly curled at the edges was served together with a jug of milk and water. During this feast Mr Quentin contrived to have a low-voiced but revealing conversation with the orphaned niece. It was uninterrupted. Mrs Ellershaw was not, despite her Christian principles, averse to a little matchmaking and she had elicited early that there was no Mrs Quentin . . . which was true enough. The niece was a pleasant companion but it would be a good thing to get her off their hands at the least expense and a penniless artist would surely not demand a great deal by way of portion; and Lucilla would be an excellent housekeeper, she had attended to that herself. She watched their exchange with a degree of complacency which would have been dispelled had she heard it.

Cartaret, with a view of gaining some form of access to Amelia, opened with some general enquiries about prison visiting and gradually drew from Lucilla a description of her first solo venture: with a surge of excitement he found hard to conceal he realised that Lucilla had most likely visited Amelia herself.

"The Head Wardress said she was docile and well-behaved and not liable to say anything that Aunt thought I should not hear and she couldn't say the same of the other prisoners and if I was to go alone it would have to be 421 or no one."

"And how did she appear to you?" Cartaret enquired, elaborately casual but with his heart beating fast.

"Oh, she was *so* nice, you wouldn't believe."

Lucilla's voice had a defiant note.

"And was she in good health?"

"She did look rather pulled," Lucilla said without reflecting that in the circumstances it was rather an odd enquiry, "but how would it be otherwise? Her hands were all swollen and chapped. They looked horribly sore."

Cartaret who had taken pleasure in drawing those hands swallowed.

"Will you visit her again?" he asked.

"If they'll let me. I expect they will if Aunt says I may. They do listen to Aunt there because she was the one who got the Female Wing built. But she thinks that I ought to visit Mrs Turnbull, 354. She wouldn't say anything she ought not because she never says anything at all, just sits and stares as if no one was there at all."

"And what has this Mrs Turnbull done?" asked Cartaret, not wishing to appear too particularly interested in one convict only.

"She killed her husband," Lucilla explained simply.

Cartaret's jaw dropped.

"She didn't mean to do such a thing," Lucilla explained. "She's terribly sorry she did it. It was just that she didn't know her own strength. They had a narrow-boat on the canal and her husband got drunk and she clouted him for leaving her to run the staithes alone and knocked him into the water and he went over the weir and he drowned. Aunt tells her that if she prays she will obtain forgiveness but I don't think Mrs Turnbull hears us much."

With an effort Cartaret returned to the matter in hand.

"I could obtain some books," he told her, "and my man could take them to the jail. What was the number you mentioned?"

"Four two one. But her real name," Lucilla confided with a wary eye on her aunt, "is Amelia. She was a governess not far from here. I am so grateful to you. I couldn't think how I was going to do it and I did promise. I have to account for all my pin-money, you see. And she was so kind to me, you can't imagine . . ."

Cartaret remembered this conversation later that night with a mixture of anger and amusement. Perhaps the true definition of *savoir faire*, he thought, was the ability to set a prison visitor at her ease.

On Monday morning a parcel was delivered to the County jail and opened in Amelia's presence by the Head Wardress. It contained Macaulay's *History of the English People*, Boswell's *Life of Johnson*, two copies of the *Quarterly Review*, a pile of much-thumbed parts of Mr Dickens' *Great Expectations*, a Bible printed in type so small that it was a menace to eyesight and five copies of the *Free Church Penny Monthly Magazine*. These treasures were handed over to her after a minute examination for files and rope ladders with the dour observation that she, the Head Wardress, didn't consider books appropriate for. female felons and if they hadn't come from that Miss Ellershaw with a message from her aunt (Aunt might have been startled to learn of this message) 421 wouldn't have been allowed to have them. After that, the menace of the review, the day's scrubbing and sewing, the silence and the repulsive scanty food, her chilblains' throb inside her ill-fitting shoes, all these seemed unimportant compared with the riches waiting for her. She blessed Lucilla fervently as she wrung out her washcloth for the fiftieth time in the evil, black scummy water in her pail.

Exercise that afternoon seemed more interminable than ever: there was a black frost which bit through the thin cotton garments supplied by Her Majesty to her involuntary guests. As she picked her way round the path, her chilblains throbbing inside her boots, she could hear Ailey's voice saying, 'A gentlewoman does not complain about a circumstance she is unable to remedy. It is a useless exercise and tedious for others.' The very idea made her smile: she wondered if Ailey would consider her present circumstances in that light and deplore complaint. In all probability she would. The wardress unaccustomed to smiles, looked at her suspiciously and wondered which of the rules she had broken.

At last the key turned in her cell door and she welcomed the sound for the first time. She took the first part of *Great Expectations* from the pile of manna on her stool and sat down under the window to read as long as the light should last. Page nine she found to have been folded inwards as if to mark a place and she straightened it carefully. Something had been written between the lines in very faint pencil:

> Kep yor pecker up the guv an me is on the job but he sez not to rite case we don do no good but i coodn leve you wivout a line them turnkeys sez no visitors wot aint relashons an no letters aloud but we are neerbi an like i say on the job yor frend poly.

Amelia stared unbelievingly at the message: it was as if a ray of sunshine had struck into the gloomy cell. She had a sudden picture of the studio as she had seen it first, aswim with sunlight. Her heart lifted and for the first time since the Governor had sent for her she permitted herself to hope . . . just a little. She was not alone. Somebody cared what was happening to her. And in the meantime, while she waited, there were books.

While she was reading Cartaret was reviewing all the evidence which he and Polly had collected. There was a small pile of signed statements, copies of ledger entries, a receipted bill for a grey hooded cloak from the Bespoke Tailor and certain other odds and ends. A grimy sketch of Bethune lay beside them. A leaner, fitter Shaftesbury in the stable below could have been witness to how far they had had to drive to collect these. Cartaret looked at them discontentedly.

"We need more," he said. "This shows him up as a bad

character and some of it is enough to cast suspicion on him, but none of it is damning enough. Counsel would make mincemeat out of it."

"It's enough to do her a bit of good," Polly maintained.

"A bit isn't good enough. If we're to get her out of that damnable place it's got to be cast-iron and lawyer-proof. It would be too cruel to have the case reopened and then when it was all over have her thrust back inside again."

"Poor little bleeder," muttered Polly. "Bad enough when you know you done summat."

"I daren't think of her," Cartaret said and began to pace restlessly round the shabby room. "When I do I get so angry I can't think properly."

"If I could get my 'ands on that Bethune . . ."

"*My* privilege," Cartaret said between his teeth.

There was a tap on the door. Polly opened it to admit Gardiner, as tidy and neat as if he had just emerged from his lodgings and had not just lighted down from the train after a long, cold and tedious journey from London. Cartaret strode to the door, hands outstretched.

"Ned! Come in! Come to the fire, you must be frozen!"

Polly who knew Gardiner's foibles, took his hat and cloak and treated them tenderly. Gardiner made for the fire and bent over to warm his hands.

"Have you eaten, Ned? Polly can go down and order you supper and see if they have a bed . . ."

"All in train," Gardiner assured him. "I brought my man with me and he is seeing to all that. I am assured of a bed. Any friend of Mr Quentin's is assured of a bed. You've been dropping the ready to some purpose round here."

"I have presented them with a portrait of the landlord's wife. What brings you north, Ned?"

Gardiner turned his back on the fire and stood warming his backside with his coat-skirts caught up over his arms. His face was unsmiling.

"Not good news," he declared gravely.

Cartaret's excitement died.

"What do you mean? Surely . . . surely they don't mean to transport her after all?"

"I think," Gardiner said quietly, "that is precisely what they mean to do."

"In the name of justice why?"

"Her sentence is to be reviewed next week."

"Next week! The law's delays are proverbial," Cartaret declared bitterly, "why hurry on this particular hearing?"

"I think it's Wheatley's doing."

"Wheatley? You mean that cousin of hers?"

"If we are to be accurate Miss Belchamber is his wife's cousin," Gardiner said.

"The misbegotten turd!" Cartaret exploded. "Why should he want to do such a dastardly thing?"

"I can think of two reasons," replied Gardiner. "The first is that he badly wants to be given the American post. He's in line for it. So is Fanshawe. A scandal would swing the good opinion away from him. And there's an election due. Think what the Radicals would make of his having a connection in jail."

"I'll see to it they know," Cartaret said grimly.

"The other reason," Gardiner went on as if Cartaret had not spoken, "is that somewhere in Wheatley House there could be one Sèvres jar, one Chinese Ming dynasty bowl, a number of priceless ivories and a Dresden shepherdess."

"Cripes!" Polly exclaimed.

"Precisely," Gardiner agreed. "He was abroad with the Trade Commission while the trial was going on and when he came back he probably realised it was his wife who had purloined those items. Better a cousin in jail than his wife, he thinks. And wouldn't it be better still to have her sent to the Antipodes where she can't make embarrassing statements about what may have happened to them. I expect he read a transcript of the trial."

"Did no one follow up what she suggested?"

"I doubt it."

"How do you know he's behind this review?"

"The Honourable Member who raised the matter of the 'over-lenient sentence' is in Wheatley's pocket. Nor was he concerned with this 'gross miscarriage' until Wheatley came back to England last month.

Cartaret was frowning.

"Surely a review will bring about the sort of damaging stuff he wants to avoid?"

"Not necessarily. A review of that nature is not a public

matter. All there will be is a small paragraph in the Law Report to say that the sentence in the case has been changed to one of transportation."

"The contemptible creature! If I could lay hands on him, I'd . . ."

"Quentin, sit down and stop pacing about like a lion in a cage. In some ways this could be turned to our advantage, don't you see?"

Cartaret threw himself into a chair and glowered.

"How?"

"Even if we had all the evidence it could take months to bring about a retrial. This way their Lordships cannot leave the matter on the shelf. What we must do is have ready a copper-bottomed, water-tight case to present them with by the middle of next week."

"But that's just what we haven't got," Cartaret exploded. "We've nothing really conclusive. Nothing out-and-out damning. The judges won't listen to chit-chat about bastards and boot-maker's bills. And Bethune's a cool customer. He won't be rushed into a confession."

"I see," Gardiner said. "I won't conceal from you I was hoping for something better. It takes time to get up a case."

"If we can't do it . . . what then?"

"Your Miss Belchamber will be on a one-way winter journey to Australia, I'm afraid, and it may take years to get her back."

"If she survives. The death-rate on the convict-transports is a scandal."

"I have been aboard one," Gardiner told him quietly. "We must make every effort."

He gathered up the papers on the table and shuffled them into a neat bundle.

"I can brood over these tonight. Tomorrow I must go back to London. There's a job which has to be done and I must arrange it while I can."

He made for the door and Polly scampered to open it for him. In the doorway he turned and looked back at Cartaret sprawled in his chair.

"By the by," he asked, "have you enquired if she can make any helpful suggestions? Miss Belchamber, herself, I mean."

Cartaret flushed with irritation.

"No visitors not of her immediate family. I don't think I could pass myself off as Lady Wheatley, do you? And she seems to be the only relative Amelia has. Even then no visits of any kind during the first six months. No letters either in or out. After that letters only from immediate relatives. I have enquired, believe me I have."

Gardiner frowned. Cartaret jumped to his feet.

"But you could see her!" he exclaimed. "You could say you were her lawyer, ask for an interview."

"I can't. No time. Even if there was time . . . no, you'll have to try to get some message to her . . . do your best. I'll be gone early but perhaps we can breakfast together. I'll explain what I've got in mind."

Gardiner had left by the seven fifteen express and was frowning over the assorted scraps of evidence in a corner of his first class compartment when Cartaret entered the Bindleton bookshop. It was not a very prosperous venture, the Bindletonians having for the most part the notion that reading for pleasure was a waste of time better spent making money. It was kept by a large gentle down-trodden man who had once been a teacher. He had had the good fortune to marry an heiress. Her inheritance had been the Bindleton Book Emporium and Circulating Library and her husband ran it according to her instructions. It was in consequence not very well run. Cartaret tinkled the bell as he opened the door and the ex-teacher emerged from the mirk and smiled mournfully at him. The advent of Mr Quentin had increased the sale of books by an appreciable amount. Cartaret wished him the time of day and asked whether he could produce any book in Italian. The ex-teacher nodded and inserted his bulk between a reef of eighteenth-century sermons bound in calf and a drift of sheet-music, making his hazardous way to the back of the shop. It was a mercy that so far he had never caused a bookslide which would overwhelm him. The back wall was lined to the ceiling with shelves so packed with books that they sagged in the middle and would have broken had it not been for the books wedged beneath them. The ex-teacher unerringly reached up to the fifth shelf, removed with his large left hand a fistful of dusty *Lyrical Ballads* and with two

175

fingers of his right hand extracted from the dusty aperture he had made a copy, battered but complete, of Dante's *Inferno*. Cartaret's eyes gleamed as he saw the trickle of stanzas through a wide expanse of page, marred only by an occasional cramped handwritten note.

"How much?"

"Two shillings," the ex-teacher said, rather apologetically.

"It could be worth more," Cartaret declared and handed him half a sovereign.

For the next two hours Cartaret was busy with pen and ink, evidently expanding the notes already made in the margins. The notes were in Italian, like the poem.

In the afternoon he took up a standing invitation to drink tea at Siloam. He was made welcome by Mrs Ellershaw and her daughters and, he was relieved to see, Lucilla. The Alderman was not there. Over the teacups he contrived to have a low-voiced private conversation with Lucilla.

"Your friend in the jail who reads," he reminded her. "She did get the books? They weren't confiscated?"

"Oh, yes. I know she did because she was allowed to send a note of thanks."

"Will you be visiting again soon?"

"Not till Christmas," she said. "This week we are inspecting the orphanage and the workhouse. Aunt is on the Board of Guardians, you know."

Cartaret could easily believe it.

"And next week we will be distributing the Christmas bundles and boxes," she went on, "and after that there will be . . ."

"I would like your friend to get this as soon as possible," Cartaret told her stemming the tide of good works, "could you get it to her?"

Lucilla's eyes gleamed with excitement.

"Are you a friend of hers too?" she asked conspiratorially.

"Yes."

"Oh, splendid! Are you trying to help her escape?"

Cartaret threw back his head and laughed aloud, attracting the benevolent attention of Mrs Ellershaw who smiled across the tea urn.

"Am I to understand," he asked as quietly as he could,

"that you would try to smuggle in a file and a ropeladder for her?"

Lucilla nodded, her eyes bright with enthusiasm.

"Well, truth to tell, escape hadn't occurred to me. What I want," he said, "is to get her out through the front gate in broad day-light and keep her out."

"You mean you don't believe she did what they say she did?"

"Exactly so."

Lucilla sipped thoughtfully at her cooling tea.

"I'll find a way, I promise. It would be . . ."

"The book's in Italian," Cartaret interrupted her, "she writes and speaks Italian. You'd be expected to know that."

"Ah," said Lucilla delightedly, "that makes it *much* easier."

"It does?"

She nodded emphatically and beamed upon him so that Mrs Ellershaw began to plan certain unostentatious wedding festivities. Lucilla's next exchange would have wiped the smile from her lips.

"Are you Amelia's lover?"

"Yes," said Cartaret firmly; he had not missed Mrs Ellershaw's approbation of their tête-à-tête and wished for no complications. Besides, it was true.

"I feel as if I was in a book," Lucilla observed happily. "Amelia the Heroine and me the Faithful Friend."

"Well Faithful Friend I hope you have a story of your own before long," Cartaret told her affectionately and slipped the little book on to her lap under the crocheted tea napkin.

Amelia was scrubbing the endless lower corridor when she was summoned to the Head Wardress's room. She had found the best way to surmount the hours of mind-numbing physical work was to try to recall verses: the tap on her shoulder came as she was trying to pin down a few errant stanzas of *Marmion*. At once her mouth went dry and she felt a trickle of ice under the bodice of her gown. Surely, surely, it was soo soon for there to be any decision from the review? When she made the regulation curtsey her heart was hammering.

"Miss Ellershaw," the Head Wardress began disapprovingly, "informs me that you can read and speak Italian."

This was so unexpected that Amelia was left speechless.

"Well, is this the case?"

Amelia cleared her throat and agreed hoarsely, trying to recall whether she had confided this unimportant detail to Lucilla and concluding that she had not. How then, had she known?

"She tells me also that you are anxious not to lose this ability as you hope to be able to obtain employment abroad . . . afterwards."

Clearly the Head Wardress did not approve of abroad.

"In the circumstances," she observed, "it is probably the best you could hope for."

"Yes, ma'am," Amelia murmured as she was apparently expected to make some comment.

"Miss Ellershaw has been kind enough to obtain for you a copy of Dante in the original," the Head Wardress informed her, referring to the letter on her desk. She pronounced the name to rhyme with saint.

"How very kind of her," Amelia said.

"I have thought about the matter," said the Head Wardress majestically, "and as you have behaved yourself in my charge I have decided you may be permitted to have it."

She handed over the shabby little volume and Amelia glanced inside it. A phrase scribbled in the margin jumped out at her: . . . as we need evidence . . ." She controlled her expression but could not control her heart which began to race with excitement.

"You may go, 421."

Amelia curtsied, thinking quickly.

"Thank you ma'am. If you please, ma'am, I would like to write a letter of thanks . . . you were kind enough to permit this before."

"I will see you have paper, pen and ink, 421."

"Thank you ma'am."

After exercise she heard the door slam and the key turn with joy and climbed up beside the window to make the most of the dying light. It did not take her long to decipher Cartaret's message which he had spread in marginal notes over most of the book. Briefly he was asking her if she could think of anything which Bethune might have done with the greater part of the money. She had no difficulty in thinking of one possible solution. It took her longer to think of a way of telling him. When the wardress came in with writing materials she found her charge intent on her Bible in the last of the daylight.

On Sunday night at chapel Lucilla caught Cartaret's eye and he realised she had news for him. After the service he moved to greet the family and shake their hands. In Lucilla's he felt a hard shape which could have been a note folded very very small. He raised her hand to his lips and succeeded in taking it into his own. With considerable difficulty he managed to refuse an invitation to supper: Mrs Ellershaw believed in striking while the iron was hot.

The note read:

Dear Mr Quentin,
    Our friend was permitted to write to me. This is what she said. I can't let you have the whole letter because it would be too big and Aunt would have to know what I was giving you. She said it was very thoughtful of me to give her what she needed more than anything and the book would give her pleasure and some much-needed mental exercise. Then she went on and said about following my excellent advice of taking a text from the Bible to think about while she was engaged on her daily tasks. I didn't advise any such thing, so I imagine it's a message of sorts. She said that yesterday she chose Psalms 20 v 7 and today it was Psalms again, 33 v 17. And then she was my friend to oblige and all that. I looked them up during the service because the note came yesterday evening and I didn't get it till morning and Aunt won't allow any business to be attended to on the Sabbath, so I had to read it in the privy. They are 'some trust in chariots and some in horses' and 'an horse is a vain thing for safety; neither shall he deliver any by his great strength'. I do hope this means something important. This is the most exciting thing which has ever happened to me.
                    Your friend to oblige you,
                        Lucilla Ellershaw.

179

Cartaret read it twice.

"Horses?" he muttered, "Horses . . ."

Polly came in with his supper-tray in time to hear this.

"What about 'orses, then?" he asked. "Thinkin' of 'avin' a flutter, are we?"

Cartaret gave vent to a whoop.

"A flutter . . . why on earth didn't I think of that. He'd all the other bad habits, why didn't I think that he might gamble as well?"

The next day, early, Cartaret set out for Shaftesbury's birthplace. Howard was, he had discovered, the district's expert on all matters equine, both hunting and racing. He arrived there to discover, somewhat to his relief, that Mrs Howard was from home and Mr Howard was in his study casting up his accounts, a task he was evidently pleased to have interrupted. He provided Shaftesbury with a snug stall, being a man with firm priorities, and then provided Cartaret with a chair by the blazing study fire and a large mug of excellent home-brewed. Cartaret, thawing, rapidly absorbed half his mug and came right to the point.

"I hear you are a racing man, Howard."

"You might say so," agreed his host cautiously. "T'aint often I miss a meeting, that's for sure, and I run my own nags from time to time."

"I suppose," Cartaret said, "if you go to the races regularly you find very much the same people at every meeting . . . the same faces . . ."

"Aye," Howard agreed.

"A fairly small group."

"Aye."

"I expect you could name most of them?"

Howard put down his ale with something of a bang.

"Now, see here, Mr Quentin, what's this about? I'm not one as has to be come at a-tiptoe. If it's work you're after, they're not the kind to want their phizzes on their parlour walls, I tell thee. If you'd paint their nags, you might come by a guinea or two."

"Bit cold for painting in the stables, though it's an idea I'll bear in mind."

"Out with it, Quentin. What are you after? I'm a man as likes things straight."

180

Cartaret decided that there was no time to beat about the bush.

"I'm after Bethune," he said. "I think he's a thief and a scoundrel."

"Bethune!"

Cartaret could have sworn Howard's eyes gleamed with interest.

"Does he go to the races?"

"Aye. He's there at all the meets. Lord knows why for he don't know a lame donkey from a cavalry charger. I think he comes to hob-nob with the swells."

"Does he bet?"

"He do," Howard looked sideways at him, "that he do."

"Does he win?"

"Some. More than he deserves."

"Does he lose?"

Howard didn't answer at once; instead he emptied his mug and set about refilling both of them from the jug on the table.

"Look'ee, Quentin, I've no mind to hide the truth. Is this owt to do with yon affair o' the governess that was turned off on his account?"

Cartaret scented something important and his belly tightened with excitement.

"Why do you ask?"

"Because I wasn't born yesterday and I hear a lot of things going about the way I do and, I'll not deceive you, I've been uneasy in my mind."

"Why?"

"Because of what happened at the meet last October."

Cartaret's heart began to thump.

"What was that?"

"He made a bet with young Jerburgh."

"That young blackguard!"

Howard looked up in surprise.

"You know him?"

"By reputation," Cartaret said hastily.

Howard snorted with amusement.

"Aye," he agreed drily. "He's a right good-for-nowt, yon sprig."

"What happened?"

181

"There'd been a deal of drinking," Howard said, "and the swells were all merry and bright, like, and Bethune was talking like he allus does with a drink in him, as if he'd been born in a stable and cut his teeth on a bit; daft stuff it was about bone and blood and blood-lines and how he had stable information. Jerburgh told him to his head he was talking balderdash and so he was any road. Bethune squared up and said he'd put money on it. Jerburgh asked, how much. Bethune said fifty. Jerburgh laughed and said that wasn't much and didn't say a lot for his faith in his fancy. The upshot was that Bethune was goaded into wagering five hundred on this sway-backed, knock-kneed bag o' catsmeat. And it came seventh."

"Did he pay?"

Howard shrugged.

"The bet was between him and Jerburgh. I don't know whether or no. How should I? But, Bethune was at the Winter Meet, large as life and swanking round with the swells as usual, and Jerburgh was there and arm-in-armly with him. So I reckon it must have been paid. And it's all that what's made me uneasy in my mind, for where would a beggarly usher like him, for all his grand connections, get the half of a sum like that, or even a tenth of it. The Canon hasn't a penny, that I do know, and if he had he'd give it all away before his son got his hands on it. Where did the money come from?"

"Quite!"

"If yon lass did take the money," Howard went on, the thoughts and suspicions of months pouring out of him, "then she must ha' given it to him and he's art and part in the business and it's bad enough that he's let her take the blame. If she didn't, then I reckon he did and he should be behind bars in her room. There! Ee, but I'm right down glad to have that off my chest. I should have spoke up before this but I hadn't that much to go on and them folks is good customers of mine. I couldn't afford to be wrong, not dealing with the nobs, I couldn't."

Cartaret got to his feet.

"I am uncommonly obliged to you, Mr Howard," he said formally. "I'd be the more obliged if you would, when called upon, swear to everything you've told me."

182

Howard made a face and then grinned.

"I'll sleep easier tonight, that I'll not deny."

Before Cartaret turned Shaftesbury's head towards Bindleton, Howard, adjusting a buckle said, almost under his breath:

"On your way home, Quentin, why don't you bait at the White Boar. Do you take a look at the barmaid's bosom. She's a great thowless lump o' a lass, but handsome I don't deny, and she's got a string of admirers. Likes presents, she do. Makes no secret of it."

Just about the time when Shaftesbury was trotting up to Howard's Farm a young man rang the bell on the tradesman's entrance at Wheatley Hall. He was pale, slightly shabby but very neat in his dress and he had arrived on foot from the station. From an inner pocket he produced a card which told of his connection with a company of art dealers, a very reputable and respectable company, and a letter in a neat clerkly hand signed with Lord Wheatley's customary scrawl which required Mr Pamplin the butler to permit the bearer to examine certain of the art treasures in the Hall with a view to valuing them for insurance. There was also a letter from the insurance company. It was a regrettable fact that both letters were forged. Lawyers have access to unconventional skills. Mr Pamplin duly admitted the bearer, treating him in the fatherly fashion he adopted to skilled craftsmen. He allocated a large footman to him in the guise of a guide to the complexities of such a great house in order to supervise the operation. Mr Pamplin opined in the Room after luncheon (beer and sandwiches had been served to the pale young man) that letters was all very well but you never knew and no one hadn't passed no remarks about valuating before his Lordship had left for London. The footman had his instructions not to let the young man out of his sight and to make sure that he did not take his leave with any suspicious bumps about his person. Later, when the pale young man had departed to catch the five seventeen up, the footman reported that he was a rum sort of cove, not interested in the pictures but in the bits and bobs and pots and that in the cabinets. He had a list, the footman said, and wanted to know the whereabouts of a red pot-affair with dragons and such all over it. The footman had remembered it for an ugly brute and told the young man that he had carried it up to the attic not a fortnight before with a whole boxful of other pots and bits, bone monkeys and faces and china figures. In the attic the young man had checked the contents of the box against his list and seemed pleased. He'd asked when the ugly brute with the dragons had come into the Hall and the footman had told him a sixmonth ago or thereabout, nearer he couldn't go. The housekeeper remembered that it had been round about the time when they had gone to London for to bury the cousin who done himself in and Mr Pamplin said it was a pity he hadn't asked her rather than the footman. After which exchange they forgot the incident. After a fortnight or so they were to be forcibly reminded of it. The station fly deposited two policemen on the doorstep, together with the pale young man looking much less shabby. To Mr Pamplin's distress and fury they presented him with a search warrant and removed, leaving him with a receipt, the box of items in which the pale young man had been so interested. Mr Pamplin, after their departure, wrote out his resignation: this was not at all the style of thing to be expected in a genteel establishment. His resignation, however, went unnoticed for when it arrived on his Lordship's desk his Lordship had other rather more serious matters to take his attention.

11

*"The truth is powerful
and will conquer."*

It would have been plain, even to a stranger, that the
Christmas holidays had begun at Blackyetts. Lights blazed
from every room downstairs, someone was banging out 'The
Holly and the Ivy' on the drawing-room pianoforte and a
raucous precarious baritone was singing words to this tune
which appeared to have little to do with Christmas but to
refer to the eccentric habits of two unlikely schoolmasters. In
the baronial hall the gloom had been dispelled by a dummy (a
bolster dressed in a frilled shirt and a frock-coat culled from
Mr Hoggett's wardrobe) hanging from the first floor gallery
and turning slowly around in the most lifelike – or deathlike
– manner above the stairwell. Round the neck was a placard,
unreadable at that height. However, this macabre decoration
cast no blight on the spirits of those taking it in turns to
hurtle down the stairs on a huge Benares brass tray which Mr
Hoggett had brought home with him from a visit to India.
They were shrieking loudly enough to shatter the stained-
glass Lily Maid of Astolat who presided wanly over the
half-landing. A large plate of mince pies stood on the oak
chest, an item large enough to hold a brace of brides but
which contained only a selection of odd gloves and galoshes
and broken umbrellas. Beside the plate, eating steadily, sat
Albert, a stony eye upon his siblings at their noisy play.
Frederick abandoned the Holly and the Ivy in favour of
sliding down four flights of banisters with an expertise which
did not permit the use of hands.

In all the hullabaloo the sound of wheels and hooves could
not be heard and the fun continued fast and furious until the

185

front door swung open to the wall and the master of the house stood staring at the sight of his heir arriving in a heap on the hall carpet having parted company with the brass tray which made a noisy arrival on its own: his second son put in an appearance immediately afterwards, careering down the banister, arms spread wide like a seagull and making very comparable noises. Mr Hoggett stared in amazement and another arrival came up behind him and stood, waiting politely to be shown in.

Mr Hoggett advanced four-square in his caped overcoat and low-crowned hat and stood with his fists on his hips. The noise gradually faded and died and his family stared incredulously back at him.

"In t'name o' Glory!" he ejaculated and pointed a finger at Albert. "You, stop feeding thi face and fetch someone to bring in t'bags. Look lively!"

Albert hirpled through the door to the servants' quarters with a martyred air and without a word. Frederick and Staneley brushed themselves down, passed their hands over their hair, straightened their Eton collars and advanced to meet him.

"Welcome home, Father," they choroused.

"Some welcome!" he glowered. "Scamps! Is that what they teach you at thi fancy school?"

"What temptation, though," remarked his companion diplomatically, his amusement very plain. "What a staircase, what a tray and what banisters! I declare I'm tempted myself."

"Oh, quite the diplomat," said Mr Hoggett and his lips twitched. "Not but what I'd give a monkey to see you at it. Staneley, lad, take Mr Scott into the library and see him comfortable till I can come."

"Yes, Father," said Staneley and went to the library door. "We didn't expect you," he added.

"That's well seen . . ."

Mr Lucas and Mr Booth and half a dozen other servants came breathlessly into the hall. The butler set his people to carry in the luggage while Mrs Lucas curtsied and said with a sincerity there was no mistaking, "I am very glad to see you come home, sir."

"And I to be here at last. A room for me guest, Mrs Lucas,

and see the sheets are well-aired. And some supper as soon as you can bring it. Soup and cold meat will do very well."

Mrs Lucas dismissed a hovering chambermaid to her duty with a flick of her finger and smiled.

"I think we can find something a mite better than that, sir. I have informed Mrs Sands of your arrival."

She swept her black skirts through the hall and out of the door as the nursery party came tumbling downstairs shouting, "Papa! Papa!"

He gathered them up into a huge hug which lifted them both off their feet.

"There's my pretty ones. And my Alice . . . and Lou . . . quite the young ladies now!"

He was fervently hugged and kissed, a ceremony watched by Albert from the service door with an expression which was almost a sneer. He heard in a pandemonium of voices all talking at once, of the new baby brother, the new foal and the kitchen cat's kittens and watched his father smiling delightedly at such a welcome.

"Eeh, but I'll need to make Mark's acquaintance right away."

Mrs Sands came majestically down the stairs with the baby in her arms.

"Here he is, sir."

Mr Hoggett inspected the latest addition to his household, prodded him in the region of the stomach with a stubby forefinger and made the obligatory clucking sounds. Master Mark stared back, sleepy and unimpressed.

"He'll do, I reckon, Mrs Sands, no need to send him back to the warehouse, eh?"

"There's a great likeness to yourself," she said and added without looking up, "You had my letter? About Miss Dorrie."

"I did," he said. "And she will be back here as soon as I can manage it."

Mrs Sands said nothing but her eyes filled and a tear trembled and fell on to the baby's shawl.

Mr Hoggett smiled, a rather grim smile and patted her on the shoulder.

"You're a good lass, Sands."

The nurse dropped a curtsy and went back up the stairs.

"Eeh, then . . ." He turned to Louisa and Alice. "Where's thi mother? In the drawing-room? Has she visitors?"

"No," said Louisa. "She's in her room, lying down. She said the boys' din gave her the headache."

"Alice, lass," Mr Hoggett looked at his younger daughter, "run and tell her I've arrived and ask would she come down and make my guest welcome. It's a Mr Scott, tell her."

Alice obediently went upstairs and her father noticed a rather startled look on the faces of Frederick and Staneley who had come out into the hall.

"What's up wi' thee?" he demanded and then his eye fell on the dummy. "Oh, aye. Well, best take it down. Thi mother won't care for that I daresay. Eeh! but it's grand to be home. There was a time . . ." he struggled out of his greatcoat and handed it to Mr Booth, "when I thowt I would never see home again. Lord, what a voyage! I wouldn't do it again for a thousand pound. Gales we had, icebergs, fog, engine failure, steering failure . . . Lord, I can't begin to tell you! I'd ha' been better waiting for the regular packet. That'll teach me to be in too much of a hurry! There. Now, fetch me over that little pigskin bag and we'll see what I've brought home for you all. And we'll go in the library or Mr Scott will think I've forgot him quite. Bring some brandy," he instructed Booth who was watching the staircase with an anxious eye.

He was shooing the excited children through the library door and beginning to introduce them to Mr Scott when Alice came running downstairs, her face white and red in patches and the tears pouring down her cheeks.

"Why, then, Alice, lass. What's up wi' thee?"

She came to a stop in the hall and looked wildly round.

"It's awful!" she sobbed out. "I didn't believe it, I didn't, I didn't . . . I couldn't believe it, but it's true. Every word of it's true! I saw . . . Oh, I can't *bear* it!"

She looked at the staring faces and gave a strange distressed little wail and then turned and ran towards the schoolroom wing. Louisa made to follow her but Mr Hoggett caught her arm.

"She's best left, I reckon. I dare say you've some notion what's overset her?"

Louisa looked mulish and stricken at the same time.

"No . . ." she mumbled and it was patently a lie.

"Aye," Mr Hoggett said grimly. "I've a notion an' all."

Just at that moment Albert lowered the dummy from the landing to lie at his feet.

"Someone's been making free with my wardrobe, I see," Hoggett said and bent down to look at the scrawled label which hung round the dummy's neck. BETHUNE BEWARE, it said, in untidy capitals surrounded by what purported to be death's heads. He pulled it off and looked at it before he crumpled it up.

"Aye," he said, "time I came home, I reckon."

About two hours before Mr Hoggett's unexpected arrival Alderman Ellershaw was disturbed in his study where he was sleeping off a civic luncheon under the *Manchester Guardian*. His niece, Lucilla, pulled off the paper gently and told him that Mr Quentin had arrived and would like a word with him. The Alderman grunted, rebuttoned his waistcoat, smoothed his bald pate and went into the morning room where his visitor was looking at an engraving with ill-concealed horror.

"Ah, Quentin. Good evening to you," the Alderman greeted him and shook hands. "I imagine you've come about the first sitting at last."

"Evening, Ellershaw. No, I came on quite another matter."

A shade of irritation crossed the Alderman's face. Formality, as he was fond of saying, lubricated social intercourse. It was monstrous to have this lanky fly-by-night dauber, not even a proper Englishman he remembered, assume himself the equal of Alderman Ellershaw JP.

"Please be seated, Mr Quentin."

Cartaret's bottom reached the chair a fraction of a second after the please. Alderman Ellershaw began to feel distinctly ruffled, even slighted.

"Now," he began taking a chair with dignity, "about this portrait, I think . . ."

"Hang the portrait," said Cartaret, "I doubt if I'll be here to do it anyway. I've come on a much more important matter."

"What do you mean, hang the portrait?" protested the

189

Alderman, "I've been kept waiting for nearly a fortnight while you painted that Hoggett . . . while you painted Mrs Hoggett."

"Yes, well, that's it," Cartaret said. "I think I've got enough now to ask you . . ."

"Enough what?"

"Enough information."

Alderman Ellershaw glared at him.

"Doubtless," he said icily, "you intend to explain yourself in time?"

"I've come about a case you heard. I think it should be reopened."

Alderman Ellershaw breathed deeply.

"Do you indeed? I presume you have a reason for making this . . . this impertinent request?"

"Of course I have or I wouldn't be here," Cartaret said impatiently. "I've been making enquiries round the district for weeks. Found some very interesting facts."

"May one enquire to which case you refer?" asked the Alderman, heavily polite. "In my position half a hundred cases pass through my hands every month."

"I would say this one slipped through your fingers," observed Cartaret. "I mean the Belchamber case."

"The Belchamber case! You must be drunk. It was an open and shut case. Never a doubt in my mind."

"Mostly shut," said Cartaret. "It seems to have escaped your attention that she was completely innocent."

"You are entitled to your opinion, sir," the Alderman told him in a strangled voice, "mine was endorsed, as doubtless you recall, by a judge and jury."

He rose and opened the door.

"That should be quite good enough for you. I'll bid you good night, sir, and have a great pleasure in informing you that I shall look elsewhere for a real artist to take my likeness."

Cartaret did not move.

"Not so fast, Ellershaw. For your own good you should hear me out."

"I will not be badgered in my own house," spluttered the angry little man. "Kindly leave at once."

"If you prefer I am perfectly ready to produce the evidence

190

of negligence – your negligence – in public," Cartaret told him calmly. "In fact I intend to do so at the first opportunity. It was just that I thought that you might prefer to know what it was before I did so."

"Negligence!" The Alderman was scarlet in the face. "What do mean, sir? I have never been so insulted in my life!"

"You surprise me. I mean that the judge and jury did not have the benefit of hearing all the facts pertinent to this case. And some of those facts you were in a position to know. Whether you did know them or not . . ."

Cartaret shrugged.

"For the sake of your wife I'm prepared to give you the benefit of the doubt. Which is why I am here tonight."

"What facts?"

"One is that Bethune and the Hoggett woman were and are lovers."

Ellershaw choked and exploded.

"Backstairs gossip, sir! I'll have you know there are penalties for slander. Severe penalties!"

"If it is a slander it is a slander pretty generally believed. And I imagine it must have come to your ears. Did it not?"

"As if I would believe . . ." stuttered the Alderman, "friends of long-standing . . . prurient rubbish . . ."

"I have copies of some interesting signed statements."

Cartaret produced a bundle of papers and laid them on the arm of his chair. The magistrate looked at them uneasily and came back into the room from his post at the door.

"Even you, with your charitable attitudes, may find these . . . suggestive. That one from the lodging-house keeper at Lowick Waters is, perhaps, the most revealing."

He riffled through the papers and produced a statement from the lodging house keeper to the effect that he had identified as Mr and Mrs Bertram who stayed at his establishment from time to time to take the Waters the two persons in the pictures. The pictures were those of Mr Bethune and Mrs Hoggett. Mrs Thackry's information had been perfectly correct.

"Even if this is true," Ellershaw stammered, "it is not in the very least relevant to the case. She was accused of larceny."

"Not relevant? It puts a rather different complexion on her

191

dismissal, don't you think? I would think a jury would find it relevant."

"I assure you that I do not find that bit of unpleasant gossip enough to . . ."

"Oh, that is just the beginning. I have a lot more. In fact I think I have discovered the real scoundrel. I have a great deal of information about him."

"About whom?"

"Bethune, of course. It was plain to the eye of a complete stranger that if the girl was innocent he was the only person who could be guilty."

"As you say, you are a complete stranger. Mr Bethune is one of a most respected . . ."

"Bethune is an unscrupulous and dissipated young rip."

Ellershaw waved his hand.

"I daresay there have been a few indiscretions. Boys will be boys after all."

"Then I hope he never casts an eye upon one of your daughters," Cartaret said grimly. "He is seven years younger than I am and you would not describe me as a boy. To my certain knowledge, well-documented . . ." He laid down more papers. "He has debauched at least one girl under the roof of Blackyetts. He paid her off . . . the date of the payment should interest you . . . and she is now respectably established. I hope she can be kept out of it, but she is willing to give evidence against him if the need should arise."

"I still don't see what all this nasty mud you are trying to stir up has to do with the theft of the money."

"Look at this date. He paid her a large sum – in gold – two days after the scene in the belvedere. Not conclusive, I admit, but very suggestive."

"All this is very dreadful but as you say, not conclusive. I see no reason to reopen the case at all."

"Well, listen to some of the facts I discovered while I was painting that woman at Blackyetts. Bethune is Mrs Hoggett's secretary as well as her stud . . ."

The Alderman blinked.

"He writes her letters, does her accounts and has continual access to her private apartments. This was not made plain at the trial. There he was made out to be a genteel and modest young man who came in by the day and had nothing to do with anything except his pupil, who is, by the way, blackmailing him."

Alderman Ellershaw collapsed into a chair.

"This is outrageous . . ." he said feebly.

"I saw him do it," Cartaret told him. "I painted the woman in what she calls her boudoir, an apartment positively aglitter with looking-glasses. Bethune was working at her writing table and I saw the little wretch come in and demand something and get it too. It was as plain as print."

"I still don't see," said the Alderman obstinately, "that you have enough to warrant . . ."

"Let us continue. Bethune was heavily in debt. Even you must know that. He was in debt to you and half the tradesmen in Bindleton. This didn't come out at the trial either. He was even in debt at Manchester. Clothes seem to be his major weakness, apart from racing, of course. You may have heard that he lost five hundred pounds at the Autumn Meeting."

"I do not attend race meetings, a man in my position . . ."

"A man in your position might learn something from his associates. There were at least two of the Bindleton Town Council at that meeting. Did you know that the five hundred was paid off less than a fortnight after Miss Belchamber's unhappy experience in the summer-house?"

"How should I know such a thing?"

"Well, perhaps not. But you almost certainly did know that he owed you twenty-three pounds seventeen shillings for you had been pressing for it. I have copies of the letters sent to him. Interestingly enough it was paid two days after the departure of Miss Belchamber from Blackyetts. I have a copy of the entry in the ledger and an affidavit from your ledger clerk to this effect."

The Alderman's face was a study in indignation and alarm.

"Did this circumstance not strike you as a little suggestive? I have a list of dates of similar payments from other tradesmen, here and in Manchester. All in all and taking into account the sum paid to the young woman in Roman Gate they amount to about four hundred and twenty pounds. An interesting total. If you add it to the five hundred lost to Jerburgh it comes to just less than the sum stolen from Blackyetts. And I don't suppose that my list of his debts is

193

exhaustive. A jury would find it very interesting, don't you agree? And this might also interest them."

Cartaret produced another piece of paper from the file.

"Bethune bought a grey cloak from you. A grey cloak exactly like the one described by that unspeakable youngster during the trial. Surely you must have known this and recalled it when the matter was mentioned. You were at the trial, I know."

"I don't keep track of all that goes on in the shop," blustered the Alderman. "I, ah, have a great deal to do with my civic and magisterial duties . . . I . . ."

"That is not the impression I receive from your manager. He is impressed by the masterly fashion in which you keep *au fait* with all that is going on in the business no matter how heavy your civic duties are. He tells me you are informed of all orders, of all bad debts . . ."

"I daresay . . ."

"I daresay, Mr Ellershaw, that you preferred to see an innocent girl jailed rather than stir up trouble among people who are not only good customers but who also had a hand in making you Alderman."

"That is not true!"

Ellershaw came to his feet. Cartaret rose at the same time and began to stuff the papers back in his pocket.

"Appearances are against you then. You will have to prove it is not true. And the best way to do that is to have the case reopened."

"I will not be bullied like this!" Ellershaw shouted. "None of these things have anything to do with the case."

"I disagree. I think put all together they point very clearly at one man. One man who paid nearly a thousand pounds worth of debts at the same time as a sum of that size was stolen, a man who had a grey cloak and who may very well have been seen going into the building where the money was at dawn . . ."

"That is pure conjecture . . ."

"So is the notion that it was Miss Belchamber!"

"I say the girl had a fair trial and was found guilty. I see no necessity to reopen the case."

"In that event," Cartaret told him, "you can take the consequences. I mean to blow the case open and if you are

194

blown with it, that is just too bad. I have no need to wish you a good night. There isn't the slightest doubt that you'll sleep well. Your conscience would appear to about as active as a lump of lard."

He walked briskly to the door and opened it to find Mrs Ellershaw and Lucilla regarding him with alarm, each with a small garment destined for a pauper infant dangling from their fingers. They did not even pretend not to have been listening.

"Was all that true?" asked Mrs Ellershaw, whose face had lost its usual high colour.

"Perfectly true, ma'am," Cartaret said and bowed. "I have been at some pains to discover it."

"You will not defile my wife's ears with the filth you have stirred up," cried the Alderman.

"Be silent, Ernest," said his wife. "I had my doubts at the time. Do you think I am a fool? I have known about Bethune and his women for ever. And the rest?"

"I have collected a good deal of evidence," answered Cartaret.

"And what might be your interest in this matter?" she asked.

"Does that signify?"

"Don't tell me that you haven't some personal interest in the case."

"I detest injustice, ma'am."

"Balderdash!" she said with great ill-humour. "I know your sort."

"That is just what I say," expostulated her husband, "I utterly refuse to . . ."

"Ernest, you are a fool," she decided impersonally. "Leave him to me, Mr Quentin. I will come to see you in the morning."

"Uncle," Lucilla said suddenly, "you've never been in the jail. You don't know how horrid it is . . ." her voice wavered and broke ". . . and to be in there and know it was not your . . . to be there for *nothing* . . . ooooh!"

She burst into tears and Mrs Ellershaw put her arm round her awkwardly.

"If ye have not charity ye become as sounding brass," she said reproachfully, but to no one in particular. "I was not thinking of the girl. I was thinking of my fool of a husband, and myself. Lucilla, you are the real Christian. I am a tinkling cymbal."

Alderman Ellershaw looked at his wife and it was clear he waited for orders. Cartaret murmured his goodbyes and left. He strode back the two miles to the hotel and went straight into the bar-parlour where he ordered a large brandy and drank it down in two gulps. Polly came in grinning from ear to ear.

"I've a bit o' news, guv," he announced. "Heard it not ten minutes since. The delo nam's back."

Cartaret stared, looked at his glass and then back at Polly.

"Who's back?" he asked faintly.

"The delo nam . . . the old man. Just a bit o' the backslang, guv. Hoggett I means. He arrived off the four ten. Took the fly and went right out to the house. They say no one was expecting him. And he's got a real swell wiv 'im, so they says."

"Hoggett's back!"

Polly nodded and grinned maliciously.

"The fur's to fly when 'e gets 'ome, they reckons."

"Harness up Shaftesbury, man. I've a notion to see it fly. We're going out to Blackyetts this very night!"

12

"Facts spread like ripples on water."

In the breakfast parlour at Blackyetts Mr Hoggett and his guest were devouring a very select supper. Owing to the difficulty of replacing her, Cook was still working her notice and she had been determined to show the Master what she could do. Louisa and her brothers sat at the table and had taken their part in the demolition of a game pie though they had left the omelettes with their crisp curls of bacon to the new arrivals. However, even Alice, her eyes red and swollen with crying, had greeted with awe the splendid pudding which had WELCOME HOME hastily spelled out on it in toasted almonds. A Gâteau Gillyflower was not to be despised even when one had lost all one's illusions about love. Alice accepted a largish portion and discovered that unrequited love had affected her appetite less than she hoped.

Mrs Hoggett, evidently dressed in a hurry for her buttons were awry and two of them unfastened, was in her usual chair though she ate nothing. She made an attempt to play the hostess by enquiring graciously of Mr Scott concerning the voyage, his welfare thereon, the fearful weather, his family (there was a family of Scotts not far from Blackyetts and she was anxious to discover whether there was a connection) and, delicately, the reason for his visit. These enquiries were, unfortunately, timed to coincide with the moments when Mr Scott had a loaded fork poised before his lips.

"Hold thi peace, Jessie, for any favour," Mr Hoggett said eventually, "let the poor man eat. Not a bite have we had since breakfast. We're clemmed both of us."

Mrs Hoggett flushed and fell into an uneasy silence during which only the clink of silver against china was to be heard.

197

At last Mr Hoggett pushed back his chair and rang for the meal to be cleared away. He led the way back to the library where the younger children were gathered arguing over the respective merits of the gifts unearthed from the pigskin bag. Albert, frowning, was absentmindedly trying to wrench off the arms of a carved wooden Indian with a real feathered head-dress.

"Right," said Mr Hoggett, "now we can get down to brass tacks."

He took the great winged armchair and unbuttoned his waistcoat in tribute to Cook.

"Amy, Jane, go to Nurse. Time you were in bed. Make your curtsy to Mr Scott, and to your mama."

They obeyed shyly and went. Mr Hoggett's eye fell upon Albert who was about to leave at their heels.

"You may stay here, young man, I've more than a notion you can throw some light on events. And Louisa and Alice, better you stay than wonder vainly what I'm about."

"Is it about Miss Lester?" Louisa asked eagerly, rushing in where the rest of the family, angelic or not, were fearing even to tip-toe.

"It is," he agreed. "And a few other matters."

The assembly found seats and sat very still looking at one another or, like Mrs Hoggett, anxiously regarding their hands. Mr Booth trod deliberately in with a tray on which were glasses and a decanter.

"Ah, thankee, Booth. Would you ask Mr Bethune to join us?"

A pin could have been heard to drop.

"I understand," Booth said without emphasis, "that Mr Bethune has returned to the Rectory. About an hour ago."

"Then ask Jem Matthews to fetch him back," Mr Hoggett said genially. "I feel he ought to be here on this happy occasion. Quite a member of the family, isn't he, my dear?"

"As you wish, sir," Booth murmured.

"You might tell Jem that I *insist* that he joins us. Do you understand?"

A smile flickered over Booth's solemn countenance as he carried a glass to Mr Scott.

"Matthews will be very happy to see to it, sir," he

observed and departed. In a very short time indeed a horse was to be heard going down the avenue at a reckless pace.

"Now," Mr Hoggett began, his glass in his hand. "I've come home at great inconvenience, markee, and even more discomfort. Crossing the Atlantic at this time of the year is no picnic, by Harry it ain't, eh, Scott? And we was brought home in a bang, both of us, by these."

From the recesses of his jacket Mr Hoggett produced a bundle of newspaper cuttings. They were easily recognisable as accounts of the trial.

"And by this . . ."

He produced two letters.

"These are letters from Mrs Sands. Now I didn't care to hear what was going on. As soon as me back's turned this household seems to go to the dogs. There's something not right here. And I want to know what it is. I want some explanations and I wants them right off. And so does Mr Scott here."

"Explanations?" said Mrs Hoggett. "Explanations of what? If you are talking about that shocking business of that governess and the thousand pounds I should have thought that the whole thing was perfectly clear. And even if it wasn't I do *not* understand what possible interest this Mr Scott can have in such a . . ."

"I was engaged to marry Miss Belchamber, at one time," Oliver explained diffidently, "and while she ended the engagement on the death of her father . . ."

"So that nonsense was true after all!" Mrs Hoggett interrupted.

". . . I still feel a marked interest in her welfare," Oliver went on smoothly. "And I felt, as our American friends would say, that she had a very raw deal at your hands."

Mrs Hoggett went an unbecoming scarlet.

"She behaved in a disgusting and immoral fashion," she declared. "I had no alternative but to dismiss her as I did."

"She did not!" Louisa bellowed. "It was all . . . all a made-up thing! She wouldn't do anything like that . . ."

"Now there," her father put in, "I'm bound to agree with you. And so does Mr Scott here. We didn't think it sounded at all like her."

"There!" said Louisa triumphantly and overcome by her emotions she put her tongue out at her stepmother.

"That'll do, Lou," said Mr Hoggett. "Mind your manners."

"You were not there!" protested Mrs Hoggett, her voice rising, "I found Miss Lester . . . or whatever her name was . . . and I must say, Mr Hoggett, I take it very ill that you should foist such a creature on me and at such a time. A criminal's daughter! Did you make no enquiries?"

"*I* knew who she was," Mr Hoggett said. "She didn't try to deceive me. I said she should alter her name and I'm right down sorry now that I did."

"That you should admit as much!" she cried. "Did it not occur to you that *I* should have been told?"

"I couldn't trust you to hold your tongue. It would have made a tender tasty morsel for you and the tea-table tabbies."

"You knew and you didn't tell me!" she accused him in fine dramatic style. "When she was to have charge of my own children?"

"And mine," he reminded her stolidly. "Including Dorrie. Poor little beggar."

Mrs Hoggett seemed to shrink into her chair.

"Her condition became much, much worse," she said sulkily. "There was no bearing with her filthy . . ."

"I know what happened," Mr Hoggett told her. "Nurse wrote and told me."

"That woman! She has always resented me!"

"You were glad of any excuse to be quit of her. Well, make up your mind to it, she's to be fetched home tomorrow."

Mrs Hoggett resorted to her handkerchief.

"You'll have more reason to weep afore I'm done," he said quietly. "Save your tears. Now, I want to know exactly what happened that night. Exactly. No beating around the bush."

"I went down to the summer-house and I caught them . . . I saw her with my own eyes."

"You went down to the summer-house? You? In the evening? Even during the day I've never seen you walk beyond the terrace. What took you to the summer-house?"

"I found a note," she admitted sullenly.

"*Did* you? Are you saying she wrote you a note telling you she was up to no good in the summer-house?"

"It wasn't to me . . . it was to Tele . . . to Mr Bethune. He had left it on my . . . he had left it lying about. I found it when I went upstairs after dinner."

"In the account of the trial," Scott put in, "Miss Belchamber said . . ."

He hunted for the piece he wanted among the sheaf of cuttings.

"Mr Bethune came into the summer-house with a note which he said was from me . . . How could it be both in the summer-house and in your quarters?"

"I thought he must have left it lying about. I suppose he just told her what it said."

"What did it say?" asked Mr Scott.

"That she was desperate, that she needed his help and he was to meet her in the upstairs room of the belvedere as she called it. And she called him dearest and darling and . . . oh, other things . . ."

"Why should she need his help?" Mr Scott wished to know.

"Because she had enticed him into the schoolroom during my absence on some trivial pretext. She was always doing it. I intended to give her notice and she knew it."

"She didn't entice him!" Louisa declared. "I was there. I know. He was always in and out but she didn't want him there. She didn't like him. Not a bit. If anyone tried to get him alone it was Alice . . . not Miss Lester."

Mr Scott cleared his throat.

"Madam, after the death of her father when she was in much greater trouble, Miss Belchamber did not even see fit to accept help from me or her relatives. I find it quite absurd that she should write such a note."

"She was infatuated with him," said Mrs Hoggett spitefully. "It didn't take her long to forget you, I must say."

"That isn't true," Louisa weighed in once more. "She detested him. You could tell."

"I have the note still," shrilled Mrs Hoggett. "I kept it. It's in my bureau. I'll show you she wrote it! Disgusting creature!"

"Sit down," said her husband, "and mind how you speak

of her. Lou, you take that key and we'll take a look at this note."

Louisa, her bosom heaving with emotion and excitement, accepted the key and some muttered instructions from her stepmama and could be heard going upstairs at a pace which shook Blackyetts to its foundations.

"Now, I have a letter too," said Mr Hoggett when her footsteps had at last died into the recesses of the house. "It's from Nurse who's a woman of sense."

"Spiteful cat!" said Mrs Hoggett. "She's . . ."

"Silence," said Mr Hoggett. "Now Nurse says," he took out his reading glass "'. . . I'll take my oath, sir, that that dratted Albert's art and part of this. He fair took against Miss Lester.'"

He laid down the letter and beckoned to Albert who advanced from his place against the wall.

"So you took against her, son? Now why?"

"Dunno," glowered Albert.

"You weren't so unsure in the trial. Spoke up like a good 'un then."

Albert said nothing.

"Come on . . . you must have had a reason."

"She was too uppity," muttered Albert. "Stepmama said she was. She didn't care for me or anybody. She laughed at me. At my hump and my leg."

"Not true!"

Staneley had been in a quiet corner playing Stone Paper Scissors with Fred until this tiresome business should be over but he came out and stood over his brother.

"She didn't laugh at you. But she wasn't afraid of you either, like the others, stupid creatures. She wouldn't toady and bootlick and call you Master Albert. *That's* why you didn't like her . . . nasty, little insect!"

"Now, Staneley . . . that'll do."

"And if you want to know what he did Fred and me'll be glad to find out."

"Enough, boy!"

"Ask him where he gets all the money?" suggested Fred from his corner. "He's got a boxful of money in his room. Pounds and pounds."

"Have you indeed?"

"They've been nosing around in my room," Albert sneered.

"You're served with your own sauce then," Staneley said bluntly, "for you do more nosing than anyone in this house."

"Money, eh?" said Mr Hoggett thoughtfully. "Now, I ask meself where you'd get pounds and pounds from sixpence a week for your pocket and threepence of that for the plate on Sunday."

Albert said nothing.

"Shall I fetch it?" asked Fred.

"I don't spend everything I get on sweetstuff and toy soldiers," Albert sneered, "or toy boats . . ."

Just at that moment, which was, perhaps, as well for Albert, Louisa came thundering back waving a piece of paper.

"Here! And it isn't in her writing. I know her writing. I've kept everything I had of hers. I'll fetch what she said about my essay, shall I?"

Mr Hoggett unfolded the note, read it in silence and handed it over to Oliver.

"Mmm," he commented drily. "Miss Amelia would appear to conduct her correspondence in schoolroom copy-plate."

He looked at Oliver.

"I'll lay you don't recognise that fist, Scott."

Oliver laughed.

"Not at all. Look, here's the last note she wrote me. Compare the two. A child could have written that one."

"Ah," Mr Hoggett observed grimly. "Happen a child did, Albert. Happen a child wrote two. One for Mr Bethune and one for his stepmama. Just your style, my son. Economical. Two birds with one stone, you thought. But you missed the other bird, didn't you? He was too downy a bird even for you. That was how it was, wasn't it, Albert?"

Albert stared defiantly and said nothing.

"But he's only a child!" Oliver exclaimed. "Surely he wouldn't be so . . . so . . .?"

"Wouldn't he," said Staneley bitterly. "If I'd a guinea for every time he'd got me into hot water . . ."

Albert's father sighed. As if the sigh had been a cue in

the theatre the sound of wheels was heard outside and a commotion of stamping feet and raised voices.

"Bethune, or I miss my guess," said Mr Hoggett. "Go and help Matthews bring him in, boys."

Staneley and Frederick looked at one another in incredulous anticipation and collided in the doorway in their eagerness. However, much to their disappointment, there was no call for their services. Bethune, looking mutinous and dishevelled and very unlike his usual tidy and elegant self was ushered in by a large red-headed man whom Mr Hoggett had never seen before. He looked about at the assembled company with an assured air, dumped his companion roughly in a chair, and bowed.

"Mr Hoggett? My name is Quentin Cartaret. I would apologise for the intrusion but that I think I have rendered you something of a service."

"Mr Quentin!" Mrs Hoggett exclaimed, "whatever are you doing here? This is the person who has been taking my picture," she explained to her husband, "I thought it would be such a charming surprise for you."

She turned back to Cartaret and her voice became a little shrill.

"If you think you can ask for more money, you are quite mistaken. You've been paid already and to my mind overpaid. I'm bound to tell you," she added petulantly, "that I think it is a wretched likeness and so do all my friends who have seen it. And I wouldn't wonder if Mr Hoggett didn't think so too. And if you think he'll want you to take his likeness, you're wrong because Mr Hoggett could easily afford a real artist."

Mr Hoggett looked from his wife to Cartaret in bewilderment.

"I have been painting your wife," Cartaret told him, "but I won't deny that my mind wasn't on it. I came to this house with quite another purpose. And when I heard tonight that you were come home, Mr Hoggett, I thought it was high time you knew what that purpose was. Lord, man, but you're arrival is *apropos*."

"I'd be uncommon grateful to know why," Mr Hoggett interjected.

"It concerns this young man here," Cartaret told him

indicating Bethune by a jerk of the head. "I was on my way here when I saw your groom. He was endeavouring to persuade Mr Bethune to accept a pressing invitation from yourself, as I understood him. I, er, added my persuasions to his. I thought you might not object."

"No objection in the world," Mr Hoggett said, "though I'd be happy to know why you had an interest."

"Your groom seemed to be under the impression that he was 'doing a bunk'. He was not, apparently, on the road to the Rectory."

"Like enough he wasn't!"

"Poppycock," drawled Bethune who had regained a little of his poise though Staneley and Fred, one on either arm of the chair into which he had been thrust, prevented his rising and he was forced to make his remarks from a semi-recumbent position. "This is perfectly outrageous. Because I am tutor here doesn't mean that I have to attend whenever I am summoned, day or night. I was on my way to visit friends and didn't wish to break my engagement."

"Friends who live in Manchester?" enquired Cartaret. "To my knowledge, and I have come to know this district extremely well, there isn't a house on that road for twenty miles."

"I find myself quite at a loss to understand this behaviour," declared Bethune. "I would like to submit my immediate resignation. I will not be treated so."

He attempted to come to his feet but was thrust back by his ex-pupils.

"Not so fast, young man," Hoggett retorted. "You've a fair few questions to answer before I boot you down my steps."

He looked across at his wife who had fallen very quiet and at Alice who had turned away her face from the sprawled figure in the chair.

"A procedure which will give me t'greatest pleasure," he added.

"If I might assist you," murmured Oliver, "I would esteem it a favour."

"Well before either of you do that," Cartaret put in, "make sure that there's a constable waiting for him at the foot of those steps. He's not only a scoundrel, he is, according to my information a criminal."

The other two turned and looked at him. Cartaret strode over to Oliver Scott and held out his hand.

"Oliver Scott, if I'm not mistaken. We met, I think, at the Academy Exhibition of two years back. I had painted your sister."

"We did," Oliver agreed and grasped the hand held out to him. "May I ask what an eminent RA is doing in this district touting for sitters? And under a false name, as I understand you."

Cartaret grinned rather wolfishly.

"Oh, correcting a manifest injustice. I have a profound interest in justice, you know. I suppose I have no need to ask what brings you here."

"No," Scott agreed stiffly. "I have a profound interest in Miss Belchamber's welfare."

"A pity you didn't indulge it rather sooner, don't you think?"

Scott scowled.

"I was not in the country and I was quite unaware Miss Belchamber was in any kind of trouble. Mr Hoggett will tell you . . . as soon as I heard I took special leave and I came."

"Left you standing, didn't she?" asked Cartaret provocatively.

"Miss Belchamber considered she would do me a disservice by marrying me . . . in the circumstances."

"And of course you agreed."

"May one enquire," Scott demanded silkily, "just what interest you might have in this matter? I recall that my sister told me that she had made the acquaintance of Mrs Cartaret."

"I told you," Cartaret returned easily, "I have a profound interest in justice. I like to know the truth, Scott, it's a known eccentricity of mine. You can't paint portraits without knowing the truth about the sitters. It makes portraiture uncommonly interesting."

He let his glance slide momentarily in the direction of Mrs Hoggett. Oliver's expression relaxed slightly and he was conscious of a wish to see Cartaret's version of Mrs Hoggett.

"Beauty is truth and truth beauty, that's all we know and all we wish to know," Louisa misquoted with stunning effect upon the company. "Miss Lester made me learn that. It's Shakespeare."

206

"No it isn't," Alice said irritably.

"Well, who is it then?"

"Shelley," returned Alice loftily and inaccurately.

Battle was joined on this score.

"In the pursuit of truth . . ." mentioned Cartaret above the din.

"And beauty, it would seem," added Oliver sotto voce.

"I think you ought to see these, Hoggett."

Cartaret handed his host the bundle of papers he had shown earlier to Alderman Ellershaw.

"You may not know that Miss Belchamber's sentence is to be reviewed in two days," he announced. "It would appear that there are those who thought it was too lenient. I think that you may agree with me that the information contained in these suggests not only that it was too lenient but that it was given to the wrong person. I have formed the opinion . . ." He went to stand lowering over Bethune and pointed at him. ". . . that the real culprit is here and not in jail. Here we have a man who paid off a number of outstanding debts within a fortnight of the affair in the summer-house. Debts for which he was being increasingly pressed for payment and which were anything up to three years old."

"A windfall," Bethune said defiantly. "I won a large sum at the races."

"No, Bethune, you did not. You lost a very large sum at the races. You lost five hundred pounds two days before the affair in the summer-house."

There was a gasp of disbelief from the watchers.

"My informant tells me that you don't often win. His exact words were that you didn't know a lame donkey from a cavalry charger. But he is fairly certain that the five hundred pounds wagered with Lord Jerburgh was paid before the Winter Meeting."

"Prove it!" sneered Bethune. "No such bet was entered in any book."

"Young Jerburgh has made a statement," Cartaret said quietly. "His father persuaded him that he should. I have it here."

He tapped the bundle of papers. Bethune seemed to shrink back into the chair.

"The judges might be interested to know how you paid

the money on a salary of a hundred pounds a year. And here is another piece of evidence you'll find hard to deny, I imagine."

He produced two folded sheets from his inner pocket and spread them on the table. The smaller was a sketch of Bethune himself which caught admirably his air of smug self-satisfaction: the larger was a pastel drawing of a plump, high-coloured girl with prominent brown eyes, a mass of brown curly hair and a fair, well-exposed bosom. She was wearing a cherry-coloured gown and displayed upon that admirable bosom was a necklace, drawn, not in pastel, but in minute detail in pen and Indian ink.

"That's Molly from the White Boar!" Louisa exclaimed. "I'd know her anywhere. Isn't he clever?"

Bethune turned a sickly colour and shrank further into the recesses of the chair.

"Have you seen this necklace before, Hoggett?"

Before he could answer Alice picked up the drawing and squealed.

"Why! It's just like poor mama's garnet necklace . . . you know, Louisa, the one that was stolen that I was to have when I was old enough. Look, there's that sort of net thing with the stones set on it and the bigger stones hanging by chains. I'd know it anywhere. Mama was always wearing it."

"She's right," Hoggett agreed gruffly. "It was a present when Alice, here, was born."

Cartaret produced a third piece of paper from his coat.

"This," he announced impressively, "is a signed statement to the effect that the necklace was given to the wearer . . . in consideration of certain favours . . . early on the morning of October the twenty-fourth."

"That's the morning after there was all the to-do," Louisa said. "The night you sent off poor Miss Lester."

She looked daggers at her stepmama whose face revealed a curious mixture of fear and anger.

"It was given to her by Bethune. He arrived at the White Boar late that night and said . . . I'll read it . . . 'there had been such a kick up at Blackyetts that the rafters were still ringing. He drank a good bit and made up to me. I said nothing for nothing in this world of woe and he said he knew where he could get me the prettiest necklet in the world and he went off and when he came back he showed me this and said I should wear it . . . !' " Cartaret looked up. "I'll spare you the rest. But just one more thing. She said that Bethune was neat as ninepence and he was wearing a grey cloak."

Mrs Hoggett turned her head from side to side and emitted a thin sound which might have been a protest. Hoggett looked at her and handed her his own big linen handkerchief. Bethune folded his lips defiantly and said nothing.

"I would suggest that Bethune came back here late that night and collected this. He was wearing this cloak and had the hood down over his face. Albert saw him and recognised him, I imagine, judging by the amount of money I am told he has amassed. And I think Ellis heard him. She heard movement in the boudoir. She said so at the trial. You took that money, didn't you, Bethune?"

"Did I? I wouldn't be so pot-sure, if I were you," Bethune flung at him.

"You needed it desperately, you knew where it was, you had the entrée to the boudoir . . . and of course after that night there was to be a handy scapegoat."

Mrs Hoggett began to weep noisily and gustily. Bethune pushed Fred aside and sat up to look at her.

"Why should I need to steal," he demanded, "when I had a source of ready money?"

There was a charged silence.

"Hadn't I, my delectable Jessamine?" enquired Bethune softly and contemptuously.

Mrs Hoggett cowered, her eyes starting like a wired rabbit's. No one spoke. Hoggett turned on the children.

"Leave the room!" he commanded harshly.

"They have something to add," Cartaret suggested.

"No!" thundered Hoggett, "out!"

The children went quickly and thankfully, Albert at their heels.

Mr Hoggett stalked over to his wife's chair.

"Is this true?" he demanded. "Did you give this scoundrel the money he needed? And then permit an innocent girl to go to jail?"

"No! No! No!" she squealed and then fell into a fit of hysterics almost falling out of her chair and grovelling at his feet. Hoggett lifted her up not ungently and put her back in her chair. She cowered there, a blowsy, plump creature with all her airs stripped from her. Hoggett looked down at her, his heavy face drawn into lines of distress.

"I should never have married you," he said harshly. "I did you as much disservice as I did myself."

He went back to the fire and stared into it for a moment. When he turned round his face was set in an expression of determination. He looked from Scott to Cartaret and then Bethune.

"Did it never occur to you," he asked his wife very deliberately, "that this creature was to blame?"

At this moment the arrival of Mr Ellershaw created a diversion which was welcome to most people in the room. To witness the humiliation of others diminishes those who watch.

Booth showed Mr Ellershaw in with his customary solemnity. However, he had greeted the opportunity to glimpse the drama behind the library door with a readiness which had made him almost hurry across the hall to announce the latest comer.

"Mr Ellershaw, sir," said Booth and his demure expression did him credit as he assimilated as much as was possible in the brief moment it took to bow in the guest and withdraw, closing the door slowly and softly. Mr Booth's dignity did not permit his even appearing to linger in earshot but as he paced back to the service door in stately fashion, his ears cocked to the uttermost he heard these electrifying words. Mr Hoggett's voice could penetrate even linenfold panelling.

"Ah, Ernest . . . I don't know what you're here for but you've come mighty *apropos*. I want to give this young scoundrel in charge . . ."

It is sad to have to relate that Booth did a neat double-shuffle on the hall carpet under the admiring and bewildered gaze of the children peering down over the banisters, clicked his fingers a number of times and then vanished through the service door at a speed which would have made his brothers of the pantry stare. That night the port circulated freely in the Hall and the Room and Cook was put to bed by Mrs Lucas and Mrs Sands who manifested a regrettable tendency to giggle as they did it. Jem once again fetched the police from

Bindleton and as they left in the first light of the winter morning there was a face at almost every window. Mr Bethune left with them.

The following day he was seen under escort on the London train. Gardiner had decided that he would be a useful presence at the review the following day. When he came back it was to be lodged securely in the County Jail to await a retrial of the Blackyetts robbery case.

13

"Anger dieth quietly with the good."

It was nearly Spring when the gates of the County Jail opened a little way, early one dull March morning and a small, rather pale figure in a grey serge cloak emerged. She was accompanied by the Governor, a bluff ex-soldier, obviously uncertain how to address an inmate in such unusual circumstances, but, nevertheless, radiating a rather apologetic goodwill, as if a short term in his prison was a trivial misfortune which might happen to anyone. The Chief Wardress who stood beside him to speed the parting guest had a resentful air as if the premature release of a prisoner in her charge was a personal slight. Amelia shook hands with both, unsmiling, and turned to face the world.

To her surprise the approach to the forbidding walls and gates was crowded with people. Once assured that this unimpressive little figure was really the Miss Belchamber who had been so cruelly put upon they began to wave and cheer and press forward to shake her hand and wish her well. It might have been a frightening experience except that the police were there to make sure she was not congratulated into a fit of the vapours. They formed an impermeable ring round her, fending off the crowd with extreme good humour even though they were the object of jeers and rude comments about having got the wrong 'un this time They brought her to a waiting cab out of which climbed a familiar, bandy-legged figure, weeping unashamedly from his one eye who ugged her to the scandalisation of the crowd who enquired she couldn't find herself something better than the organ-rinder's monkey.

"They're all awaitin' for you at the Station Hotel," he said

212

when he remembered himself and let her go. "The guv sez you'll want to dress and such before you meets them all and there's that Miss Ellershaw in the cab. She got your bags as I packed up and a new dress wot the guv 'ad made. Come on, do, miss . . ."

The crowd pressing close understood that there were to be celebrations and they approved, waving and cheering as she was handed into the cab and driven off. Behind her the gates of the County Jail closed again. Inside the cab Lucilla, speechless, hugged her also and Amelia wept.

There was another gathering at the Station Hotel, equally pleased to see her and equally vociferous. Inside, the manager presented her with a bouquet of spring flowers and his heart-felt congratulations and good wishes: a positive corridor of smiles extended up the stairs to the door of the private sitting-room engaged by Mr Hoggett for the great occasion as the staff of the hotel, the newest and smartest in the town, crowded to see her. However, some confusion was evident; Lucilla stifled a giggle when she heard a plaintive voice ask, "Which one's 'er?"

"That'll teach you to keep doubtful company," Amelia whispered. "Who can touch pitch and remain undefiled?"

The private sitting-room was a mass of flowers and presents and food and drink with a confusing number of familiar faces among the decorations. Amelia whose world for the past many weeks had been one of silence began to feel tired and bewildered by the noise of so many voices. She saw Cartaret first and smiled at him: it was a little disconcerting when he did not immediately smile back. Amelia had not had the benefit of a looking-glass for a long time and she had been dressed as if she was a helpless child by Lucilla and Mrs Ellershaw. She did not know how she had altered. Cartaret had not been north for Bethune's trial. He saw her face thin and pale, her eyes shadowed and her hair for all Lucilla's efforts, limp and dull. He was shocked and could not smile and so her smile wavered and disappeared. She looked away and Louisa came at her in a rush, nearly knocking her over, and hugged her, blubbering.

"The beasts! The beasts! You don't look like yourself . . . you're so thin! Oh, Miss Lester . . . dear, Miss Lester, I'm so glad . . . so glad . . ."

213

She began to cry in good earnest and was drawn away by Lucilla who plied her with handkerchiefs and soothing sounds. Mr Hoggett presented himself next with a bone-crushing handshake which made her wince visibly and barked, "By gum, I'm mortal pleased to have you out of that place at last . . . and here's someone you'll be glad to see again, I don't doubt . . ."

Amelia, dazed, saw Oliver looking at her. She submitted docilely to a more considerate handshake and a kiss on the cheek. Cartaret was at his shoulder, his face pinched and angry.

"Your hands!" he exclaimed in a harsh, shaken voice and took them into his own.

The rest looked in dismay for they were bluish-red and swollen, with open sores and splits on her fingers. Amelia drew them away and hid them as best she could in her skirts.

"It was the water," she said apologetically, "I suffer from chilblains . . ."

Cartaret made a curious sound and strode to the door where he bellowed for the page who scurried up, resplendent in bright brass buttons and gold braid.

"Go to the apothecary and buy something soothing, some ointment for . . ."

"Algonicum Balm," mentioned Lucilla at his elbow.

"Algonicum Balm . . . and a pair of soft white cotton gloves . . ." He thrust a half-sovereign at the boy. "Keep the change, but *hurry* . . ."

Meanwhile Mr Hoggett had shown Amelia to a chair, looking mystified as if he did not know quite how he should behave to her.

"Try a morsel of this ham," he entreated, evidently deciding that food was what she chiefly needed. Amelia's mouth was watering at the array of dainties on the table. Commonplace articles of diet like soft bread rolls, butter, fruit, eggs, milk and cheese had come to seem like unspeakable luxuries. Hoggett heaped her plate high and brought the rest of them to order by commanding them to sit down and leave off staring at the poor lass as if she had two heads.

When the meal was over and Amelia's health had been drunk Mr Hoggett coughed.

"Now," he declared, "there's decisions to be made. I'll

214

say my piece first. And I'll start by saying downright it was my fault."

He looked about defying anyone to contradict this admission but nobody did.

"I took on that Bethune in good faith," he went on. "The missus was mad to have a Lord's cousin for a tutor and he was well-recommended, that I'll say, mind you, but I should have looked a bit further than his father and his cousin, Lord or no. Nor I shouldn't have gone off to America and left you to stand buff . . . not that I thought for a moment that you'd have more to put up with than Albert's mischief and Mrs Hoggett's everlasting interference . . . but there it is. Now, I can't say fairer than that . . ."

He glowered round the table.

"There's nothing can be done to make up to you for what's occurred," he went on, "and Stan Hoggett's not fool enough to think there is. And to know that Bethune's waiting to be transported doesn't neither . . . nor the bit o' bother your cousin's got herself into. Other folk's troubles don't make yours any better."

"No," Amelia agreed. "Will they really transport him? I thought the colonists were trying to put a stop to that?"

"I wouldn't blame them trying to stop Bethune going there," said Mr Hoggett grinning. "That creature's like a cat. He'll fall on his feet there . . . you mark my words."

"I can only hope you're wrong," said Cartaret. "Give me your other hand."

He smoothed the balm on gently and drew the glove over her hand as if she had been a child. "And let me tell you if it does you no good to know that Bethune's in the hulks at Chatham, believe me it gives your friends a lot of pleasure . . ."

"Hear! Hear!" said Oliver.

"Hear! Hear!" bellowed Louisa and hiccoughed.

"Now," Mr Hoggett went on and he looked round the table as if he was conducting a board-meeting: Mr Hoggett was accustomed to board-meetings and did not so much chair them as sit on them. "What I proposes is this. Mrs Hoggett is going to make a long stay with her mama. They are going into the country. Later they'll be going to Harrogate for to drink the waters. Mrs Hoggett's nerves have suffered from all this," he added thinking of the revelations of Bethune's trial, "and she don't feel up to society and won't for a while. There's a home for you at Blackyetts for as long as you need it and if you'll have an eye to the children while you're there it will be more than they deserve. Eh?"

"Oh, please, say you'll come," Louisa begged. "Everyone would be so happy!"

"Even Albert?" Amelia could not forbear to enquire.

"Albert," said Albert's father grimly, "is going to school. The Grammar School at Bindleton where I can keep a very sharp eye on him. Albert needn't worry you . . ."

"Albert could be your partner one day," Amelia said. "He's a clever boy."

"Too damned clever by half," Mr Hoggett snapped. "I warmed his backside for him, hump or no hump and he's been no trouble since I warrant you. And I'll thank you not to wish a partner on me who forges letters."

"I think Albert wants . . ."

"Never mind what Albert wants," Mr Hoggett said in exasperation.

"But you must," Amelia told him earnestly. "I thought about him a lot when I was in that place . . ."

"You never thought about Albert?" exclaimed Louisa. "How awful!"

"I wondered why he hated me so, for he did hate me, you know."

"Albert doesn't have to have a reason," Louisa declared. "He hates everyone."

"Albert wants to have people . . . consider him," Amelia said awkwardly, her tongue jibbing at the word 'love'. Love and Albert did not seem to fit in the same sentence. "He pretends that he doesn't care that everyone dislikes him, makes believe he enjoys it. But the more I thought about it the more I thought you will have to pay him some attention. Do you know, the first thing he said to me was, 'I expect they told you I killed my mother.' That's a heavy burden to lay upon a child."

She looked anxiously at Mr Hoggett.

"I'll attend to him, never you fear," said Mr Hoggett. "But at this moment I want to attend to you and I haven't said all I mean to say."

216

Like all good chairmen Mr Hoggett rarely lost sight of the main point.

"When you get wed as I don't doubt you will, I'll settle ten thousand on you, same as I'll do for my own daughters. There . . . I can't say handsomer than that."

He looked down the table at Oliver as if Scott were the manager of the marriage department and it was his role to defend its performance. Oliver, taken very much aback at this departure, cleared his throat, smoothed his moustache and murmured in diplomatic accents, "How very generous. But no more than Amelia deserves."

Amelia bowed her head looking at her hands in the loose cotton gloves, conscious of the sting of the balm in her sores. Mr Hoggett, obviously disappointed at this pale response, jogged the marriage department again.

"Surely Mr Scott has something to add to that, eh?"

Oliver felt as if the ceiling had fallen in. Since he had encountered Mr Hoggett in the New York shipping office he had felt continually as if he had been swept up into a millrace from which he would have been very glad to escape. His descent on the shipping office had not been motivated by enduring love but by an impulse of indignation that something so horrible should happen to someone he liked very much. Then he had believed that Amelia had no friends and it behoved him to do what he could to help. He had a certain amount of influence and was prepared to pull every string at his disposal to have her case reopened and her sentence either quashed or reviewed. When he found during that interminable voyage across the Atlantic that Amelia was very far from being friendless he would have been quite content to withdraw and simply make certain that nothing was left undone that he might do. Mr Hoggett, however, had refused to permit this, having like many hard-headed, practical men a streak of romanticism a yard wide. In Oliver Scott he had seen a happy ending as satisfying as the double line drawn under the final figure in an audit. Thus it was at his most pressing invitation that Oliver had come north to be present, albeit reluctantly. Had he had the slightest inkling of Mr Hoggett's intentions he would have fled the country.

However, in all honour, he could not draw back; he could not even hesitate. He could only rely upon Amelia's good sense. With as good a face as he could he laid his career on the block. He rose and came round the table to where she sat.

"Amelia," he began, and if his face was a little grim for a man about to propose marriage no one noticed except Amelia. "I have great pleasure in renewing my offer of marriage. It was a blow to have my congé last year and my feelings have not changed."

He waited to hear her response and wondered rather angrily how he could have permitted himself to be inveigled into such a tight corner. Some diplomat you are, he sneered at himself. Something of this escaped into his expression and Amelia was looking at him closely. He smiled hastily.

"Well?" Mr Hoggett prompted, grinning like a turnip lantern.

"You are both very kind," Amelia replied almost inaudibly.

"Kindness be hanged," muttered Cartaret under his breath, just loud enough for her to hear.

"However," she went on, "nothing has really changed since I wrote you that letter in July. I am still Belchamber's daughter and now I have been a jailbird to boot."

"Innocent as a lamb," Mr Hoggett blustered, "Innocent as the babe unborn!"

"Mud sticks," Amelia insisted quietly, "and that is what people will remember, the scandal and the jail. No, Oliver, you're kind and generous but too much has happened for me ever to marry you. It would not do. And my feelings have changed. I am not the person you asked this time last year."

There was a long pause: Oliver was conscious of a burden lifted from his shoulders and despite that a certain regret. He had never liked her better than he did at that moment. Briefly, he wondered whether he wouldn't do better to press his suit and brazen out his marriage, but he knew he did not possess the calibre for that. He bowed and went back to his seat.

"Then you'll stay with us!" Louisa exclaimed into the puzzled silence and she galumphed over to put her arms round Amelia. "You'll stay with us for ever and ever!"

The meeting dissolved into considerable confusion as Louisa's protestations of devotion, Mr Hoggett's forcibly expressed disappointment in the performance of the marriage department and a general release of tension were blended into a hub-hub at which Amelia accustomed to almost perpetual silence over the past months flinched and looked down at her hands, fighting to keep her composure.

"Now look here!"

Cartaret rose to his considerable height and quelled the babble with a glare.

"I did not masquerade around this benighted town drawing simpering worthies and listening to interminable gossip just to provide Scott with a wife. You go and choose one in Town, Scott. You'll find dozens of spaniel-eyed wenches there ready to diplomatise with you and do it much better than Amelia. It would bore her to extinction. As for you Hoggett . . ." He turned on the chairman. "I appreciate that you mean well, but my intention was not to provide you and your family with a tutelary deity or a surrogate mama. I can imagine no worse fate than being mama to Albert. Keep your ten thousand pounds, or, better still, give them to Albert. If you do he'll be a nabob before he's fifty . . . or Chancellor of the Exchequer. Now I come to consider, he has all the talents of the politician."

His indignant gaze turned to Amelia who was sitting very still, her gloved hands in her lap and a faint smile on her face.

"I require my housekeeper," he said abruptly, "immediately."

He sat down and the meeting thereupon fell into considerable disorder.

Some three months later Cartaret, bearing a newspaper, came down into Polly's kitchen kingdom and found Amelia crying.

"Oh, Lord!" he exclaimed. "Have you had a look at *The Times* already?"

Amelia wiped her eyes and sniffed while he hovered rather helplessly over her.

"Why should *The Times* make me cry?" she asked.

"What is the matter?" he demanded, "you never cry."

"Not often," she agreed. "It was Mrs Snaith."

"What did she do?" he enquired fiercely. "If she said anything to upset you I'll turn her out this minute!"

"No! No, she didn't say a word. She is a dear," Amelia said hastily. "And such a hard worker. It was just that she was scrubbing the floor."

She pointed at the damp flags under her feet.

"Why the blazes should that make you cry?" asked Cartaret, baffled.

"For sheer thankfulness," Amelia said and the tears welled up again. "If it hadn't been for you and Polly I'd still be scrubbing. When I think of those miles of corridors and acres of stone floors and the filthy smelly water . . ."

"Well, don't think of them," he instructed her reasonably. "Think of something more cheerful. Have you had a letter from Lucilla?"

"She is to come to London with Mrs Ellershaw and Miss Cosgrave on the nineteenth."

"Miss Cosgrave?"

"*Study of a Gentlewoman.*"

"Good Lord! Is that her name?"

Study of a Gentlewoman had been well hung at the Summer Exhibition.

"And will they be permitted to visit this house of sin?" he enquired.

"Luke fifteen, verse two," Amelia murmured.

"Very likely," he observed acidly. "I find this habit you and Lucilla have of conversing in chapter and verse exceedingly unenlightening."

" 'The Pharisees and Scribes murmured saying, This Man receiveth sinners and eateth with them.' "

"I take it they are coming to dinner."

"Mrs Ellershaw disliked being a tinkling cymbal and doesn't wish to be thought a Pharisee."

"I take it also that she has swallowed the fact that you have turned your back on respectability and become my mistress."

"I have not become your mistress."

"No, alas. But she thinks you have. The good always believe the worst of anyone."

"True," Amelia agreed. "Lucilla says that her aunt is convinced that Mrs Hoggett took the money for Bethune, just as he claimed."

"Mrs Ellershaw is an ignorant, prejudiced, bigoted

woman and as shrewd a customer as I met all the time I was up there."

Amelia looked up from her bowl of peas in surprise.

"Do you agree with her?"

"I do."

"You mean that Bethune didn't steal the money, after all?"

"Why should he?" Cartaret asked indifferently. "She was besotted enough to give him anything he asked for."

"But . . . he's been transported."

"I wouldn't have lifted a finger to stop him being hanged!"

"Quentin!"

"He was content to hold his peace, spend the money and let you take the blame. He knew all her affairs. He knew where the money came from. Do you know why it all happened as it did? Hoggett's letter to say he might be home for Christmas after all arrived the same day that Bethune 'borrowed' five hundred to pay Jerburgh. Bethune could not find the money to repay all that he'd 'borrowed' so she had to do something to account for what was missing. Getting rid of you got rid of a rival and provided a likely culprit."

"But the ten sovereigns?"

"She didn't want you on the doorstep, starving and making awkward statements."

"All the same," breathed Amelia doubtfully, "transportation . . ."

"Don't concern yourself for him," Cartaret said harshly. "He wasted none on you. Nothing's happened to him that he didn't deserve."

"How must *she* feel?"

He gave her a look of affectionate scorn.

"Profoundly relieved that Hoggett stood by her, I imagine . . . look, if you think that vain silly lump is torturing herself imagining her lover in gyves being seasick under hatches, you're quite beside the mark. Her feelings are reserved entirely for herself, you may be sure."

"Hoggett knows?"

"Of course he knows," Cartaret said bitterly. "Her kind can always depend on his kind. It wouldn't be good for business to have a wife in jail. It hasn't done Lord Wheatley much good to have one who escaped going there by the skin of her teeth and every string her husband could pull."

He went to the window and stared out at the garden where Polly was bent double planting lettuces.

"If you look at that newspaper you will find that your rather less than devoted Oliver is betrothed," he said suddenly and harshly, "to a Miss Lamberton. I expect you have met her. She is a suitable wench with a face like a spaniel . . . a King Charles spaniel."

"I wish them both very happy," Amelia said calmly and resumed shelling peas.

"Is that all? You've no regrets? You could have gone back into your old milieu, you know. All this would have been forgotten in time."

"I've no regrets."

"You're quite sure?"

"Quite sure," Amelia said. "We would not have suited one another in the least."

Cartaret did not turn round.

"You wanted to marry him at one time."

"The girl who did has gone," Amelia told him. "I wouldn't know her if I met her."

"You didn't refuse him just for his sake, then?"

"No. It was quite as much for mine."

Cartaret came away from the window and stood beside her watching her hands as she shelled peas, luscious little peas, the first fruits of Polly's garden.

"I want to paint you," he said brusquely. "Leave those damned things and come up to the studio."

"No," Amelia protested, "I've half a hundred things I must do this morning."

"I am your employer and I say they can wait. Come along!"

He took her by the wrist and pulled her, half-laughing, half-protesting up the three flights of stairs and into the studio where the early summer sun flooded the room. He gave her an easy pose, reclining on the huge couch, leaning against one arm, one hand on the back and the other lying in her lap. She laughed up at him as he chose a canvas from the store.

"Too mean to pay a model's fee," she upbraided him, "that's all it is."

He didn't reply but stood in front of her holding the blank canvas.

222

"Amelia . . ." he began and then stopped, frowning.

"Well?"

"Take your clothes off . . . please."

"Now, you know my views," she said firmly. "Paint me as much as you like but you endure the dust and the mess and I keep my clothes on."

He said nothing in answer to this but moved across the studio to clamp the canvas to the easel and angle it for the light.

"Who would you take your clothes off for?" he demanded suddenly and glared at her under his eyebrows. "For your husband? Or would you have him come to you in the dark?"

Amelia, startled and confused, blushed and put her hands to her cheeks.

"You're beautiful. I want to *see* you. Dammit, girl, I'm a painter, I *live* through my eyes, you know that. If I had to live in the dark I'd cut my throat . . ."

He strode over to the couch and stood looking down at her.

"I can't be your husband," he shot at her, "but I can be better than that . . . I can be your lover. Husbands are dull creatures, I tell you. The shine went out of me when I was a husband. I'll be your lover until . . ."

He stopped and ground his teeth at her in a mock rage.

"You make me sound like a lady-novelist," he complained. "Till the day I die, indeed. Threadbare stuff. What is this love that makes us inarticulate, awkward . . ."

Amelia looked down, unable to meet his eyes, and he bent over and grabbed her chin as he had done the first day, forcing her to look at him.

"I can't imagine being without you now," he muttered. "Think of that, blast it!"

He let her go and went back to the easel.

"Forget it!" he said savagely and rummaged for his charcoal. "Forget it all. I shouldn't have said it."

He peered out at her around the easel.

"I suppose you'll walk straight out after this and try to find another post. Well, if you do I'll give you a character that'll bring you straight back. Be warned."

Amelia had begun to regather her wits. She smiled at this

threat and then sat up slowly. She unbuttoned her close-fitting pink bodice. Underneath she was not wearing more than a fine silk camisole for it was a hot day. She stood up and let her skirt slip to the ground with her petticoats. Cartaret looked up, ready to start the outline, to find her standing naked, shivering a little and looking anxiously at him.

"Lord," he said reverently.

"Now," she said and a quiver of amusement livened the question, "which will you do first, sir? Paint me? Or lie with me?"

"Oh, Amelia . . ." He was laughing as he came towards her. "I never do know what you will do. Here?"

"Here, in the light. I used to dream about the light in this room. And about you," she admitted. "Waking up in that dark cell was hideous . . . worse than anything."

He plunged over to the door and locked it, muttering something about Polly, and came back to find her standing in the sunshine, arms outstretched, as if she was bathing in light.

"I feel like Zeus," he said, looking at her through narrowed eyes.

"Another thoroughly disreputable, overbearing character," she murmured and held her arms out to him.

He gave a great laugh and snatched her up, holding her high to the sun so that she was dazzled.

"Our first child," he decided, "is about to be conceived."

"What do we call him? Perseus?" she asked, rather shakily.

"That's my literary love," he chuckled. "No. You're done with monsters. We shall call him Luke . . . light."

"Or Lucilla," she reminded him, hiding her face in his shoulder.